RAVES FOR JAMES PATTERSON

"WHAT DO WOMEN WANT? AT THIS POINT IN HIS CAREER, MR. PATTERSON PROBABLY HAS A BETTER ANSWER THAN FREUD DID."
—*New York Times*

"A MASTER OF POPULAR LIT."
—*Publishers Weekly*

"THE MAN WHO CAN'T MISS."
—*TIME*

"PATTERSON MAKES READERS CARE."
—*Winston-Salem Journal*

"PATTERSON HAS MASTERED THE ART OF WRITING PAGE-TURNING BESTSELLERS."
—*Chicago Sun-Times*

"A MUST-READ AUTHOR…A MASTER OF THE CRAFT."
—*Providence Sunday Journal*

"PATTERSON IS A MASTER."
—*Toronto Globe and Mail*

First Love

First Love

JAMES PATTERSON

AND EMILY RAYMOND

GRAND CENTRAL
PUBLISHING

NEW YORK   BOSTON

Copyright © 2014 by James Patterson
Hot Winter Nights copyright © 2016 by Codi Gary

Hachette Book Group supports the right to free expression and the value of copyright. The purpose of copyright is to encourage writers and artists to produce the creative works that enrich our culture.

The scanning, uploading, and distribution of this book without permission is a theft of the author's intellectual property. If you would like permission to use material from the book (other than for review purposes), please contact permissions@hbgusa.com. Thank you for your support of the author's rights.

Grand Central Publishing
Hachette Book Group
1290 Avenue of the Americas, New York, NY 10104
grandcentralpublishing.com
twitter.com/grandcentralpub

Originally published in hardcover in January 2014
First trade paperback: November 2014
First mass market: July 2017

Grand Central Publishing is a division of Hachette Book Group, Inc.
The Grand Central Publishing name and logo is a trademark of Hachette Book Group, Inc.

The publisher is not responsible for websites (or their content) that are not owned by the publisher.

The Hachette Speakers Bureau provides a wide range of authors for speaking events. To find out more, go to www.hachettespeakersbureau.com or call (866) 376-6591.

ISBNs 978-1-4555-8500-7 (mass market), 978-0-316-31536-4 (ebook)

Printed in the United States of America

OPM

10 9 8 7 6 5 4 3 2 1

For Jane—

In the fall of 2010, I turned in the outline for First Love *to my editor, but the story actually began many years before. I was in love with a woman named Jane Blanchard. One morning we were out for a walk in New York City. Seemingly out of nowhere, Jane suffered a violent seizure. She was sick with cancer for nearly two years after that, then died at a young age. Far too young. Janie, I miss your smile. I hope it lives on in this book, this love story that reminds me of our time together (though I don't remember stealing any cars).*

—J.P.

First Love

prologue

one

OKAY, I MAY NOT BE PUTTING MYSELF IN THE BEST possible light by admitting this, but let me say right at the start that I was such a straight arrow, such a little do-gooder, that skipping my last two classes that day (AP physics and AP English) made me so insanely, ridiculously jittery that it actually occurred to me this whole crazy plan wasn't going to be worth it.

Looking back on it now, I can't believe I was *this close* to backing out of the most beautiful, funny, painful, and life-changing experience I will ever have.

What an idiot I was.

I was at Ernie's Pharmacy & Soda Fountain, and I had about five hundred butterflies throwing an epic party in my stomach. The toes of my vintage Frye cowboy boots kept knocking against the counter, until Ernie—who's about a million years old and pretty much a total grouch—told me to quit it. Ernie is one Nickelback concert away from complete deafness, though, so I took my boots off and kept knocking away.

I was glad he didn't ask why I was sitting in his ancient shop, drinking a giant coffee (which I needed like I needed a hole in the head), instead of two blocks down the street at Klamath Falls High School, listening to Mr. Fox blather on about the space-time continuum. Because what would I have said?

Well, Ernie—Mr. Holman, I mean—I'm waiting for a boy I could never date, and I'm about to ask him to do something so major that it's going to either save our lives or completely destroy us.

Ernie doesn't care much for teen angst, which is probably why practically no one I know ever comes to his shop—that and the fact that all his candy has dust on it and the Snickers bars are hard enough to use as crowbars.

But I don't mind. And neither does the boy I mentioned. Ernie's is *our* place.

That boy had sent me a note earlier in the day. He'd somehow gotten it inside my locker, even though he doesn't go to my school anymore and we have Navy SEAL–type security guards to protect us against God-knows-what (rioting due to sheer small-town boredom, maybe).

Axi—

So, you got earth-moving news, huh?

I'm shocked you think you can surprise me—or

surprised you think you can shock me.

Or something like that.

You're the word nerd.

Well anyway, can't wait to hear it.

Ernie's. 1:15.

Yeah, that means <u>cutting class</u>.

No excuses.

—Your favorite "scalawag"

That's Robinson for you. I'd jokingly called him a scalawag once, and he'd never let me forget it. He's almost seventeen years old. My best friend. My partner in crime.

I heard the front door open and could tell he'd arrived by the way Ernie's face perked up like someone had just handed him a present. Robinson has that effect on people: when he walks into the room, it's like the lights get brighter all of a sudden.

He came over and clapped a hand on my shoulder. "Axi, you dope," he said (affectionately, of course). "Never drink Ernie's coffee without a doughnut." He leaned in close and whispered, "That stuff will eat a giant hole in your guts." Then he straddled the stool next to me, his legs lanky and slim in faded Levi's. He was wearing a flannel shirt, even though it was late May and seventy-five degrees outside.

"Hey, Ernie," he called, "did you hear the Timbers fired their coach? And can we get a chocolate cruller?"

Ernie came over, shaking his grizzled head. "Soccer!" he groused. "What Oregon needs is a pro baseball team. That's a real sport." He put the doughnut on an old chipped plate and said, "On the house."

Robinson turned to me, grinning and pointing a thumb at Ernie. "I love this guy."

I could tell the feeling was mutual.

"So," Robinson said, giving me his full attention, "what's this crazy idea of yours? Are you finally going to apply for your learner's permit? Have you decided to drink a whole beer? Are you going to quit doing your homework so religiously?"

He's always getting on me for being a good girl. Robinson thinks—and my dad agrees—that he's such a bad boy because he quit high school, which he found "insufficiently compelling" and "populated by cretins" (*cretins* being a word that I taught him, of course). Personally, I think he has a point there.

"I'm probably going to fail everything but English," I said, and I wasn't exaggerating. My GPA was about to take a nosedive, because finals were coming up, and with any luck, I wasn't going to be around to take them. A week ago, knowing that would have kept me up at night. But I'd managed to stop caring, because if this plan worked, life as I knew it was about to change.

"Knowing you, that seems highly unlikely," Robinson said. "And so what if you're a little distracted and you—God forbid—get a B plus on something? You're busy writing the Great American Novel—*ow!*"

I'd swatted him on the arm. "Please. Between school and taking care of dear ol' Dad, I haven't had *any* time to write." My dad hit a rough patch a few years ago, and he's been trying to drink his way out of it. Needless to say, the strategy isn't working that well. "Can we focus on the matter at hand?" I asked.

"Which is . . . ?"

"I'm running away," I said.

Robinson's mouth fell open. By the way, unlike yours truly, he never had braces and his teeth are perfect.

"And FYI, you're coming, too," I added.

Two

"DID YOU HEAR THAT, ERNIE?" ROBINSON CALLED. I'd have told him he sounded gobsmacked, but he'd never let me forget that particular vocabulary word, either.

Of course, Ernie hadn't heard anything, not even Robinson's question. So Robinson pushed away the doughnut and stared at me like he'd never seen me before. It's not often I can surprise him, so I was enjoying this.

"Did you ever read that copy of *On the Road* I gave you?" I demanded.

Now Robinson looked sheepish. "I started it..."

I rolled my eyes. I'm forever giving Robinson books and he's forever giving me music, but since he's distractible and my iPod is dead, that's usually about as far as it gets. "Well, Sal—who's really just Jack Kerouac, the author—and his friends go all over the country, and they meet crazy people and dance in dive bars and climb mountains and bet on horse races. We're going to *do* that, Robinson. We're leaving this dump behind and taking an epic road trip. Oregon to New York City—with stops along the way, of course."

Robinson was blinking at me. *Who* are *you?* the blinks were asking.

I sat up straighter on my stool. "First we're going to see the redwoods, because those things are totally mystical. Then we'll hit San Francisco and Los Angeles. East to the Great Sand Dunes in Colorado. Then Detroit—*Motor City*, Robinson, which is so right up your alley. Then, because you're such a speed addict, we'll ride the Millennium Force at Cedar Point. It goes, like, a hundred twenty miles an hour! We'll go to Coney Island. We'll see the Temple of Dendur at the Metropolitan Museum of Art. We'll do anything and everything we want!"

I knew I sounded nuts, so I spread out the crumpled map to show him how I'd figured it all out. "Here's our route," I said. "That purple line is us."

"Us," he repeated. Clearly it was taking him a while to wrap his head around my proposition.

"*Us.* You have to come," I said. "I can't do it without you."

This was true, in more ways than I could admit to him, or even to myself.

Robinson suddenly started laughing, and it went on so long and hard I was afraid it was his way of saying *No way in hell, you totally insane person who looks like Axi but is clearly some sort of maniac.*

"If you don't come, who's going to remind me to have a doughnut with my coffee?" I went on, not ready for him to get a skeptical, sarcastic word in edgewise. "You *know* I have a terrible sense of direction. What if I get lost in LA and the Scientologists find me, and suddenly I believe in Xenu and aliens? What if I get drunk in Las Vegas and marry a stranger? Who's going to poke me in the ribs when I start quoting Shakespeare? Who's going to protect me from all that? You can't let a sixteen-year-old girl go across the country by herself. That would be, like, morally irresponsible—"

Robinson held up a hand, still chuckling. "And I may be a scalawag, but I am not *morally irresponsible.*"

Finally, the guy says something! "Does that mean you're coming?" I asked. Holding my breath.

Robinson gazed up at the ceiling. He was torturing me and he knew it. He reached for the plate and took a thoughtful bite of cruller. "Well," he said.

"Well, *what?*" I was kicking the counter again. Hard.

He ran his hand through his hair, which is dark and always a little bit shaggy, even if he's just gotten it cut. Then he turned and looked at me with his sly eyes. "Well," he said, very calmly, "hell yes."

part one

1

IT WAS 4:30 AM WHEN I WOKE UP AND PULLED my backpack out from under the bed. I'd spent the last few nights obsessively packing and unpacking and repacking it, making sure I had exactly what I needed and no more: a couple of changes of clothes, Dr. Bronner's castile soap (good for "Shave-Shampoo-Massage-Dental-Soap-Bath," says the label), and a Swiss Army knife that I'd swiped from my dad's desk drawer. A camera. And, of course, my journal, which I carry everywhere.

Oh, and more than fifteen hundred dollars in cash, because I'd been the neighborhood's best babysitter for going on five years now, and I charged accordingly.

Maybe there was a part of me that always knew I was going to split. I mean, why else didn't I blow my money on an iPad and a Vera Wang prom dress, like all the other girls in my class? I'd had that map of the US on my wall for ages, and I'd stare at it and wonder what Colorado or Utah or Michigan or Tennessee is like.

I can't believe it took me as long as it did to get up the guts to leave. After all, I'd watched my mom do it. Six months after my little sister, Carole Ann, died, Mom wiped her red-rimmed eyes and took off. Went back East where she'd grown up, and as far as I know, never looked back.

Maybe the compulsion to run away is genetic. Mom did it to escape her grief. My dad escapes with alcohol. Now I was doing it...and it felt strangely *right*. At long last. I could almost forgive Mom for splitting.

I slipped on my traveling clothes and sneakers—saying good-bye to my favorite boots—and hoisted my backpack onto my shoulder, cinching the straps tight. I was going to miss this apartment, this town, this *life*, like an ex-con misses his jail cell, which is to say: Not. At. All.

My dad was asleep on the ugly living room couch. It used to have these pretty pink flowers on it, but now they look sort of brownish orange, like even fabric plants could die of neglect in our apartment. I walked right by and slipped out the front door.

My dad gave a small snort in his sleep, but other than that, he never even stirred. In the last few years, he'd gotten pretty used to people leaving. Would it really matter if another member of the Moore family disappeared on him?

Out in the hallway, though, I paused. I thought about him waking up and shuffling into the kitchen to make coffee. He'd see how clean I'd left it, and he'd be really grateful, and maybe he'd decide to come home from work early and actually cook us a family dinner (or a what's-left-of-the-family dinner). And then he'd wait for me at the table, the way I'd waited so many nights for him, until the food got cold.

Eventually, it would dawn on him: I was gone.

A dull ache spread in my chest. I turned and went back inside.

Dad was on his back, his mouth slightly open as he

breathed, his shoes still on. I put out a hand and touched him lightly on the shoulder.

He wasn't a horrible father, after all. He paid the rent and the grocery bill, even if it was me who usually did the shopping. When we talked, which wasn't often, he asked me about school and friends. I always said everything was great, because I loved him enough to lie. He was doing the best he could, even if that best wasn't very good.

I'd written about eight hundred drafts of a good-bye note. The Pleading One: *Please try to understand, Dad, this is just something I have to do.* The Flattering One: *It's your love and concern for me, Dad, that give me the strength to make this journey.* The Literary One: *As the great Irish playwright George Bernard Shaw wrote, "Life isn't about finding yourself. Life is about creating yourself." And I want to go create myself, Dad.* The Pissy One: *Don't worry about me, I'm good at taking care of myself. After all, I've been doing it since Mom left.* In the end, though, none of them seemed right, and I'd thrown them all away.

I bent down closer. I could smell beer and sweat and Old Spice aftershave.

"Oh, Daddy," I whispered.

Maybe there was a tiny part of me that hoped he'd wake up and stop me. A small, weak part that just wanted to be a little girl again, with a family that wasn't sick and broken. But *that* sure wasn't going to happen, was it?

So I leaned in and kissed my father on the cheek. And then I left him for real.

2

ROBINSON WAS WAITING FOR ME IN THE BACK booth of the all-night diner on Klamath Avenue, two blocks from the bus station. Next to him was a backpack that looked like he'd bought it off a train-hopping hobo for a chicken and a nickel, and his face made me think of a watchdog resting with one eye open. He looked up at me through the steam rising from his coffee.

"I ordered pie," he said.

As if on cue, the waitress delivered a gooey plate of blueberry pie and two forks. "You two are up early," she said. It was still dark. Not even the birds were awake yet.

"We're vampires, actually," Robinson said. "We're just having a snack before bed." He squinted at her name tag and then smiled his big, gorgeous smile at her. "Don't tell on us, okay, Tiffany? I don't need a stake through my heart. I'm only five hundred years old—*way* too young and charming to die."

She laughed and turned to me. "Your boyfriend's a flirt," she said.

"Oh, he's not my boyfriend," I said quickly.

Robinson's response was almost as quick. "She asked me out, but I turned her down."

I kicked him under the table and he yelped. "He's lying," I told her. "It's the other way around."

"You two are a comedy act," Tiffany said. She wasn't that much older than we were, but she shook her head like we were silly kids. "You should take that show on the road."

Robinson took a big bite of pie. "Believe me, we're gonna," he said.

He shoved the plate toward me, but I shook my head. I couldn't eat. I'd managed to keep a lid on my nerves, but now I felt like jumping out of my skin. When had I ever done anything this crazy, this monumental? I never even broke my curfew.

"Hurry up with that pie," I said. "The bus to Eureka leaves in forty-five minutes."

Robinson stopped chewing and stared at me. "Pardon?"

"The *buuuuus*," I said, drawing it out. "You know, the one we're getting on? So we can get the heck out of here?"

Robinson cracked up, and I considered kicking him again, because it doesn't take a genius to tell the difference between being laughed *with* and laughed *at*. "What's so funny?"

He leaned forward and put his hands on mine. "Axi, Axi, Axi," he said, shaking his head. "This is the trip of a lifetime. We are *not* going to take it on a Greyhound bus."

"What? Who's in charge of this trip, anyway?" I demanded. "And what's so bad about a bus?"

Robinson sighed. "*Everything* is bad about a bus. But I'll give you some specifics so you'll stop looking at me with those big blue eyes. This is *our* trip, Axi, and I don't want to share it with a dude who just got out of prison or an old lady who wants to show me pictures of her grandkids." He pointed a forkful of pie at me. "Plus, the bus is basically a giant petri dish for growing superbacteria, and it takes way too long to get anywhere. Those are your two bonus reasons."

I threw up my hands. "Last I checked, we don't have a private jet, Robinson."

"Who said anything about a plane? We're going to take a car, you dope," he said. He leaned back in the booth and crossed his hands behind his head, totally smooth and nonchalant. "And I do mean *take* one."

3

"WHAT ARE YOU *DOING?*" I HISSED AS ROBINSON led us down one of the nearby side streets. His legs are about twice as long as mine, so I had to jog to keep up with him.

When we came to an intersection, I grabbed his arm and whirled him around to face me. Eye to eye. Scalawag to Ms. Straitlaced.

"Are you serious about this?" I said. "Tell me you're not serious."

He smiled. "You took care of the route. Let me take care of the ride."

"Robinson—"

He shook off my grip and slung his arm around my shoulder, big brother–style. "Now settle down, GG, and I'll give you a little lesson in vehicle selection."

"A lesson in *what?* And don't call me that." It stands for Good Girl, and it drives me absolutely nuts when he says it.

Robinson pointed to a car just ahead. "Now that, see, is a Jaguar. It's a beautiful machine. But it's an XJ6, and those things have problems with their fuel filters. You can't have your stolen car leaking gas, Axi, because it could catch on fire, and if you don't die a fiery death, well, you're definitely going to jail for grand theft auto."

We walked on a little farther, and he pointed to a green minivan. "The Dodge Grand Caravan is roomy and dependable, but we're adventurers, not soccer moms."

I decided to pretend this was all make-believe. "Okay, what about that one?" I asked.

He followed my finger and looked thoughtful. "Toyota Matrix. Yeah, definitely a good option. But I'm looking for something with a bit more flair."

By now the sun was peeking over the horizon, and the birds were up and chattering to each other. As Robinson and I walked down the leafy streets, I felt the neighborhood stirring. What if some guy stepped outside to grab the newspaper and saw us, two truants, suspiciously inspecting the neighborhood cars?

"Come on, Robinson," I said. "Let's get out of here." I was still hoping we'd make the bus. We had ten minutes left.

"I just want the perfect thing," he said.

At that moment, we saw a flash in the corner of our eyes. It was brown and fast and coming toward us. I gasped and reached out for Robinson.

He laughed and pulled me close. "Whoa, Axi, get a grip. It's only a dog."

My heart was thrumming. "Yeah, I can see that...now."

I could also now see it wasn't likely to be an attack dog, either. He was a small thing, with matted, shaggy fur. No collar, no tags. I took a step forward, my hand extended, and the dog flinched. He turned around and went right up to Robinson instead (of course) and licked his hand. Then the darn thing lay down at his feet. Robinson knelt to pet him.

"Robinson," I said, getting impatient, "Greyhound bus or stolen car, the time is now."

He didn't seem to hear me. His long, graceful hands gently tugged on the dog's ears, and the dog rolled onto his side. As Robinson scratched the dog's belly, the animal's leg twitched and his pink tongue lolled out of his little mouth in total canine ecstasy.

"You're such a good boy," Robinson said gently. "Where do you belong?"

Even though the dog couldn't answer, we knew. He was skinny and his fur was clumped with mud. There was a patch of raw bare skin on his back. This dog was no one's dog.

"I wish you could come with us," Robinson said. "But we have a long way to go, and I don't think you'd dig it."

The dog looked at him like he'd dig anything in the world as long as it involved more petting by Robinson. But when you're running away from your life and you can't take anything you don't need, a stray dog falls in the category of Not Necessary.

"Give him a little love, Axi," Robinson urged.

I bent down and dug my fingers into the dog's dirty coat the way I'd seen Robinson do, and when I ran my hand down the dog's chest, I could feel the quick flutter of his heart, the excitement of finding a home, someone to care for him.

Poor thing, I thought. Somehow, I knew exactly what he was feeling. He had no one, and he was stuck here.

But we weren't. Not anymore.

"We're leaving, little buddy. I'm sorry," I said. "We've just got to go."

It was totally weird, but for some reason that good-bye hurt almost as much as the one I'd whispered to my father.

4

WE LEFT THE DOG WITH ONE OF ROBINSON'S sticks of beef jerky, then headed to the end of the block, where Robinson pulled up short. "There it is," he whispered, with real awe in his voice. He grabbed my hand and we hurried through the intersection.

"There *what* is?" I asked, but of course he didn't answer me.

If things went on like this, we'd have to have a little talk—because I didn't want a traveling companion who paid attention to 50 percent of whatever came out of my mouth. If I wanted to be ignored, I could just stay in Klamath Falls with my idiotic classmates and my alcoholic father.

"There is the answer," Robinson said finally, sighing so big you'd have thought he just fell in love. He turned to me and bent down in an exaggerated bow, sweeping his arm out like a valet at some superfancy restaurant (the kind of place we don't have in K-Falls).

"Alexandra, milady, your chariot awaits," Robinson said with a wild grin. I rolled my eyes at him, like I always do when he does this fake-British shtick with my full name.

And then I rolled my eyes again: my so-called chariot, it turned out, was actually a *motorcycle*. A big black Harley-Davidson with whitewall tires and yards of shining chrome, and two black leather side bags decorated with silver grommets. There were tassels on the handlebars and two cushioned seats. The thing gleamed like it was straight off the showroom floor.

Robinson was beside me, whispering in some foreign language. "Twin Cam Ninety-Six V-Twin," he said, then something about "electronic throttle control and six-speed transmission" and then a bunch of other things I didn't understand.

It was an amazing bike, even I could see that, and I can hardly tell a dirt bike from a Ducati. "Awesome," I said, checking my watch. "But we *really* should keep moving."

That was when I realized Robinson was bending toward the thing with a screwdriver in his hand.

"Are you out of your *mind?*" I hissed.

But Robinson didn't answer me. Again.

He was going to *hot-wire* the thing. *Holy s—*

I ran to the other side of the street and ducked down between two cars. Adrenaline rushed through my veins and I pressed my eyes shut.

There was no way this was happening, I told myself. No way he was going to actually get the thing started, no way this was how our journey would begin.

I had it all planned out, and it looked nothing like this.

Then the roar of an engine split open the quiet morning. I opened my eyes and a second later Robinson's feet appeared, one on either side of the Harley.

We're breaking the law! I should have screamed. But my mind simply couldn't process this change in plans. I couldn't say anything at all. I just thought: *He's running away in cowboy boots! That is so not practical!* And: *Why didn't I bring mine?*

"Stand up, Axi," Robinson yelled. "Get on."

I was rooted to the spot, my chest tight with anxiety. I was going to have a heart attack right here on Cedar Street, in between a pickup and a Volvo with a MY OTHER CAR IS A BROOM bumper sticker. So much for my great escape!

But then Robinson reached down and hauled me up, and the next thing I knew I was sitting behind him on the throbbing machine with the engine revving.

"Put your arms around me," he yelled.

I was so heart-and-soul terrified that I did.

"Now hang on!"

He put the thing in gear and we took off, the engine thundering in my ears. My dad was probably going to wake up on the couch and wonder if he'd just heard the rumble of an early-summer storm.

We shot past the Safeway, past the high school football field, past the Reel M Inn Tavern, where every Friday night my dad hooked himself up to a Budweiser IV, and past the "Mexican" restaurant (where they put Parmesan cheese on top of their burritos).

Yeah, Klamath Falls. It was the kind of place that looked best in a rearview mirror.

Seeing it flash past me, feeling the rush of the wind in my face, I suddenly didn't care if we woke up the entire stinking town.

Eat my dust! I wanted to shout.

Robinson let out a joyful whoop.

We'd done it. We were free.

5

THIS WASN'T ANYTHING LIKE THE MOPED I RODE
once. It wasn't like anything I'd ever felt before. We
weren't even on the highway yet, but already it felt like we
were flying.

Then above the roar of the engine I heard Robinson's
voice. *"I don't want a tickle/'Cause I'd rather ride on my
motorsickle!"* It was an old Arlo Guthrie song. I knew the
words because my dad used to sing them to me when I was
a little girl.

*"And I don't want to diiiiie/Just want to ride on my
motorcy...cle,"* I joined in, even though I can't carry a tune
to save my life.

Robinson leisurely steered us past strip malls on the out-
skirts of town. He was whistling now (because if you ever
want to blow out your vocal cords, try singing loudly enough
to be heard over a Harley). He was acting like it was no big
deal to be zipping away on a stolen motorcycle.

My God, what in the world did we think we were doing?
We were supposed to be on a bus, and instead we were on a

stolen motorcycle that cost more than my dad made in two years. Escape was one thing, but robbery took it to another level. Suddenly I couldn't stop picturing the disappointment on my dad's face when he posted my bail, or the headline in the *Klamath Falls Herald and News*—GOOD GIRL GONE BAD—next to an unflattering mug shot that washed out my blue eyes and pale skin.

I tried not to imagine a cop around every bend as we headed south of the Klamath Falls Country Club, where my mom used to go for sloe gin fizzes on Ladies' Poker Night. And I kind of freaked out when we were actually acknowledged by another motorcycle rider, heading into town. As he passed, the biker dropped his arm down, two fingers angling toward the road, and Robinson mirrored the gesture.

"Don't take your hands off the handlebars!" I yelled. "Ever!"

"But it's the Harley wave," Robinson hollered.

"So?"

"So it's rude not to do it back!"

Of course, manners are useless when you're flat on your back in the bottom of a ditch....I didn't say that to Robinson, though, because I had to admit, Robinson was driving the motorcycle like he'd done it a thousand times before. Had he? Didn't a person need a special license to drive a motorcycle? And what about the hot-wiring? It would've taken me that long to figure out how to start the motorcycle with a key. Yeah, we had a few things to talk about, Robinson and me.

Past the Home Depot and Eddie's 90-Days-Same-as-Cash, Robinson yelled something, but the roar of the engine swallowed his voice. I think it was "Are you ready?" I didn't know what he was talking about, but whatever it was, I was probably *not* ready. Then I noticed that the speed limit went up to fifty-five, and Robinson pulled back on the throttle.

This may be obvious, but the thing about being on a motorcycle is that there is nothing between you and the world. (Or between you and the hard pavement.) The wind roars in your face. The sun shines in your eyes like a klieg light. There is no windshield. There are no seat belts. We were going sixty-five now, and the little white needle was rising. I tightened my arms around Robinson's waist.

"What are you doing?" I yelled.

Eighty, and the roar of the wind drowned out the sound of my screaming.

Ninety, and tears were streaming from my eyes. I clung to Robinson for dear life.

One hundred, and I might as well have been on a rocket ship blasting into the stratosphere.

Adrenaline coursed through us like liquid fire. We were charged. Dangerous. The motorcycle shuddered and gained even more speed, and the wind was like a giant's merciless hand trying to push me off the back of the bike.

My life flashed before my eyes—my small, sad life.

Good riddance!

The fear was electrifying. It was terrifying and amazing, and if I'd thought I was having a heart attack before, I was *definitely* having one now.

And I was totally, dizzyingly, thrillingly loving every second of it.

In those brief moments, I shed my small-town good-girl reputation like an ugly sweater, and I burned it in the flames of the Harley insignia. We were runaways. Outlaws. Me and Robinson. Robinson and me.

And if we died in a fiery crash—well, we'd die happy, wouldn't we?

6

BUT WHETHER IT WAS LUCK OR FATE OR ROBIN-
son's driving skills, we didn't die. We rode for hours along
twisting back roads, until I felt like I'd molded myself to
Robinson's back. Like I'd become some kind of giant girl-
barnacle he'd need to pry off with that screwdriver of his.

At lunchtime we finally stopped in the town of Mount
Shasta, California. It was tucked into the lower slope of a
mountain, a giant, snow-streaked peak that's supposedly
some kind of cosmic power center.

Yeah, you heard me right.

If you believe local legend, it's home to an ancient race of
superhumans called Lemurians, who live in underground tun-
nels but surface every once in a while, seven feet tall and decked
out in white robes. In other words, Mount Shasta is totally
unlike Klamath Falls, which is the world's capital of monotony
and is home to guys with names like Critter and Duke.

Also, UFOs have allegedly landed on Mount Shasta. And
that's just the tip of the bizarro iceberg.

Even the smiling attendant at the Shell station was

wearing a giant amethyst crystal around his neck and had a chakra diagram on his T-shirt.

Robinson returned the attendant's blissed-out grin, but his didn't come from Mount Shasta's cosmic power rays. It came from the Harley. He struck a pose, one hand on the gas tank, a thumb hooked in his belt loop, and offered me a goofy Hollywood sneer. "Am I James Dean or what? *Rebel Without a Cause*?"

I squinted at him. Though I would never admit it, Robinson kind of looked like he could be a movie star. Sure, he was a little on the skinny side, but that face of his? It belonged on a poster tacked to a tween girl's bedroom wall.

"James Dean died in a car crash. You know, because he was *speeding*," I said. My legs were trembling so much I could barely stand. The thundering rumble of the engine had burrowed into my bones.

"I only sped once," Robinson countered. "I had to see what this bad boy could do."

"Once was plenty," I shot back, trying to sound stern. I'd loved it, sure. Because *ohmygod* it felt like flying. But I was pretty sure that—like paragliding or jumping out of an airplane—going 110 on the back of a stolen Harley was the sort of thing you only needed to do once.

Robinson walked into the station to pay for the gas and emerged with two Vitaminwaters and a Slim Jim, which, if you ask me, is like eating a pepperoni-flavored garden hose. But Robinson had loved horrible food for as long as I'd known him.

We took a little stroll into the town center. There was a guy wearing a sandwich board that read ARE YOU SAVED? But instead of a picture of Jesus or angels, there was a drawing of a green-skinned alien holding up two fingers in a peace sign. Robinson stopped to talk to him. Of course.

I ducked into a health food store that smelled like patchouli and nutritional yeast and got some vegetables for our dinner. When I came outside, Robinson was reading a flyer that the man had given him.

"We could go on a spirit quest," he said. "Meet our Star Elders."

"No way, Scalawag," I said, snatching the pamphlet from him and tossing it into a recycling bin. "As fascinating as that sounds, I spent months planning this trip, and last I checked, communing with our so-called Star Elders was not on the to-do list."

"Well, neither was stealing a motorcycle, and look how well that turned out."

He looked pretty proud of himself for that comeback.

"Okay, fine," I acknowledged. "It's been great so far. But we can't ride a hot bike across the country. For one thing, we'll get caught. And for another, I don't think my butt can take it."

Robinson laughed. "You actually look kind of annoyed right now. Are you?"

"No," I lied. "But next time, *I* pick the ride."

"Oh, Axi—" he began.

"I don't want this trip to be a huge mistake, okay?" I interrupted. "I'm not interested in jail time."

Robinson leaned over and plucked a swirly glass orb from the sidewalk display in front of the Soul Connections gift shop. He waved it in front of my face. "By everything that is cosmic and weird and awesome, I banish all doubts from your mind." He glanced at the price tag. "Only five ninety-five. A bargain!"

He dashed into the store and a moment later reappeared with the orb nestled in a purple velvet bag. He placed it in my hands. "This is magic," he said. "It will keep you from ever being annoyed at me again."

"Don't count on it," I said drily. But I couldn't help smiling at him. "Thanks. It's really pretty."

"Axi," Robinson said, his voice softer now, "if this trip is a mistake, it's the best one we'll ever make."

And somehow, by the look he gave me then, I knew he was right.

7

BY THE TIME WE STOPPED AT A CAMPGROUND IN Humboldt Redwoods State Park, we'd been driving for seven hours. Robinson had stuck to the back roads, and I wasn't complaining. My fear of getting pulled over by cops looking for a black Harley with an Oregon plate hadn't completely disappeared, but I was thinking about it less as we got farther and farther from home.

The sun was low above the horizon when we pulled into the park, and it vanished completely as we entered the green canopy of trees. Robinson let out a low whistle as the shadows enveloped us.

Old-growth redwoods. How can I even describe them? They towered above us darkly, and they felt *alive*. Not alive like regular trees, but alive like they had souls. Like they were wise, ancient creatures, watching with only the faintest hint of interest as two road-weary teenagers walked beneath them. The air was cool and slightly damp, and the silence was profound. I felt like we were in church.

"I totally understand the whole Druid thing now," Robinson whispered.

"I think the Druids actually worshipped oak trees," I noted. "They didn't have redwoods in ancient Ireland."

"Smarty-pants," Robinson said, poking me.

I put my hand on a rough, cool trunk. "Majestic tranquillity," I said softly, seeing how the words felt in my mouth. A little too pretentious: I wouldn't be writing that down in my journal. But there were *real* writers who'd seen redwoods like these, and I could steal from them, couldn't I? " 'They are not like any trees we know, they are ambassadors from another time,' " I said.

"Huh?" said Robinson.

"John Steinbeck wrote that in *Travels with Charley.*"

He sighed. "Another one of the books you gave me—"

"That you didn't read."

Robinson used to pretend he felt guilty about ignoring the stacks of books I passed to him, but eventually he stopped bothering. "I thought I was supposed to read *East of Eden* first," he said.

"Let me know when you get to it," I said. "I won't hold my breath."

"Well, you can let me know when you listen to that Will Oldham CD I got you."

"I put it on my iPod but, as you know, it's broken," I pointed out. "Your eyeballs work just fine."

We found our campsite then, a small clearing surrounded by a ring of redwoods, with a picnic bench, a fire pit, and a spigot for cold, clear water. I unhooked my tent from the backpack. It was an army-green miracle of engineering: big enough to contain two people and their sleeping bags, it weighed less than a pound and, folded up, fit into a bag the size of a loaf of Wonder Bread. Robinson eyed it, impressed.

"Watch how I set this up," I directed. "Because tomorrow night it's your job."

"I thought it was the woman's job to keep house and the man's job to hunt for food," he said, grinning slyly.

I snorted. "Are you planning to kill an elk with your screwdriver? Good luck."

"I was thinking more along the lines of a squirrel," he said, but even that was ridiculous, because Robinson would never hurt anything. I mean, the guy had to grit his teeth to kill a mosquito.

I unpacked the veggies I'd bought, plus a hunk of aged Gouda and a bag of lavash, the thin flatbread I love and couldn't get in Klamath Falls because apparently it was too *exotic*.

"Well, well, well," Robinson said as he watched me skewer mushrooms and peppers on sticks I'd stripped of their bark. "I guess you'd do all right on *Survivor*."

I rolled my eyes at him. "I paid for this stuff, Robinson. I didn't forage for wild green peppers and cheese. Now, are you going to gather some sticks for the fire or what?"

"You couldn't buy firewood, too?" he asked, but he ambled good-naturedly into the brush to find things to burn.

Soon we had a nice fire going, and we roasted our kebabs over the flickering flames. I stuck slices of cheese between pieces of lavash, wrapped them in foil, and set them near the fire until the cheese melted. When everything was ready, we leaned against a fallen log that was covered with springy green moss, which made a surprisingly comfortable backrest. We didn't have plates, and the vegetables were a bit burned in places, but it was the best dinner I'd ever had. It tasted like freedom.

Robinson complimented my cooking, but within the hour he was raiding my backpack for junk food, claiming to be suffering from vitamin overdose.

"What else do you have in here?" he demanded. "I know you're keeping Fritos or Oreos or something terrible and delicious from me." I watched as he pulled out the map, two feather-light rain ponchos, my Dr. Bronner's, my toothbrush, and my journal.

"Open that on pain of death," I warned.

Finally Robinson held up a chocolate bar, triumphant.

"Half for you, half for me," he said.

"A *quarter* for you and a *quarter* for me," I corrected. "I'm rationing."

Robinson laughed. "You're a planner, I know. You always have everything figured out. But do you really think there's a shortage of chocolate bars on the West Coast?" He reached out and handed me a small piece of chocolate. When our fingertips touched, I twitched as if I'd been shocked. It surprised both of us.

"You're jittery all of a sudden," he said. "We're safe here, Axi. No one's going to find us." He walked over to the bike and lovingly patted its seat. "Or the hot Harley."

While Robinson fondled his new toy, I tried to calm down, breathing in that "sweeter, rarer, healthier air," as old Walt Whitman would say. Night was coming, bringing darkness and deeper silence. It seemed like in all the world, there were only the two of us.

I'd always told Robinson pretty much everything I thought about, but I couldn't tell him this: I wasn't nervous about being discovered. I was suddenly nervous about something else.

Sleeping arrangements.

INSIDE THE TENT, I UNROLLED OUR SLEEPING bags. There wasn't an inch to spare. We were going to be *thisclose* to each other, Robinson and me.

He was still outside the tent, throwing leaves into the fire and watching them curl and blacken. "Do we need to string up the packs? You know, to protect them from bears?" he called.

"There aren't any bears around here," I assured him, smoothing out my bag. It was pink camo. Hideously ugly, but it'd been on sale. "Only elk. Spotted owls. That sort of thing."

Robinson poked his head inside the tent. "Do you know that for real?" he asked. "Or are you just saying it to make yourself feel better?" He looked me right in the eyes. He knew me too well.

"I'm, like, sixty percent positive," I admitted. "Or less."

Robinson was unsurprised. "I'm stringing up the packs, then."

He ducked back out and I heard him rustling around.

He took a long time, whether because he was new to the demands of camping or because he was sneaking more of the chocolate bar... well, that could be his secret.

When he popped his head in again, he was grinning. There was a tiny spot of melted chocolate in the corner of his mouth. "Cozy in here, isn't it?"

Then he slipped off his boots and climbed all the way inside, and cozy became something of an understatement. I felt weirdly shy. Like suddenly my body was bigger and more awkward—and more *female*—than it had ever been before. I wondered if I smelled like motor oil and BO. I noticed that Robinson smelled like campfire, like soap, like *boy*.

Robinson could have had his pick of girls from our high school. Even after he dropped out (which for everyone else who'd done it was the social kiss of death), all the cheerleaders and the student council girls still wanted to take him to prom. Sometimes I pictured them hanging off his arms, like those little game pieces in Barrel of Monkeys, brightly colored and plastic.

"I'm not interested in them," he'd say. Eventually, I'd gotten up the nerve to ask: who—or what—was he interested in? He'd laughed and slung his arm around my shoulders the way he did sometimes.

"I'm interested in you, GG," he'd said lightly. As if that settled it.

But what did that mean, really? Because as far as I could tell, he wasn't interested in me in *that* way. We'd held hands a few times, like when we were in the movie theater watching *Cabin in the Woods* or *Paranormal Activity*. And once when I'd drunk three-quarters of a beer, I had kissed him, sloppily, good night.

But that was all, folks.

Now we lay side by side, staring at the tent ceiling only

three feet above our heads. I listened to the wind in the tops of the trees and the sound of Robinson's breathing, and for the first time considered what traveling together would mean in practical terms. Where was I supposed to change? What if I wanted to sleep in my underwear? What would Robinson think when he saw me in the morning, mussed and sleepy, with tousled hair and flushed cheeks and breath that could kill a small animal?

Not that that was the problem. No, the problem—or, at the very least, the Thing That Mattered—was that we would be sleeping right next to each other. Alone. Not even a stuffed teddy bear between us.

Robinson shifted, trying to make himself comfortable. No doubt he was realizing the same thing I was. I cleared my throat.

"Before you say anything," Robinson said, "here's the deal."

I could almost hear my heart doing a tiny shuffling dance.

"Stealing is—well, it's not a good thing, Axi, but it's not necessarily that bad, either. I mean, we're taking good care of the bike. And this guy's going to get it back."

That dancing ticker of mine slowed. I'd thought we were going to talk about *us*. Honestly, I was already over the stealing. *Regret is a waste of time*, my mom used to say. She'd served up that platitude a lot before she split town. Maybe it made her feel better about leaving.

"And if for some reason he doesn't get it back," Robinson went on, "his insurance covers the loss and he gets a brand-new one."

He made it sound so simple. And maybe it was. In some ways it was simpler than talking about *us*.

Robinson rolled over so he was facing me. His nose, I noticed, was sunburned. His chin was covered in faint dark stubble. I watched his Adam's apple move as he swallowed. Our eyes met, but I quickly looked away.

He reached out and brushed a piece of hair from my forehead. I held my breath.

Suddenly I understood that running away was all the thrill I could stand today. If Robinson touched any other part of me, I might explode into a million pieces.

But he didn't touch me again. He smiled. "Sweet dreams, Axi Moore," he said softly. Then he rolled back over.

Inside I ached a little, but I wasn't sure what for.

9

I STARED INTO THE DARKNESS FOR A LONG TIME, feeling the contrast between the cold, hard ground beneath me and the soft warmth of Robinson beside me. Thoughts raced through my mind endlessly: *What if Robinson and I get caught? Or if we chicken out and go back home? Or if we keep on and each night lie side by side, chaste as children? If we kiss? If we whisper the word* love, *or if it remains unsaid forever?*

It would probably only matter to me. I didn't know if it would matter to Robinson. I tentatively put my head on his shoulder, but he didn't move a muscle.

When I finally slept, I dreamed we were on the edge of a cliff, peering down. Dream-Robinson was holding my hand. "Don't worry," he said. "It only looks like a cliff. It's actually a mountain, and the way is up, not down."

Even in dreams, he was an optimist.

By the time Robinson stumbled out of the tent the next morning, looking rumpled and adorable, I'd packed our bags and plotted our route to Bolinas, a tiny town nestled between the California hills and the Pacific Ocean. I wanted to see it mostly because the town is supposed to be a secret. The people who live there are always tearing down the road signs that point to it. But that wasn't going to stop me from discovering what the big deal was about this place.

"Maybe," Robinson said teasingly as he mounted the bike, "buried deep inside the Good Girl, there's the heart of a rebel."

"Haven't I already proven that to you by suggesting this crazy trip?" I climbed up behind him and commanded, "Now, *drive.*"

Naturally, we missed our turn the first time, but when we finally got there, we were a little mystified.

"*This* is what they want to keep to themselves?" Robinson asked.

The downtown consisted of two intersecting streets. There was a restaurant called the Coast Café—which, FYI, did not overlook the coast—and an old-fashioned-looking bar. I had to agree: Bolinas didn't seem particularly inspiring.

But the adjacent beach was beautiful. We kicked our shoes off and sat down in the sand, staring at the blue water and feeling the sun on our shoulders. Tanned, half-wild children ran around us, throwing rocks at seagulls. Robinson started digging his toes in the sand, and more than once I caught him looking at me, an unreadable expression on his face.

"So... what are you thinking about?" I finally asked. I hoped he didn't detect the slight edge of apprehension in my question.

"Corn dogs," Robinson answered without missing a beat.

Sometimes I could just kill him.

He could have been thinking about me, about *us*, but instead his mind had settled on wieners encased in corn batter.

We ducked into Smiley's Schooner Saloon, and Robinson walked up to the bar like it was the counter at Ernie's. "Good afternoon, sir," he said. "Two Rainiers, please, and a corn dog."

I swear, if Robinson ever had to pick a last meal, it'd be corn dogs, French fries, and a deep-fried Twinkie.

"ID?" the bartender said.

Robinson fished out his wallet. The bartender's eyes darted from Robinson's fake license to Robinson's face and back again. "Okay . . . *Ned Dixon*." Then he turned to me.

I shrugged. "I wasn't driving, see, so I left my license back—"

The bartender crossed his meaty arms. "Listen, *kids*, how about you head across the street and get yourself a nice ice-cream cone at the café."

"Actually, I'm lactose intol—" Robinson began, but I interrupted him.

"Oh, *I* get it!" My voice came out surprisingly fierce. "We can fight in Afghanistan, but we can't have a beer and watch the sunset?" My hands gripped the edge of the bar and I leaned forward, hostility coming off me in waves. I had no idea where this was coming from, but it actually felt kind of good to be angry with someone. Someone who didn't matter, someone I would never see again.

I probably would have yelled more, but Robinson dragged me outside. Then he bent over, practically choking with laughter. "Fight in Afghanistan?" he wheezed. "Us?"

"It just came out," I said, still not sure what had just happened. I started to giggle a little, too.

Robinson wiped his eyes. "You don't even like beer."

"It was a matter of principle. A lot of people die in Afghanistan before they're allowed to buy a six-pack."

"A lot of people die every day, Axi. They don't go off

on bartenders in secret towns about the unfairness of the drinking laws. I can't wait to see what you come up with next," he said, still laughing at my outburst as he strode ahead of me.

His flip tone made me stop short in the middle of the sidewalk. Yeah, people *do* die every day. Some people, like Carole Ann, die before they even learn to tie their shoes. Others die before they graduate from high school.

Hell, either one of us could die on this crazy trip.

There were so many more important things to do than buy a beer before that happened. I hurried to catch up with Robinson, who was turning the corner to where we'd parked the motorcycle in an empty lot behind the saloon. But now there was a man in a leather jacket and chaps standing right beside it, giving it a long—and much-too-close-for-my-comfort—look.

"Nice bike," the guy said. "Got a cousin in Oregon who has one exactly like it."

My lungs felt like bellows that someone had just squeezed shut. I took a step backward. Should we just run?

But Robinson didn't flinch. "Your cousin has good taste," he said. He glanced at the bike behind Chaps. "You riding a Fat Boy these days? I love those, but my girl here likes a bigger bike." His voice had taken on an easy drawl, like he and Chaps were two dudes who'd see eye to eye over a Harley.

Chaps was still sizing Robinson up: Robinson was taller but about a hundred pounds lighter. Me, I was still thinking about running—and about how Robinson had called me his girl. That sounded...interesting. But did he mean it, or was it just part of his act?

"Happy hour's almost over, y'know," Robinson said.

Chaps gave him one long, last look, then shook his head and went inside.

I was already reaching for paper and pen.

Thanks so much for letting us ride your motorcycle, I wrote. *We took really good care of it. We named it Charley.*

Robinson read over my shoulder. "We did?"

"Just now," I said. "Charley the Harley."

I'm sorry we didn't ask you if we could borrow it, but rest assured that your bike was used only for the forces of good. Sincerely, GG & the Scalawag

I tucked the note into the handlebars. "Come on. Time to find another ride," I said, like I'd been stealing cars my whole life. In all of downtown Bolinas there were only about five cars, though.

"That one," I said, pointing to a silver Pontiac.

Robinson nodded. "Dead boring," he said. "But sensible."

I could feel the tingling beginning in my limbs. Robinson took a quick look around and then got in. I ducked into the passenger side, mentally thanking the owner for leaving the doors unlocked.

From his backpack Robinson removed a small cordless drill and aimed it at the keyhole. I watched as glittering flecks of metal fell onto the seat.

He packed a drill? I thought.

A grizzled surfer was looking right at us. I smiled and waved.

"Hurry up," I hissed at Robinson.

He produced his screwdriver and inserted it into the mangled keyhole. "One more minute."

The adrenaline tingle was growing more intense. Painful, even.

"I had to break the lock pins," Robinson explained.

As if I cared! I just wanted the engine to turn on. I sucked in a deep breath. Any moment we were going to be racing out of town, and everything would return to normal—my *new* normal, that is.

That was when two people came out of the Coast Café—and began heading toward their silver Pontiac. I met the woman's eyes, saw her jaw drop open. The man started running. "Hey," he shouted. *"Hey!"*

His arms flew forward, and he was just inches from us when the engine suddenly roared to life. Robinson slammed the car into reverse and we shot backward into the street. A moment later we were blazing out of town, going fifty in a twenty-five zone.

"I'm going to miss Charley," I said, my heart pounding.

Robinson nodded. "Me too."

"But not Bolinas," I added.

"That was *your* idea," Robinson reminded me with a smirk.

I shrugged and let out a deep sigh of relief. The sun was flashing deep vermilion over the blue ocean, calming me as I watched it slip lower and then vanish before my heart rate had even returned to normal.

Amazing how beauty can be so fleeting.

10

WE DROVE ACROSS THE GOLDEN GATE BRIDGE
that night, gliding over a dark San Francisco Bay into the
narrow streets of the Presidio. Since the car offered a solid
roof over our heads—and since cops apparently frown
on urban camping—we decided to spend the night in the
Pontiac.

I curled up in the backseat, and Robinson folded himself,
with difficulty, into the front. There was no question of us
touching (or, as the case may be, not touching) with all that
upholstery in the way. A tiny part of me felt relieved, but a
larger part of me longed for the so-cozy-it's-claustrophobic
tent.

That was my realization for the night: I was capable of missing Robinson when he was less than two feet away from me.

I was starting to develop a theory about missing things
in general. It had started when we left Charley the Harley
behind, and I hadn't stopped thinking about it the rest of the
drive. If I practiced missing small things—like the rumbling
ride of a motorcycle, or the faint murmur of my dad talking

in his sleep, or now sleeping right next to Robinson—maybe I could get used to missing things. Then, when it came time to miss something really important, maybe I could survive it.

We listened to the radio for a while, Robinson humming along and me keeping my tuneless mouth shut until we drifted off. In the morning, fog rolling in from the bay blurred the streetlights into soft orange halos. I peered over the seat at Robinson's tangled limbs.

"Rise and shine," I sang. He opened one eye and gave me the finger.

Not everyone is a morning person.

"There's someone I want you to meet," I told him.

"Now?" Robinson asked. But I simply handed him his shoes.

There was one book I'd gotten Robinson to read in the last six months. *The Winding Road* was a memoir about growing up as the daughter of an alcoholic father (I could seriously relate) and a beauty-queen mother (ditto) in a small town in southern Oregon. The author, Matthea North, could have been me, which is maybe why I found her story so fascinating. A couple of years ago, I wrote her a fan letter. She wrote me back, and an epistolary friendship—I guess you could call it that—was born.

(*Epistolary:* a word I'm not going to use in front of Robinson.)

You must stop by for a visit sometime, Matthea had written. *We'll drink tea and ponder the vagaries of love, the secrets of life, the mysteries of the universe...*

If ever there was a time for that conversation, it was now.

Matthea's house was on Nob Hill, at the top of an impossibly steep street. I rang the bell and we waited nervously on the stoop. Robinson didn't even know what we were doing here, and I refused to tell him. If you ask me, a person doesn't get enough good surprises in life. Birthday, Christ-mas...that's only two times a year to count on.

But when the front door opened, I was even more sur-prised than Robinson. Since Matthea North and I had so much in common childhood-wise, I guess I thought she'd look like an older version of me: slender, medium-sized, with the full lips and wide-set eyes of a beauty-queen mother somehow diluted into a slightly less remarkable prettiness.

Matthea looked like Bilbo Baggins. In a Gypsy costume. Under five feet tall, bedecked in scarves and necklaces, she reached up to take my hand. "You must be Axi," she said. Her green eyes, set deep in rosy cheeks, positively twinkled at me.

I swallowed. "Yes!" I said brightly. "Robinson, this is... the one and only Matthea North."

He turned toward her, smiling his wide, gorgeous grin. "Hey, you wrote that book—the one about the town even worse than ours." If he was fazed by her clothes, he didn't look it.

Matthea laughed. Older ladies love Robinson.

We followed her into the darkness of her home, and already she was chattering about how Mark Twain never said the famous line about how the coldest winter he ever spent was a summer in San Francisco, but he should have, because it was absolutely Arctic today; how birdsong had evolved over decades to compete with the sound of traffic, and weren't those sparrows outside just deafeningly loud; how she'd gotten a bad fortune in her cookie from Lucky Feng's, but did we know that it was the Japanese who'd actu-ally invented the fortune cookie?

She motioned for us to sit on a dusty-looking Victorian couch. "I loved your short story about that old deli, Axi," she said, "the one about that girl and boy who are best friends but maybe something more—"

"Oh, yeah, thanks," I said hurriedly, not wanting to cut her off but needing to.

Robinson cleared his throat. I could practically hear him thinking: *You wrote a story about Ernie's? And us?*

I ignored him. Of course I'd written about him. He was my best friend, wasn't he? The one who knew me like no other. The one I thought about approximately 75 percent of my waking hours, if not more.

"Thanks for letting us come over," I said. "I really wanted Robinson to meet you. I can't get him to finish any book, ever, but he read yours in a night."

"It gave me...insights," Robinson said, looking pointedly at me.

Matthea laughed. "Axi and I share certain background details, don't we? But Axi's much smarter than I was at her age."

"She's ornerier," Robinson said. "That's for sure."

I kicked him in the shins—lightly.

Matthea produced a pitcher of iced tea and a plate of lemon cake, and Robinson helped himself to two slices.

"So, how's the writing going, Axi?" Matthea asked.

"Um, not much at all lately," I admitted, reaching for my own slice of cake. "Please tell me there's some secret to keeping at it. Not giving up. Believing in yourself. That kind of stuff." I tried to keep the desperation out of my voice.

Matthea sighed and began to braid the fringe on her scarf. "My dear, there is no universal secret. There's only the secret each writer discovers for herself. The path forward."

I could feel my shoulders slump. Of course. There's no such thing as a magic bullet. Who doesn't know that?

"Are you aware that European kings used to have their hearts buried separately from their bodies?" Matthea asked.

"Um...no," I said, and I saw Robinson raise his eyebrows

with that slight grin I loved. Clearly, he was amused by my weirdo writing mentor.

"It was a way of offering their hearts, literally and figuratively, to their country. Forever." Matthea sighed. "Macabre practice, if you ask me. But I like it as a metaphor. You give your country—which, in this case, is your story—your heart."

"Oh," I said. "Okay." No wonder I hadn't written the Great American Novel yet. My heart was still firmly planted in my chest. Wasn't it?

"Be patient," Matthea said gently. "Keep writing, but keep dreaming, too. Remember that inspiration struck the brilliant mathematician Archimedes when he was in the bathtub."

And inspiration struck the brilliant physicist Richard Feynman when he was in a strip club, I thought. (I may be failing AP physics, but I did learn a thing or two.)

That's pretty much how the rest of the conversation went. We didn't ponder the unpredictability of love or the mysteries of the universe, but since we touched on everything from the mummified hearts of European kings to Einstein's theory that creativity was more important than knowledge, I felt like it was time well spent.

After a fourth piece of lemon cake, though, Robinson excused himself, saying he needed to get a bit of fresh air. I watched his retreating back, feeling a vague sense of unease. My body gave an involuntary shiver, and Matthea looked at me piercingly. We continued our chat, but later, as we were leaving, she put her hand on my shoulder. "Are you all right?" she asked.

For one tiny millisecond, I wanted to tell her everything. The real reason behind what Robinson and I were doing, which I hadn't even wanted to admit to myself this whole time. It didn't actually have anything to do with me escaping my boring life in Klamath Falls. But I couldn't tell her.

"I'm great," I said.

"And your friend?" She squinted toward Robinson, who was leaning against the car, staring down the hill toward the bay. He brought his arms up and almost seemed to hug himself, as if he were cold. Or as if, for a moment, he felt the need to reassure himself about something.

"He's great, too," I insisted. *Why are you lying, Axi?*

Matthea picked a yellow flower from one of the vines around her door and tucked it behind my ear. "Give your story your heart," she repeated.

It sounded reasonable enough. But when I looked at Robinson, I knew I'd already given my heart to something—to someone—else.

11

IF I DIDN'T KNOW IT WAS MEDICALLY IMPOSSI-
ble, I'd say that Robinson was born with a wrench in his
hand. Or that as a baby, he sucked on a spark plug instead
of a pacifier.

This gearhead gene was why I was taking him to Torrance, California, next—because it certainly wasn't my kind
of place. Torrance breeds NASCAR drivers and semiprofes-
sional cage fighters. (Ugh.) It has a racetrack, a giant rock 'n'
roll car show, and about five hundred stores that sell car parts.

In other words, for a guy like Robinson, it's the Promised Land. The kind of place he had to—he *deserved* to—
experience.

When we pulled into the parking lot of the Cal-Am
Speedway the following afternoon, Robinson sucked in his
breath and gave me his crooked, perfect grin.

"Axi Moore," he said, "you are greatest person I have ever
known."

"You just wait," I said, smiling back.

I steered him away from the glass atrium entrance and

toward a side door propped open with a rolled-up copy of *Car and Driver*.

Brad Sewell was waiting for us in the pit. "Alexandra," he said, stepping forward to give me a bear hug. "Long time no see, kiddo."

Robinson clearly wanted to know how this beefy dude with a Dale Earnhardt tattoo and I were acquainted. But I simply said, "Robinson, this is Brad. Brad, this is my friend Robinson."

"Nice to meet ya," Brad said. "Let me walk you through a few things, and then we'll get you in the cockpit."

It was only then that Robinson understood what he was actually here for, and he looked like he might spontaneously combust from excitement.

He turned to me. "It's like *Some Kind of Wonderful*," he whispered.

We'd watched that old movie a hundred times. One of the best scenes is when the geeky main character takes his reluctant date, one of the Beautiful People, to an art museum after hours. He can do this because he's friends with the museum guard, and because he's hung a painting of the Beautiful Girl in one of the galleries.

Today was my museum moment for Robinson, but better. I'd bribed Brad with a chunk of my savings, and I'd shamelessly pulled the "I knew you when our sisters were in the cancer ward" card.

Brad began talking gibberish to Robinson, something about "initial turn-in" and "apex of the curve" and "neutral throttle on the corner." But Robinson was nodding confidently, and then he was climbing into a flame-resistant Nomex suit, and Brad was fitting him with a radio helmet and snapping him into a five-point harness.

"Any fool can speed on the straightaway; it's the curves that make a racer," Brad said over his shoulder.

"Oh, sure," I said. Like I knew what he was talking about—I couldn't even drive to the grocery store.

Robinson revved the engine and then pulled out of the pit. He didn't go that fast at first, but he must have gotten the hang of it after a while, because the engine got louder and the car became a green blur flashing past us again and again.

"So how's your little sister?" I asked Brad.

"She's in remission. Two years now."

"That's fantastic," I said. Lizzie Sewell had been really nice to Carole Ann. Lizzie, it seems, was one of the lucky ones.

"And what about you?" Brad asked, and I pretended not to hear. Fortunately, just at that moment, the bright green car came screeching to a halt on the track outside the pit, and Robinson opened the door.

"Axi, you have *got* to get in here!" he yelled.

I looked over at Brad. I was hoping he'd tell me that the other seat belt was broken or that he was fresh out of helmets.

"There's a suit over there that'll fit you," he said.

And that's how I found myself in the passenger seat of a custom Chevy race car, outfitted like Danica Patrick and quivering with excitement.

"On your mark, get set, go!" yelled Robinson, and we peeled out onto the track, zero to sixty in about a millisecond.

The g-force slammed me against the seat, and the stunning, brain-shaking roar of the engine filled my ears. I could feel the noise as much as hear it. It vibrated in my chest and shook me deep in my guts.

I couldn't help it: in joy and terror, I screamed.

I stopped, though, because I couldn't even hear myself. And then I screamed some more.

We came toward the first curve, and I noticed the tall chain-link fence that arced inward over the track. Somehow I understood—even though I was totally incapable of higher thought, of abstract things such as words—that the fence was to keep us from splattering our body parts all over the bleachers in a crash.

The car had thick mesh netting instead of windows, so the wind came rushing in, hot and smelling like asphalt and oil. I couldn't see how fast we were going, and I didn't want to know.

We banked around the curve, the engine squealing.

As we pulled into the straightaway and Robinson hit hard on the throttle, suddenly my vision seemed to narrow. It was like looking through a tunnel. Everything on either side of me blurred and faded, and all that mattered was the airspace in front of us, and how lightning fast we were going to blast through it.

My body was singing with fear and happiness and an incredible feeling of being completely alive in the moment. I was no longer Alexandra Jane Moore—I was a supernova strapped into a bucket seat.

Go, go, go! I thought wildly. Because screaming, after all, was useless.

We took three more sound barrier–shattering laps, and when we finally slowed, I turned to Robinson with wide and no doubt crazy-looking eyes.

"Oh my God," I said, pulling off my helmet and shaking out my sweat-drenched hair. "Oh. My. God."

Robinson cackled madly. Brad came over and said, "Whaddja think?"

It took Robinson a moment to answer, probably because he had to wait for his brain to stop vibrating. Then he said, "I might have just had the best time of my life."

I started laughing like an idiot, because that was exactly what we'd come for, what I'd wanted to give him.

Carpe diem. Because today, after all, was all we knew we had.

12

"I'M STANDING ON TOM CRUISE," ROBINSON yelled. "Take my picture!"

"You're on his *star*, Scalawag," I said. But I snapped the photo anyway: dark-eyed Robinson, handsome as any movie star, dressed like a hipster lumberjack. Even in Southern California, he couldn't give up the flannel.

We were fresh off the Cal-Am racetrack, still hopped up on the experience. Hollywood was a hop, skip, and a jump up the 110 from Torrance, so that's where we went next.

Of course we had to go straight to the Walk of Fame. While Robinson ogled the street performers (buskers, hustlers, and dudes dressed like Iron Man and Captain Jack Sparrow), I dashed around taking photos of the names I knew and loved: Marilyn Monroe, Audrey Hepburn, James Dean… and, okay, Drew Barrymore and Jennifer Aniston, because it's 2013, people, and not all good movies are in black and white.

"This place is nuts," Robinson said, hopping over to Snow White's star. "Look, now I'm on top of a fairy tale."

"'I used to be Snow White, but I drifted,'" I said. Then I

cocked a hip and gave my best sultry wink—like Mae West, whose line I'd just stolen.

Then I turned, and together we walked up Highland Avenue, toward the golden Hollywood Hills and the giant, iconic white sign. Our destination: the Hollywood Hotel. Robinson didn't know it, though, because I wanted to keep surprising him. The delight on his face—the way his eyes went wide when he was taken aback—I wanted to keep seeing that for as long as I possibly could.

The fact that we would be alone together in a hotel room had nothing to do with my decision.

(Quit laughing!)

When Robinson saw me striding up to the reservation desk, he said, "Do we have enough money for this?"

I wasn't sure if we did, but it didn't matter. "My back can't take another night in the car, and I am *not* camping out with those shirtless dudes I saw in the park." (If I couldn't tell him the truth, didn't that seem like a good enough reason?)

"I thought that guy with the python looked nice," Robinson joked. "But hey, I'm down with creature comforts. Are we gonna get room service?"

I shook my head. "Nice try," I said. "Spendthrift. Profligate."

"I totally don't know what those words mean," Robinson said, "but I'm not the one who booked us the expensive hotel room."

We rode the mirrored elevator to the fifteenth floor in silence. We didn't meet each other's eyes, either in person or in our reflections. Did Robinson feel shy, the way I suddenly did? I didn't know, because I couldn't look at him.

A minute later, we opened a door onto a spacious cream-colored room, with a giant flat-screen TV, floor-to-ceiling windows, a little seating area, and one giant boat of a bed.

I felt my breath catch in my throat. Robinson and I had slept in a tent, as close together as spoons. And this bed was so stupidly huge that we could be on either side of it and not touch at all. And yet—it felt way more intimate.

I went to the sink to wash the racetrack grit from my face. In the mirror was a girl I hardly recognized. For one thing, she desperately needed a shower. For another, she looked... well, *wild* was the word that came to mind. Certainly she did not resemble a *straight arrow* or a *do-gooder,* which were the kinds of nouns I was used to.

I met her pale blue eyes and smiled faintly at her. *Who are you? What do you want?* I mouthed. But she only offered me that strange smirk.

When I came out of the bathroom, Robinson was already in bed, though it was barely after eight. He was wearing an ancient Bob Dylan T-shirt and pressing buttons on the remote. The TV was on but muted.

"Axi Moore," he said, smiling at me, the blue light from the screen flickering on his handsome face.

"Robinson," I said, barely above a whisper.

"What do you want to do now?" he asked.

I almost cracked up. That was the question to end all questions, wasn't it?

For a moment I stood there, caught between the hallway and the bed, between fear and desire. On the one hand, I wanted to sink into Robinson. Reach my fingers into his hair. Feel his lips on my neck. Hold his smooth skin close against mine.

But then I thought of the dream I'd had among the redwoods—how something could be both perfect and terrifying, both mountain and abyss. *What was the right thing to do?*

"Hey, look," Robinson said suddenly, his voice brightening. "It's *Puss in Boots.*"

Just like that, the tension in the air snapped. We loved that movie, even though it's for kids. Robinson insisted—I think seriously—that it was Antonio Banderas's best role.

So the fuzzy orange cat with the big boots and the Spanish accent banished my questions and doubts until another day. I crawled under the covers next to Robinson. The sheets were silky white and smelled like bleach. I took a deep breath, and I scooted right up against his side. Then I tipped my head onto his shoulder.

Robinson seemed to stiffen. I froze, too. My heart sank in my chest, and my eyes closed in shame. Had I read the situation so wrong? I told myself I would count to five and then pull away to the far side of the giant bed.

But then I felt Robinson's body shift. He curved toward me. And he leaned down and kissed the top of my head. Under the covers, his hand found mine. Our fingers intertwined.

That's enough, I thought. *That's all I need.*

For now.

13

OVER BREAKFAST THE NEXT MORNING, ROBINSON told me he had something to confess.

We were in Starbucks, eating microwaved Artisan Breakfast Sandwiches, which, FYI, have nothing artisanal about them. At the table next to us, a Stormtrooper and an unconvincing Michael Jackson sipped venti dark roasts before taking up their posts along the Walk of Fame.

"Spill it," I said. I felt a slight fluttering beneath my rib cage. *He's going to say he's sorry, that he should have kissed me last night.*

"I want to see where Bruce Willis lives." Robinson looked up at me from underneath his bangs, his expression only slightly sheepish.

I felt like knocking my head against the table. Why did I keep expecting some profound declaration from him? Sometimes he made me wonder if the human adolescent male was a completely different species from the human adolescent female. (Different as in significantly less evolved.)

But this was his trip as much as mine, and I wanted to be

a good sport. So after breakfast, we flagged down the nearest open-top tour van. The guide promised it would give us an *incredible* look at the stars' *jaw-dropping* homes, and a *secret window* onto their *enviable* lives.

I thought it might make me feel like a Peeping Tom, but Robinson had no such worries.

"If you don't want strangers staring at you, don't get famous," he said.

"I guess I should cancel my *American Idol* audition, then." I began to sing "I Will Always Love You"—a tough song for a good singer, and a devastating one for someone like me.

Robinson yelped and covered his ears.

Since we'd bought tickets for the Deluxe Route, we took our time on the tour, getting off one van, wandering around, and then hopping back on the next. We drove along the shopping districts of Melrose and Rodeo Drive; we passed beneath the towering palms of the Sunset Strip; we saw the La Brea Tar Pits and the Petersen Automotive Museum (which included a Hot Wheels Hall of Fame I never thought I'd pull Robinson away from).

It was late in the afternoon when we finally wound our way up into the hills.

"We're getting close, Axi," Robinson said, grinning. "Good ol' Bruce is going to invite us in to dinner."

"Sure," I said snidely. "Then we'll have dessert at Jennifer Aniston's house."

Robinson looked hurt. "Sarcasm doesn't become you, GG." But then his irrepressible smile shone again. "I bet Jen makes a wicked crème brûlée. She probably makes nice coffee, too, which is cool, because I like coffee with fancy desserts." He sounded utterly, completely sincere.

Crazy as it was, I loved this about Robinson: how he was

capable of believing in something he didn't *actually* believe in. Does that make sense? He knew what he wanted to be true, what he felt should be true, and for a certain amount of time, by the power of his will (or his humor, or his stupid, boyish hope), it was true.

Believing in believing. Robinson was exceptional at that.

"On the left you will see the house formerly owned by Arnold Schwarzenegger," the tour guide called, interrupting my thoughts about Robinson and, no doubt, Robinson's thoughts about dessert.

Robinson leaned in close to me and whispered Arnold's most famous line: " 'I'll be back.' "

" 'Come with me if you want to live,' " I hissed—an Arnold quote from *Terminator 2*.

"Wait, I've got one—" He slapped his forehead, unable to recall it.

" 'Hasta la vista, baby' ?" I asked, smiling smugly.

"Gaah, it was on the tip of my tongue!" Robinson reached out and tickled me in the ribs, which made me squeal.

The tour guide kept talking, but we'd stopped listening. We drove through lush green neighborhoods, peering past iron gates and elaborate landscaping to catch glimpses of enormous mansions. The air smelled like roses . . . and money.

The driver slowed down around a particularly steep curve and then stopped to let a group of cyclists pass.

I grabbed Robinson's hand. "Let's split."

He turned to me, uncomprehending.

"Over the side," I whispered. And because he still didn't seem to get it, I showed him. I swung a leg over the edge of the open-top van and dropped down to the street.

If the other passengers noticed, they didn't say anything. A second later, Robinson landed beside me, looking utterly baffled. The van started up again and pulled away.

"So what's the brilliant plan now, Axi?" Robinson's hands were on his hips. "We don't know where Bruce Willis lives, and we're probably ten miles from our hotel."

I only smiled. "Follow me," I said. And I led him toward what I'd seen: a FOR SALE sign and a gate left open.

"Oh, duuuude," Robinson whispered, sounding suddenly like a K-Falls cretin. "Really?"

I looked up and down the street. Except for a lone gardener, whose back was to us, it was utterly deserted. We crept up the driveway, then alongside the vacant house to the back gardens. Whoever had lived in this ornate Mediterranean (estimated asking price: a cool five to ten mil) was gone, but the pool was still full, its water glassy and aquamarine blue.

The sun was on its way down and the sky was the color of persimmons. Robinson turned to me. "GG...," he began.

I threw my arms out and spun around. "If *this* hasn't proven to you I'm not a GG anymore," I asked, "what will?"

Robinson didn't say anything, but I already had an idea.

In one fluid motion, I stripped down to my underwear, tossed my clothes in a heap, and dove into the pool. I swam all the way to the bottom before rocketing back up in a cascade of glittering water droplets.

"Come in if you dare," I called to Robinson. *"Scalawag."*

He hesitated for a moment, but Robinson could never back down from a challenge. He took off his shirt, revealing his broad, pale chest, his flat stomach, and the low V of muscle there. I'd never seen that much of his skin before, and the ivory smoothness of it was startling.

Seeing him on the lip of the pool, naked now but for his boxers, I thought of Michelangelo's *David*. Not because Robinson had a perfect *David*-like body (though it was very nice) but because he had that combination of power and vulnerability that Michelangelo had given his sculpture. See, Michelangelo didn't show David triumphant, the way every other sculptor did. He showed David before he fought Goliath—when David believed he was doomed and went into battle anyway.

Robinson reached up to plug his nose, and he no longer looked remotely like a Renaissance hero. "Cannonball," he yelled on the way down. He came up spluttering. "Oh my God, it's cold!"

I laughed. "You mean invigorating," I said. "Revitalizing."

Robinson rolled his eyes at me. "Nerd. I can still call you *word nerd*, can't I?" Then he swam toward me, smiling, and he put his hands on my shoulders. Suddenly I was sure he was going to kiss me. He was so close, and his fingers were on my skin, and there was nothing—*nothing*—but water between us (and some flimsy, soaking-wet clothes).

He moved forward another step, and then he stopped. He opened his mouth like he was going to say something. But then he vanished under the water. The next thing I knew, he was picking me up and tossing me backward into the deep end, and I was squealing, gasping, laughing, and he was saying, "Shhh, shhh, we don't want the cops to come."

We swam as evening fell and distant lights from the inhabited houses flickered on through the trees. I looked over at Robinson, who was floating on his back in the shallow end, and I wondered what it would be like to live in one of these castles.

I'd have everything money could buy, but it wouldn't be the same as having everything I wanted. Not even close.

14

WE WERE LUCKY THAT NIGHT. NOT ONLY DID WE get away with trespassing, we got a ride home. The gardener from across the street had seen us emerge, wet and shivering, from the gate, and offered to drive us back to town.

"*Estás invadiendo*," he said, smiling. "*¿Si?*"

Robinson nodded. "*Si*," he said. "*Somos traviesos.*" He turned to me. "That means 'we're naughty.'"

I was pressed up against his side in the front seat of the truck, trying to find the warmth of him through our damp layers of clothes. "See? You totally can't call me GG anymore," I said sleepily.

"Maybe BG," he suggested. "For Bad Girl."

My eyelids were so heavy, and then they were closing. "Or MB. Mixed Bag...," I murmured.

And honestly, that was the last thing I remember. I must have fallen asleep in the truck, and Robinson must have carried me up to the room and laid me down on our shared bed. Maybe he fluffed up the pillows for me, and maybe he even kissed me. But if he did, I'll never know.

I woke several hours later to find him staring at me.

"Before we leave, we should actually see a *star*," he said. "Not just a pink symbol on a sidewalk, or the house where one lives."

I burrowed under the covers. "Why can't we just turn on the TV? There're plenty of them there."

"We need to see one in real life," he insisted.

But this isn't real life, the old Axi Moore insisted. *This is a crazy adventure. And as great as it is, it can't last.*

Of course, as both the old and the new Axi well knew, real life didn't necessarily last, either.

I peeked my head out from the blankets, then ducked it back under again. Robinson was at the end of the bed, and he suddenly yanked the covers off me. I tried to grab them, but he was too strong. "Did you bring a nice dress?" he asked, raising one dark eyebrow at me.

I scoffed. "Runaways tend not to pack formal wear."

"Well, put on whatever you've got, because we're hitting the red carpet."

I assumed Robinson was pulling my leg, but I rose and took a quick shower, then put on the Forever 21 wrap dress I'd packed just in case. I put on a little mascara, too, and a dab of lipstick.

His eyes lit up when he saw me emerge from the bathroom. "You clean up good, Axi Moore," he said. Robinson did, too. In a slightly rumpled oxford and a clean pair of jeans, he looked like an ad for Levi's 501s.

He led me down the hall and out to the street, where we hopped into a cab. "Now it's my turn to surprise you," he said. And then he held his hand over my eyes until we pulled up in front of the Hammer Museum. "Ta-da!" he said.

Ahead of us snaked a long line of black limos. There was red carpet laid over the sidewalk, and a bunch of people milling around, and a giant banner that said CHILDREN'S HOSPITAL LOS ANGELES ANNIVERSARY GALA.

I saw the word *hospital* and my stomach suddenly felt like it was full of stones. "What is this?" I asked.

"A benefit," Robinson said brightly. "A party. Major star power, because as you can imagine, no one in Hollywood wants to be accused of not helping sick kids." He climbed from the cab and held out his hand. "Come on, let's go inside."

"*You* are a sick kid, Robinson," I said. "Mentally, I mean. They don't just let randoms crash the red carpet."

"But we're not randoms, as you so ungenerously characterize us. We are Axi and Robinson, the G-rated Bonnie and Clyde." He lifted me into the sunshine and smiled his dazzling smile. "If we don't belong here, who does?"

What could I do but laugh? "I think stealing a Harley ought to at least earn us a PG," I said.

"I'm in complete agreement," Robinson said. Then he held up a finger, signaling me to wait. "As the kids say, BRB."

He walked up to the nearest gatekeeper, a middle-aged woman dressed all in black. I watched as men in suits and women in jewel-colored cocktail dresses filed past her through the doors. The gatekeeper was trying to ignore Robinson, but I knew she wouldn't last. When Robinson turned on the charm ray, few could withstand it.

Sure enough, a moment later, she nodded and beckoned me over. As I approached, she looked at me with . . . concern, or maybe even pity. I shivered under her gaze. What exactly had Robinson told her? "You two go in over there," she whispered, and pointed toward a side entrance.

And then we were inside, and there were famous people *everywhere*. I saw Matt Damon talking to Mark Wahlberg by a potted fern, and Tina Fey posing in front of a giant stand of paparazzi. Camera flashes popped like fireworks, and in a matter of seconds, I was no longer worrying about what Robinson had said to the gatekeeper. All around us were bona fide superstars, talking and laughing and guzzling free drinks, just like regular people.

"I'm seeing a lot of excellent facial work," Robinson noted. Somehow he'd gotten his hands on a flute of champagne.

"'I love Los Angeles. I love Hollywood. They're beautiful. Everybody's plastic, but I love plastic,'" I said.

"Huh?"

"Andy Warhol said that."

Robinson held out his arm, and I tucked my hand in the crook of it, as if we were on our way to prom. He leaned in close, and I could feel his breath in my hair. "I told you we'd get in, didn't I?"

"And you were right," I said.

"Which makes you...?" He waited, an expectant smile teasing the corner of his mouth.

I sighed. "Wrong."

He laughed and pulled me close. "Axi admits fallibility," he said. "I'm going to treasure this moment forever."

My cheek pressed against his shirt, I smiled up at him. I would, too, I thought, but for a wholly different reason. Just days earlier we were in Klamath Falls, and now we were on the red carpet. What couldn't we do, as long as we were together?

15

THERE IS A LIMIT TO THE SUCCESS OF ANY partnership—and we discovered ours later that evening, when Robinson decided it was time to teach me to drive.

I said, "Robinson, I can't learn how to drive in a stolen car."

He shrugged. "It's just like any other car. Gas pedal on the right, brake on the left. Four gears forward, one reverse."

He was always so confident. But maybe that was because everything came easily to him: he could hot-wire a Harley, sweet-talk just about anyone, and play whatever musical instrument he was given. His free-throw percentage was ridiculous, and no matter where he was, he could always find true north.

Me, I was not so sure of myself. About anything. "I don't know how I feel about this," I said softly.

Robinson reclined the passenger seat and pretended to close his eyes. "I feel good enough for the both of us. Time for me to relax and enjoy riding shotgun."

I clenched my hands on the steering wheel. *You can do*

this, Axi, I told myself. *You've played Grand Prix Legends!* Then came the other voice: *Yeah, and you sucked at it. You always crashed right out of the starting gate.*

"Ready?" Robinson asked.

I nodded, even though I wasn't. Robinson had to lean over and start the car, because I didn't know how to work the screwdriver.

"Okay. So check your mirrors and see if it's clear. Then you're going to step on the brake and shift into drive." He made it sound so easy, like I wasn't behind the wheel of a two-ton death machine.

I must have said this out loud, because Robinson said, "That is a *slight* exaggeration. We're in an empty parking lot, Axi. How much damage can you do?"

"I don't know," I said grimly. "We'll see."

For a second I thought of my physics class, the one I'd skipped the day I met Robinson at Ernie's dusty old counter. *A body at rest will remain at rest unless an outside force acts on it.* That's Newton's First Law. In other words, I was totally safe—until I stepped on the gas.

But I took a deep breath and somehow successfully shifted gears. When the car didn't explode, I forced myself to lightly press the gas pedal. The car moved forward. Slowly. Jerkily. But it moved. "Oh my God, I'm driving," I said.

Robinson grinned. "And the prize for stating the obvious goes to...Alexandra Moore!"

"Shut up," I squealed.

Robinson laughed. "Sorry—I couldn't resist. You're normally a much more subtle thinker."

"I hate you," I said, but I was laughing, too.

I was going twenty miles an hour and it felt like flying. I was also quickly nearing the edge of the parking lot. "What do I do now?"

"Why don't you try turning," Robinson suggested. "So we don't, I don't know, go barreling into traffic?"

I slammed my foot on the brake and whirled to face him. Sure, I'd had a good thirty seconds of decent driving, but some things just weren't funny yet. "This is hard for me, you know!" I yelled.

Robinson reached over and put his hand on my arm. It was…calming. "Axi," he said gently, "is it really hard for you? Think about it before you answer."

I frowned. It was scary, yes. Unfamiliar. But hard? Well, not really. It was like Robinson said: gas pedal on the right, brake on the left. Four gears forward, one reverse.

All I needed to do was move forward.

It was almost as if Robinson could see the fear leaving my body. He gave my arm a squeeze. "See?" he said. "You get it. You're going to be fine."

And I was fine. I drove around the parking lot for almost an hour while Robinson, the human karaoke machine, sang driving songs: "On the Road Again," "I Get Around," and "Mustang Sally." I practiced turning, accelerating, and even parallel parking.

Finally Robinson said, "I think you're ready for the street."

I said, "I think I'm ready for you to stop singing."

"Deal."

So at the edge of the lot, I looked both ways—and then I pulled into traffic.

"Pedal to the metal, Axi!" Robinson said.

I was giddy, thrilled, scared. I was behind the wheel of a car, in fantastic Los Angeles, with the boy who was possibly the love of my life sitting next to me.

"Whoa, you cut that guy off there," Robinson said.

"I did?"

"Don't drive like you own the road; drive like you own the car."

"That's funny," I said, checking my mirrors and accelerating, "because I don't own it, and neither do you."

"If I can just get off of this LA freeway/Without getting killed or caught," Robinson sang—it was some old country song.

Wasn't he supposed to not sing? "It's not a freeway," I pointed out.

And it was a good thing it wasn't, because what happened next would have been a lot worse.

The other part of Newton's First Law? *A body in motion will remain in motion, unless acted upon by an outside force.*

In this case, the outside force was a parking meter.

I don't know how it happened. One minute everything was fine, and the next minute we were at a dead stop and blood was pouring out of my nose.

16

DIZZY AND OVERWHELMED, I STARED OUT THE window with a T-shirt held to my face as Robinson hurried us onto the 10. He'd handed me the shirt as he slid into the driver's seat. We had to leave the scene quickly—there were witnesses.

"You're okay, right?" he asked.

"I think so." My voice came out very small. I wasn't worried about my nose—I was worried about having smashed up a stolen car.

"Don't worry," Robinson assured me. "The LAPD's got way bigger fish to fry."

But his voice sounded sort of shaky. As if maybe he didn't have any idea what he was talking about. And he kept glancing in the rearview mirror, like he was watching for flashing lights.

"I'm sorry," I whispered. But I don't think he heard me.

His eyes darted from road to mirror and back again. "Well, Axi, in the immortal words of Dale Earnhardt Senior, 'You win some, you lose some, you wreck some,'" he said.

"Every path has its puddle, you know? Nothing ventured, nothing gained! You can't make an omelet without breaking some eggs. And who wants to live in a world without omelets? Besides chickens, of course. I mean, I'm sure they'd be totally fine with it, ecstatic, really—"

"Robinson, you're babbling," I said.

"What?" He turned to me, his eyes flashing.

I took the shirt away from my face and felt a trickle of blood make its way down my lip. It tasted like salt. "You're babbling," I said. "Are you freaking out?"

His eyes widened. "Who, me? No! I'm not freaking out. Nope, no way! Not me."

"The fellow doth protest too much, methinks," I said, feeling suddenly woozier. Robinson was usually so calm; seeing him flustered definitely didn't make the situation better.

Robinson said, "Huh?"

"A slight modification of a *Hamlet* quote," I said weakly. I realized I was tapping my feet really quickly on the floor— almost like I was trying to run away inside the car.

"Are you speaking English?" he demanded. "Like, even now?"

I clenched my hands. It was my first real moment of doubt. Deep, profound doubt. As in: What were we *doing?* Was this whole trip the worst idea I'd ever had in my life?

I guess I must have said that out loud, too, because Robinson almost instantly calmed down. He took a long, deep breath, then leaned over and squeezed my knee. "We had a little adventure, and now it's time to be moving on," he said gently. "This trip is a brilliant idea, Axi. The best."

"Are you sure?" I asked. "Are we about to get caught?"

"No," Robinson said, this time sounding certain. "We're fine. Although we're missing a headlight and you have blood on your chin, which looks weird. Like maybe you're a vampire or something. But seriously. We're fine. We're better than fine. We're invincible. What's next on our itinerary?"

I couldn't believe how fast his mood had changed. But if Robinson felt confident again, I would try to, too. Because if I didn't trust him, what was I doing driving across the country with him?

"Well… Vegas, actually," I said. Yes, we were in over our heads—I understood that. But maybe things would still work out for us.

Robinson pounded the steering wheel. "Vegas, baby, here we come!"

I could hear the happiness in his voice. Part of me wanted to shake him, and the other part adored him for his unfailing optimism. How many times had I been in the pits of despair, only to have Robinson reach down and haul me up into the sunlight? More than I cared to remember.

"It's all your fault, you know," I said, dabbing at my nose and chin.

He snorted. "I'm not the one who crashed."

"But you're the one who tried to teach me to drive."

"It's a life skill, Axi. I'm not going to be able to chauffeur you around forever." He turned to smile at me then. Maybe it was a trick of the light, but it seemed there was a new glimmer of melancholy behind his smile.

"Yes, you are," I said softly. But Robinson didn't reply.

17

WE DROVE ON THROUGH THE NIGHT. THE DARK shapes of the Los Angeles hills gave way to flat nothingness, and then, after a few hours, an orange glow blossomed in the sky. It grew steadily brighter, and when the highway began its gentle slope downward, suddenly a vast ocean of glittering lights stretched out below us.

"*Oooh, Las Vegas ain't no place for a poor boy like me,*" Robinson sang. Then he turned to me. "That's Gram Parsons," he said. "Did you listen to that album I gave you?"

I hunched down in my seat, shaking my head minutely.

Robinson laughed. "Doesn't matter. I can sing the whole damn thing for you."

"And you probably will," I said.

Humming, he drove us down the Strip, which was lit up like Christmas times a million. It was as bright as day on the street, even though it was after midnight. We passed signs for the Bellagio, Bally's, the MGM Grand—casinos I knew from *Ocean's Eleven* set in a landscape I knew from Hunter S. Thompson's *Fear and Loathing in Las Vegas*.

"So we have to gamble, right?" Robinson asked.

I nodded, suddenly resolute. "I believe it's required."

I cleaned myself up in a 7-Eleven bathroom while Robinson ate his ten thousandth Slim Jim. Then we went to the Luxor, mostly because it was shaped like a pyramid. It even had a giant Sphinx out front—an absurdity we just couldn't resist.

The moment we stepped inside, we were in yet another world. The sound of pinging slot machines, the smells of air-conditioning and sweat, the flashing lights above the pits: it was total sensory overload.

Robinson put his arm around my shoulders. "You want to win big?" he asked.

"Yeah, we've got twenty bucks to blow."

"Is that what your budget tells you? Well, that's two games of blackjack with a ten-dollar buy-in." He grinned. "That's assuming we don't win, which we will."

"Twenty dollars'll last longer at the slots," I said, because sitting in a semicircle with a bunch of strangers and trying to decide whether to tell the dealer to "hit me" was more than I was up for.

Robinson eyed the blackjack table longingly. He probably thought he could charm the cards into falling the way he wanted them to. Not me. Maybe I wasn't GG anymore, but I'd never be the gambling type. Because it was my baby-sitting money we were talking about, and I'd wrangled some serious brats to earn it.

Maybe it was just as well that a burly guy in a black vest came up to us as we headed for the slot machines. He wanted to see our IDs.

"Well, you see—" Robinson began.

The guy cut him off. "Save it. If you got an ID, you can play. If you don't, scram."

"Go on," I said to Robinson. "Now you can play a hand of cards. I'll wait outside."

He shook his head. "No way, Axi, we're in this together."

I liked the sound of that a lot. "Okay, what do you want to do now?"

Robinson yawned so deeply I decided not to wait for an answer. I said, "Let's go find a place to sleep."

So we pulled into the nearby parking lot of Treasures, which at first I thought was a gift shop. "Why's it open so late? Who needs a snow globe at two AM?"

Robinson laughed—*at* me, not with me. "It's a strip club, you dope. This is Sin City, remember?"

I was too tired to take offense. I settled down in the backseat and pulled my sweatshirt over me. Robinson snaked his hand around his seat in the front, and I reached out and took it. Here we were in the car again, three feet of air and eight inches of foam between us. *Why* hadn't I made a move at the hotel?

"Tell me a bedtime story," Robinson said.

"Sing me a bedtime song," I retorted.

"Flip a coin," he said.

I agreed, and he lost. So I fell asleep to Robinson singing, drumming lightly on the dashboard.

> *There was a girl named Axi*
> *who was a runaway.*
> *Instead of taking a taxi*
> *she tried to drive around LA.*
> *She crashed her car and hurt her nose*
> *and I don't mean to brag*
> *but who should rescue Axi*
> *but a charming scalawag?*

It was a pretty good lullaby, all in all.

* * *

The sound of ringing laughter woke me at 4 AM. A handful of dancers were leaving the club, done with their shift for the night.

One passed by the car and spied me in the backseat. "Hey, girl," she said, leaning in so close I could smell perfume and sweat. "You can't sleep here. They'll tow your car and take you and your friend here to the pound."

Robinson sat up, rubbing his eyes. "Huh?"

"Y'all need to be getting on home," said another. I could hear her smacking her gum. "Wherever that is."

Robinson leaned out the window and smiled at them like they were long-lost friends. "That is excellent advice," he said. "And I thank you for giving it. But unfortunately it is not possible for us to follow it at this time."

The women burst into laughter. One nudged the other with her bony hip. "Look at them! They're as cute as kittens. Chrissy, you take 'em home with you."

The blond one called Chrissy looked us over. She spent an especially long time looking at Robinson. "My car's the white Chevy over there," she said finally. "Y'all follow me out."

18

SUFFICE IT TO SAY THAT I DID NOT WANT TO GO.
What if Chrissy was an ax murderer?

But Robinson said that for one, the chances of that were
very slim; and for two, being killed with an ax was con-
ceivably more appealing than spending another night with
the emergency brake poking into his side. So we followed
Chrissy toward the old Las Vegas Strip (the place they used
to call Glitter Gulch) and into a modest apartment complex.

"Here we go," she said, pointing toward a sagging red couch
in the middle of a dingy living room. Neon lights from the signs
outside reflected on the bare walls. "You sleep in there, and your
boyfriend can have the floor in the kids' room. It's carpeted."

"He's not my boyfriend," I said, out of habit. I could see
Robinson getting ready to deliver his line—*She asked me out,
but I turned her down*—so I quickly added, "He's not my type."

Chrissy raised one thin, painted eyebrow. "Oh yeah?
'Cause looks to me like he'd be everyone's type."

Robinson, who seemed ready to fall over from exhaustion,
made a show of kissing his biceps. He was such a beautiful
goof—of *course* he was my type.

"Dork," I said.

"Nerd," he retorted.

Chrissy cackled. "God, you two are seriously the cutest things ever. If you aren't together, I don't know what your problem is."

Then she handed Robinson a pile of blankets and shoved him toward the door of a bedroom. "The kid on the left snores," she said. "Fair warning."

She gave me one last tired, vaguely maternal smile and disappeared into her bedroom. I lay on the soft couch and thought about what she'd said: that if Robinson and I weren't together, she didn't know what was wrong with us.

I didn't know, either. I mean, there was plenty wrong with us. But was that the thing keeping us apart?

I couldn't sleep, thinking about it. About him. Close to dawn, I tiptoed into the room where he was sleeping. He lay on his side, his hand tucked under his cheek. I watched him for a long time, counting his slow breaths and imagining I could hear the strong beat of his heart.

It sounded ridiculous even to me, but I couldn't stand not being near Robinson—especially now that I'd gotten to spend every night with him since we started this totally-insane-but-also-the-best-thing-ever trip. He made me feel the kind of joy I hadn't felt since I was a kid and my family was whole. And he also made me feel...a kind of rush I'd never felt before in my life.

How could I ever go back to being by myself—being without him—now that I knew these feelings were possible?

Before I knew what I was doing, I crept forward and lay down beside him, matching my breathing to his. Whether or not he wanted me the same way I wanted him, we were in this together—that was what Robinson had said. It had never occurred to me before what a complicated word *together* was.

19

I WOKE UP GASPING. THERE WAS A WEIGHT ON my chest, crushing my heart, squeezing the air from my lungs. *So this is it*, I thought, *this is what it feels like to die.*

Next: *Oh my God, I haven't kissed Robinson yet. Except for that one time, ages ago, when I had that beer, which didn't even count...*

I clawed at the covers, my lungs screaming. My desperate fingers felt something hard and round—a small, bony knee.

There was a shriek, a high giggle, and suddenly the weight was gone. I sat up, dazed and blinking. There was a boy on the floor, gazing up at me with giant green eyes.

"My name is Mason Drew Boseman," he said pertly. "I'm four."

"You must weigh fifty pounds," I gasped, rubbing my sternum, where he'd just been sitting.

Then a small girl wandered in, clutching a dirty stuffed bunny. "That's Lila," Mason said. "She's two and she doesn't know how to use the potty."

"I'm...Bonnie," I said, my breath finally returning to normal. "Nice to meet you both."

Mason ducked his head, suddenly shy, like he hadn't just nearly killed me. Lila simply stared, then slowly brought her thumb up to her mouth and began to suck.

"Maybe I'll get up now," I said, untangling myself from the clean but ratty blanket. Still they stared.

I walked into the kitchen, following the smell of coffee. "Morning—" I began to say.

But I stopped. Because Chrissy, who was barefoot and in a silky red nightgown, had Robinson pressed up against the counter—and she was kissing him.

And it looked for all the world like he was kissing her back.

I turned around and stood shaking in the hall. Had I really just seen that? Was there a chance I was still dreaming? Mason looked up at me questioningly.

I counted to twenty, then coughed and tried to make it sound like I was coming down the hall to the kitchen. I heard the shuffling of feet, the screech of chair legs against linoleum.

This time when I rounded the corner, Robinson was at the kitchen table, reading the paper like he was the man of the house. "Morning, sunshine," he said, pushing a mug of steaming coffee toward me. He needed a shave, and there was a smudge of dirt on his cheek.

"He changed my oil, can you believe that?" Chrissy asked me. Her cheeks were flushed.

"That's not a metaphor for something, is it?" I asked, looking pointedly at Robinson.

He chose to ignore the question. "I woke up early. Thought I'd do a friend a favor."

That was Robinson. He never missed an opportunity to

help someone out. Apparently, he also never missed a chance to kiss someone—unless that person was me.

Chrissy had hopped up onto the counter, and she was looking at him like she was ready to ask him to move in. She might have two kids, but she was probably only a few years older than we were.

Mason tugged at my leg. "Did you know that dead squirrels can eat you? They have very sharp teeth. Dead squirrels are cool. Also dinosaurs are cool, and Batman, but Spider-Man is better because he got bitten by a spider." Mason began hopping up and down, narrowly missing my foot. "Superman can go into space because he can fly, but not Spider-Man because he needs a web and he can't shoot it in space because there's no buildings up there." His hopping had progressed to a wild bouncing.

Chrissy giggled. "I swear I don't give him coffee."

"He's charming," I said—through gritted teeth.

"I'm not charming. I'm starving!" Mason said.

I took a step forward. "Will you let me cook breakfast?" I asked. "So you can relax?"

Chrissy looked at me in surprise. "Uh...okay."

"You took us in—it's the least I can do." The fact was, I didn't know what to do with my hands, and cooking would calm me down. So I made omelets for everyone, with cheddar cheese and snippets of chives from a pot that Chrissy kept on her windowsill. I thought about undercooking her omelet and putting bits of eggshell in it, but I reminded myself that she wasn't really the wrongdoer. I'd told her Robinson wasn't my boyfriend, so as far as she knew, he was available.

Not that I totally forgave her.

"Wow, I lucked out bringing you two home," Chrissy said, her mouth full of eggs. "This is the best omelet I've ever had."

"I've made a lot of them," I said. "I'm no gourmet or anything."

Robinson pointed his fork at me. "Not true. She can cook anything. She'll make someone a good little wife someday."

"Watch it," I warned.

"It's a compliment," Robinson insisted.

"I didn't take it as one," I said.

"You guys bicker like a brother and sister," Chrissy said, giggling. Then she looked serious again. "Do your parents know where you are?"

I turned back to the stove. "We plead the Fifth."

"We're on vacation," Robinson said.

Chrissy sighed and leaned back in her folding chair. "Okay," she said, "I won't pry. Everyone's entitled to their secrets. But here's a piece of advice: get out of Las Vegas, okay? Because you come here and you just get stuck."

She gazed toward the window then, the one that looked out over the Neon Boneyard, where old signs go to die. Something told me that getting stuck was exactly what had happened to her.

I looked at Robinson, who was dumping sugar into his coffee. We'd never get stuck anywhere, not even if we wanted to. There was an undeniable reason for that—but it was one of our secrets.

20

"I DON'T WANT TO TALK ABOUT IT."

So said Robinson when I asked him what he was doing tonsil-diving with a Las Vegas stripper at nine o'clock in the morning. (As if it would have been just fine later in the day.)

"Well, I want to talk about it," I said. I had dragged him and our few belongings outside as soon as breakfast was over, trying to avoid giving Chrissy a chance to ask us to stay.

Robinson looked at me for a moment, his expression unreadable, and then he turned and walked away. He wound through the cars parked near the Neon Museum, shaking his head and seemingly talking to himself.

I felt so helpless. Was I crazy? Had I imagined the romantic tension between us? What if Robinson had never wanted anything from me but my friendship? If that turned out to be true, then it was too bad Chrissy wasn't actually an ax murderer—because I was going to die a long, slow death of humiliation.

I wiped a bead of sweat from my lip. It was 10 AM and already hot. I sat down on the toe of a giant metal high-heeled shoe, which used to be part of the sign for the Silver Slipper Saloon.

I *hated* Las Vegas.

"What are you doing?" I finally called to Robinson.

He didn't answer—he was still pacing. I wasn't about to follow him up and down the street, so I stared at all the dead signs. There was one that said WEDDING CHAPEL and another right next to it that said SIN.

I thought about all the people who had come to Vegas looking for love or money, and what a minuscule percentage of them must have actually found it.

Robinson appeared at my side, and even though he was finally saying something, it wasn't anything I was interested in. I'd listen when he explained the kitchen kissing. In the meantime, I'd keep looking at the signs: GOLDEN NUGGET, JOE'S LONGHORN CASINO . . .

Then Robinson grabbed my arm and turned me toward him. He said, "The thing about a Boxster is, it eats tires. Especially if you dump your clutch. But since we aren't in this for long-term ownership . . ."

I scrutinized the shoe's peeling paint. "I don't know what you're talking about."

Robinson sighed, exasperated. "I'm talking about a Porsche, Axi, because we're taking one." He pointed to a low black shape a hundred yards off. "It's an older model, so it won't have a tracking system. Hard to steal cars that send out little beacons to the LVPD, you know?"

Finally I looked at him. "We have a car already."

"I'm sick of it," Robinson said. "We need a better one." He kicked at the tip of the shoe.

"I don't want to steal another car," I said.

"Oh, my beloved Aximoron—*you* don't have to," he said. He flashed me his beautiful grin, then bounded away.

I clenched my fists and stared up at the white desert sky. Robinson was crazy—*He kisses some girl and then calls me his beloved? What gives?*

There was a screech of tires as Robinson pulled up in front of me. "Get in," he ordered.

If I didn't, would he drive off without me? Honestly, he looked like he might. It was times like these when Robinson seemed like the bad boy my father always claimed he was.

I barely had my seat belt on before Robinson gunned the engine and peeled out into the street. He was going sixty-five before I even blinked.

"That's what I meant by dumping the clutch," he said calmly. "In case you wondered."

I stared out the window, refusing to look at him. "I didn't," I said.

We were heading out of town, leaving the glittering lights and broken promises of Las Vegas behind us. Quickly.

"Slow down," I told him.

Robinson only laughed. "Speed never killed anyone! It's suddenly becoming stationary...that's what gets you."

I crossed my arms. "Yeah, if a thousand other things don't get you first," I huffed.

But it was Robinson's turn to ignore me. He began to whistle Bruce Springsteen's "Born to Run," and he kept on doing it, over and over, until I was ready to beg him to stop.

Then he saw the flashing lights coming up behind us, and suddenly I didn't have to.

21

OBJECTS IN MIRROR ARE CLOSER THAN THEY APPEAR.
That's what your car's side mirror will tell you, but
I am here to say that the minute you can make out that
the object you see is a police car, it is already way too
close.

"Robinson," I hissed, panic rising in my voice.

"Maybe they're not after us," he said. "I was only going…
hmm, twenty miles over the speed limit. Heck, it's practically a crime to go any slower around here. This is Las Vegas,
baby—everything's legal but good behavior."

I could tell by the sound of his voice that Robinson didn't
believe this but wanted me to. He didn't want me to be afraid.
He never had, for as long as I'd known him.

"Pull over to the right-hand shoulder." The amplified,
crackling voice came through a megaphone mounted on the
side of the police car.

Robinson glanced down at the speedometer as if checking to see how high the numbers went. Like he was wonder-
ing if he should try to outrun the guy.

"Don't even think about it," I warned. "Do what the policeman says."

"You don't sound much like Bonnie," he said reproachfully.

"For God's sake, this isn't a movie. This is life! *Pull over!*"

I was reaching for the wheel to yank it to the right when Robinson slowed, flicked on his turn signal as polite as you please, and eased onto the right shoulder.

"See? I can follow directions," Robinson said. He tried to keep his tone light.

But it didn't matter now. I put my face in my hands. We were caught. I saw the headlines, the court-appointed lawyer, the hideous orange jumpsuit they'd make me wear. Was I old enough to be tried as an adult?

"It's going to be okay," Robinson said quietly.

Liar, I thought.

The officer approached Robinson's window. From my angle I could see only his belt and the soft, round stomach above it. "License and registration," he said gruffly.

Not even a "please."

"Sir," Robinson began, "is there a problem?"

The officer's hand shot out. "License and registration," he said again.

Robinson smiled ingratiatingly. "I believe I was going the speed of traffic—perhaps it was a trifle fast—"

"License and registration."

Robinson turned to me, his eyes wide. "He seems to have a somewhat limited vocabulary," he whispered, and to my horror, I almost burst into giddy laughter.

I covered my mouth as Robinson made a show of rooting around in the glove compartment. "It's in here somewhere," he said.

The cop began tapping impatiently on the roof of the car. Then he leaned in and looked at both of us carefully. He had small, mean eyes and an angry mouth. "Not many kids got a car this nice," he said. "You'd think their folks'd teach 'em how to drive it. But spoiled little rich kids—they don't listen to their parents much, do they?"

It was the first time in my life anyone had ever mistaken me for rich.

"I liked him better when he didn't talk," I whispered to Robinson.

Robinson pulled out the registration and handed it over. The cop inspected it. "License," he said.

"Sir, this is all a mistake," Robinson said. "I'm very sorry for speeding. If you'll just let us go with a warning, I promise I'll never do it again."

The cop barked out a laugh. "I heard that one before. There's a sucker born every minute, son, but you're not looking at one." He stared philosophically down the highway and then turned back to us. "See, these rich kids," he went on, his eyes narrow and cold, "if their folks can't teach 'em things, the law has to. The law just loves to give lessons."

Robinson was so used to charming people. I'd seen him talk his way out of detentions, and into a Hollywood party, and everything in between. So now he looked as though he couldn't believe what he was hearing. But he nodded. "Of course, sir. I understand. I'm going to have to get out, though. I keep my wallet under my seat, and I can't reach it from in here. May I step out, sir?"

The cop backed away. Robinson reached over and grabbed my hand. Hard. "Bonnie," he whispered.

"What?" I asked. But he was already out of the car, and I could still feel the pressure of his fingers on my skin.

I saw it all through the window. At first Robinson kept his

hands in the air, to show the cop he meant no harm. But the next thing I knew, there was a flash of movement, a grunt, and then a holler of rage.

Robinson yelled, "Get out, Bonnie, I need you!"

Without thinking, I obeyed. And that was when I saw the love of my life—car thief, trespasser, and kisser of strippers—pointing a gun in a young cop's face.

I nearly fell to my knees. I reached out to the hood of the Porsche to steady myself. The metal of the gun glinted in the desert sunlight. *This can't be happening*, I thought. *This is definitely a dream or a scene from a movie—or a hallucination or something.*

Robinson half-turned to look at me and, I swear to God, *winked.*

My jaw dropped. If I'd thought he was a little crazy before, now I was sure he'd gone utterly insane. Then I saw that tiny smile flicker at the corner of his mouth. That smile I knew better than my own. It said to me: *This is all a game, Axi. No one's going to get hurt.*

I took a step toward them, and I prayed that he was right.

"I'm really sorry that I have to do this," Robinson said, turning back to the cop, "but you gave me no choice."

The cop's face was red and glistening. He was silent, full of brutal but impotent rage. He seemed to have lost the power of speech altogether.

I looked up and down the road, watching for traffic. Never had I been gladder that Robinson stuck to the back routes.

"Bonnie," Robinson said, "you take his cuffs and put them on him."

Fumblingly, I did as I was told. When I snapped the metal around his wrist, the cop flinched. "I'm so sorry," I blurted. "Are they too tight? I don't want them to be too tight, but I don't exactly know how to work them."

The cop merely turned redder in the face.

Robinson was jittery, like he might jump out of his flannel. Even on a back road, someone could drive by at any moment. "Again, I'm really sorry about this, sir. It's just that we're on a mission. We have to keep moving. It's a life-or-death situation."

The red-faced cop cleared his throat like he was going to say something. But then his mouth contorted and opened, and he spit. A whitish glob of mucus landed right on the tip of Robinson's cowboy boot.

"Well, that was rude," Robinson said, sounding shocked.

As if the cop should be more polite. I wondered if Robinson had somehow hit his head in our fender bender and the blow had knocked his conscience out of whack.

"You kids have no idea the trouble you're going to be in," the cop suddenly bellowed. His anger and his scarlet face frightened me. I could hardly look at him.

Maybe it wasn't the cop who was the problem—maybe it was us. The teen outlaws.

Maybe I was kind of terrified of who we'd so quickly become. We'd just threatened a police officer with his own gun and locked him up with his own handcuffs!

How had our trip gotten so out of control after I had mapped it out to perfection?

And why…didn't I care anymore?

I suddenly felt exhilarated. Unstoppable. This was the moment to make a real choice about the rest of my life, no matter how afraid I was to do it.

I steeled myself and dragged my eyes up to meet the cop's. "We're not going to get caught," I said.

I said it softly but firmly. It was a promise. A prayer. A wish.

22

ROBINSON TOOK A STEP BACK FROM THE COP, using the gun to point toward the door of the police car. "Bonnie," he said to me, "you're going to need to drive the cruiser." He turned to the cop. "I haven't taught her how to drive a stick yet," he explained.

By now I was nearly numb with shock, but I climbed into the driver's seat of the black-and-white. Gas pedal, turn signal, ignition. Everything looked to be in pretty much the same place. Meanwhile Robinson was gently shoving the cop into the back. Thank goodness for the glass between us, because, even cuffed, that guy petrified me. If looks could kill, Robinson and I would have been goners.

"You gonna be all right?" Robinson asked me, poking his head in the front window.

I put both hands on the wheel, one at ten and one at two. I tried to seem like I wasn't having a small heart attack. "Well, there aren't any parking meters to hit."

He gave me a crooked smile. Maybe it was totally inappropriate, but I needed it.

"Awesome, you're good to go, then. Now follow me," he said. He got into the Porsche, drove a little way, then took a dirt road off to the left. We followed it for a couple of miles, passing nothing but dirt and scrubby sage.

I refused to look into the rearview mirror because I could practically feel the death glare the police officer was giving me. I was so on edge from the last fifteen minutes that I knew if I met his eyes I was going to freak out completely, crash, and end up killing us both. I was gripping the steering wheel so tightly that my fingers were turning white.

When Robinson stopped, I braked too hard and scrambled out of the car, barely remembering to put it in park.

"Whoa," Robinson said, catching me by the elbow as I stumbled toward him. "Everything okay? He's all locked up in back?"

"No, I let him out," I snapped, yanking my arm away. *Breathe*, Axi. "Sorry. Nerves."

"Let's get out of here."

"But—" I glanced at the police car. The cop was sitting motionless in the back, but I thought I could hear him cursing.

"Someone will find him, don't worry," Robinson said, pointing into the distance at what looked like tract houses— or a mirage. Everything was flat all around us. The desert was so empty. There wasn't even a cactus.

Robinson took my arm again and led me toward the Porsche. When we were strapped in, he gunned the engine, and we shot out of there in a great cloud of dust that billowed up so high it hid our crime completely.

"We've got to ditch the Porsche," Robinson said as he pulled onto the main road. For some reason he was heading back into town.

Suddenly I began to shake. My legs jumped and twitched

and even my teeth were chattering. Had we just done what I thought we did? "Robinson—" I said.

"What?" He looked at me, concerned.

"I can't steal a car right now. My nerves can't take it."

"No problem," Robinson answered. "We can go back to Axi's Plan A."

"I don't even remember what that *is*," I moaned.

"The bus, of course—petri dish for superbacteria. Because I don't know about you, darlin', but I'm just itching for some kind of dreadful infection." Then Robinson grinned maniacally.

"Tell me—honestly. Have you lost. Your. Mind?"

As usual, Robinson ignored my question and instead pulled into a bus station on the edge of the city. "There it is! Our ticket to bacterial meningitis."

We got our backpacks and left the Porsche in a fire lane. I just wanted to be gone. I didn't have time to write a thank-you note to the owner, but it was probably just as well. Now that we were bona fide criminals, we should try to leave fewer clues behind.

Inside the station, it was dark and cool and grimy. All my adrenaline-fueled courage had faded, and I wanted to curl up in a ball in the corner. "Where do we go? We were supposed to see the Great Sand Dunes next," I whispered.

Robinson scanned the departure board. "Interesting," he said. "Because these famous dunes of sand happen to be near Alamosa, Colorado, correct?"

I frowned in confusion. "How did you know that?"

"My dear, that bus leaves in moments. See?" Robinson pointed. "The luck of the traveler is with us." He was already walking toward the ticket booth, one hand reaching for his wallet.

Could it really be that simple? "I thought it was luck of the Irish," I called weakly.

He turned around and shrugged. "Who cares? We've got our ride. But for your information, my grandma was an Irish rose from County Cork."

I looked at him in surprise, because Robinson never, ever talked about his family. "Okay, but what about the cop?" I asked, hurrying up to him. "We can't just leave him. We have to call someone."

"I thought you weren't GG anymore," Robinson said.

I couldn't tell if he was joking or not. "Just because I want to make sure someone doesn't die of heatstroke?" I found an old pay phone and fished in my pockets for change. I told the woman who answered that I'd been out riding my horse when I'd come upon a cop car in the middle of nowhere. I made myself sound young and stupid, but I gave all the necessary details.

She wanted to know my name. "Carole Ann," I said.

"You did a good thing, Carole Ann," she said.

Lady, if only you knew.

23

THERE'S AN OLD SAYING ABOUT HOW ONLY THE guilty sleep well in jail. The innocent man stays awake all night, freaking out, while the guilty one sleeps like a baby. He figures he's finally where he belongs and he might as well get some shut-eye.

Robinson and I weren't in jail, of course—we were on a Greyhound. But it was uncomfortable and smelly and confined, the way I imagined jail to be. And we hadn't been on the bus more than five minutes before Robinson leaned over, put his head on my lap, and fell asleep.

Guilty, I thought. *We're both so guilty.*

For a while I stared out the window, watching the flat, dry land go by. I still couldn't believe the way things had turned. A few hours ago, Robinson making out with someone else was just about the worst of my problems. Now? Try felony assault, grand theft auto, and who knew what else.

Back in the moment, of course, what we'd done made perfect sense. We'd *had* to do it. A stolen Porsche, a hijacked gun, and suddenly cuffing and abandoning a cop seemed like a fine idea because, hey, it would keep us out of juvie.

For now, I thought darkly.

Reality came down on me with a crushing weight. What in the world had we done? This was supposed to be a road trip—a lark—and it was turning into a crime spree. What would we do next? Steal a kid's lunch money? Rob a bank?

In the seat ahead of us an old lady was knitting. I could hear her needles sliding and clicking. Every once in a while she'd turn around and smile at me. At first I smiled back, but then I started to get nervous. Was it possible she knew something? Could she read the guilt on my face? Did the Nevada police employ undercover agents old enough to collect Social Security?

I shook Robinson awake. He sat up, rubbing his eyes, and gave me a grumpy look.

"We can never do anything like that again," I said quietly. "Ever."

Robinson ran his hand through his tousled hair and sighed. "I know, Axi. Do you think I wanted it to happen like that? You know that's not me. But we couldn't let him stop us." His dark eyes, with their heavy lashes, searched my face. He wanted to be sure I knew he'd done the only thing he could. "I don't want this to end," he said. "Not yet. Do you?"

I shook my head. I wanted to go on like this with him forever, except I wanted more kissing and less crime. "What if we'd—" I began, but Robinson held up a hand.

"There's no point in what-ifs. What's done is done."

"You sound like my mother," I said. "Who, I have lately realized, was usually full of BS."

Robinson grinned, then faced forward and said hi to the old lady, who'd turned to look at us again. "It was total insanity, I admit that," he whispered to me when she turned back around. "But it's over, okay, Axi? Everything is going to be fine. In the words of Irving Berlin, one of the greatest songwriters of all time, from here on out, there's nothing but blue skies."

Maybe I'm an idiot—actually, I'm definitely an idiot—but hearing him say that made me feel better.

Robinson reached out and brushed a piece of hair from my cheek. "I never want anything bad to happen to you, Axi," he said quietly. "And while I have not yet been in one, I suspect that jail is bad."

"You think it's worse than a pediatric cancer ward?" I blurted.

Robinson seemed to pale. Then he laid his head on my lap again. "I promise," he said, "we'll never do something like that again."

"Pinkie swear," I said, holding out my little finger.

We shook on it.

"And Axi?" He looked up at me from below, his eyes wide and deep enough to drown in.

"What?"

"I'm sorry about Chrissy. Honestly, she came on to me. It took me by surprise. And I didn't want to be rude."

I sighed. Robinson was the only guy in the world who could deliver that line and actually have me believe it. "Yeah, I know how much you dislike rudeness," I said.

"I do," Robinson said, closing his eyes. His voice grew sleepy again. "Rudeness is so…rude…"

I smiled. And then I rested my head against the greasy bus window and fell asleep.

24

WE GOT OFF AT THE ALAMOSA STOP AND STUCK
out our thumbs, trying to look wholesome and innocent.
When that didn't work, Robinson told me it was time for
me to show some leg.

"*You* show it," I countered. "You're the one who always
charms everyone." (Also? I hadn't shaved since we left
home.)

"Except that cop," he said ruefully.

Eventually, a nice old man in an El Camino pulled up. We
told him we were headed to the Great Sand Dunes National
Park, and he nodded approvingly and drove us right up to
the visitors' center. He wouldn't even take ten bucks for gas.

Instead, he slipped me a twenty as I was pulling my backpack from underneath the seat. "Go out for dinner tonight,"
he urged. "Y'all need some meat on your bones." For a
moment he gazed wistfully at the sand dunes, gleaming
golden at the base of blue, snow-capped mountains. "If my
Meg was alive, I'd call her up and tell her to put a roast in the
oven." His eyes seemed to film over. Then he snapped back

to the present. "Take care of yourselves, all right?" And then he drove away.

I tried to shake off the strange, sad feeling his good-bye had given me. I looked over at Robinson, who was waving at me from the edge of a creek that cut along the base of the dunes.

"It's like someone picked up a piece of the Sahara and put it down in Colorado," he said when I approached.

"It's amazing," I said, snapping a picture that I knew wouldn't do it justice. "Why do people end up in towns like K-Falls when there are places like this in the world?"

"That's an excellent question," Robinson said. He flung his arms out wide, as if he could hug the whole huge vista. "We should probably never go back." He looked pretty pleased by that idea.

We began walking up a ridge to the top of the dunes. It was tough going—the sand was loose, and our feet sank deep into it. I could hear Robinson breathing hard behind me. As we neared the top, the wind picked up the sand and flung it, stinging, against us.

"It's like full-body exfoliation," Robinson said, wiping the grit from his face. "There are people who pay good money for this."

"The glass is always half-full for you, isn't it?" I asked. I would have smiled, but I'd have gotten sand in my teeth. Optimism was one of his best qualities.

Stinging sand aside, we arrived in a spot that was breathtakingly beautiful. On nearby dunes we saw some people hiking up and others sliding back down on what looked like snowboards. Their delighted shouts carried through the air, which was already shimmering with heat.

Robinson began to strum an imaginary guitar: *"Even castles made of sand…"* Then he looked at me somewhat sheepishly. "Jimi Hendrix."

"I know," I told him. "My dad has that album." I squinted into the distance. Beyond the dunes, the prairie was full of yellow wildflowers. I held my camera at arm's length and took a picture of us squinting and grinning, on top of the world.

We might have hiked back down then, but I turned and saw an old plastic sled half-buried in the sand. I pointed, and Robinson's eyes lit up. "Are you thinking what I'm thinking?" I asked, but I knew he was, so I didn't wait for an answer.

I climbed onto the front of the sled, and Robinson stood behind me, his hands on my back. He began to run, pushing me, and then he leapt in. He wrapped his arms around my waist and buried his head in my hair as we raced down the slope. The wind whipped the sand into my face, but I didn't care—I screamed with delight.

At the bottom of the dune, we lay on the sand, breathless.

"Wow," Robinson said.

"Who needs snow?" I yelled, flinging up my arms. "Want to go again?"

Of course he did.

We spent a giddy, thrilling hour hiking up and then racing down, after which we were so hot and tired we could barely move.

"I'm dying of thirst," Robinson said, collapsing at my feet. "Also I think my nose is fried."

" 'What makes the desert beautiful is that somewhere it hides a well,' " I said.

"Huh?" Robinson asked, rubbing his nose.

"It's a line from *The Little Prince*."

"You and your books," he said teasingly.

"It wouldn't kill you to read one."

He raised a dark eyebrow. "You never know. It might," he said, and smiled. "So where's that well, then?"

I tossed him a water bottle from my backpack, but it arced

wide. He scrambled to get it, then opened the lid and drained the liquid in about two seconds.

"You're lucky I've got another one for myself," I chided. "Otherwise that would've been very greedy. Very scalawag-ish."

He snorted. "I know you, Axi. Of course you have extra water. Now I'm going to close my eyes. Wake me in ten." Then he put a shirt over his face and fell asleep, just like that, at the bottom of a sand dune.

We washed off the grit in cold, clear Medano Creek, and we set up our tent at a nearby campground. After dinner—canned chili heated over the fire—we stored our food and packs in the metal bearproof box on the edge of the campsite.

Night came suddenly, as if someone had blown out the sun like a candle. And then the stars burst from the sky, more than I'd ever seen in my life. I stared up, dazzled, and by this point almost too spent to speak.

Robinson looked up, too. "There's something I wanted to say to you that I never got a chance to," he said.

I knew not to get my hopes up by now. "What's that?" I asked.

"You throw like a girl."

"You are such a jerk," I said, laughing. I picked up the rinsed-out chili can and took aim. "I'll show you throwing like a girl!"

"I'm kidding. Those are the last lines from the movie *Sahara*," he said. "Since we spent the day in the desert and all."

I put the can back down. I was too exhausted to throw, anyway. Instead, I took a deep drink of water. And I looked at the long, lean shape of Robinson through the darkness, thinking that there were many different kinds of thirst.

25

WE STOLE A PICKUP JUST AFTER DAWN, AS THE sun was rising golden over the mountains.

Isn't it crazy, how matter-of-factly I can say that?

Well, Your Honor, we ate breakfast, and then we stole a truck. Granola bars and a Chevy, sir, if specifics matter to the court.

If I ever meet that judge, I'm sure he'll ask me, "Did you two think you were invincible?" And I'll look him right in the eyes. "No, sir," I'll tell him. "In fact, I thought the opposite."

The engine of our borrowed truck was loud and rattling, and the radio played only AM stations. "This thing needs a new muffler," Robinson said, frowning. "The exhaust manifold could be cracked, too."

"Awesome, a broken getaway car," I said. "And wow, are we listening to *Elvis* right now?"

"*Love me tender, love me true,*" Robinson sang. Then he stopped abruptly. "It's not like I had time to give it a checkup before I stole it." Was it just me, or did that sound a little...

huffy? "Anyway, variety is the spice of life, and we can trade up at the next stop. Would you care to tell the chauffeur where that is, Ms. Moore?"

I shrugged. The next stop I'd planned was Detroit, four-teen hundred miles away. "I don't know. The world's big-gest ball of stamps? Carhenge? The Hobo Museum?" We were driving northeast, toward Nebraska, heading into what residents of the East and West Coasts liked to call flyover country.

"Carhenge?" Robinson asked, sounding interested. "I bet that's like Stonehenge, but with cars."

"Wow, ten thousand points for you," I said. He gave me a hurt look. "I'm sorry," I mumbled.

I was irritable because I'd been awake most of the night. And it wasn't the claustrophobic tent or the hard ground; it was Robinson. What was I supposed to do about him? About us? We'd been through so much together—and our journey had started well before the trip began. Wasn't it time for me to tell him how I felt (even if I wasn't exactly sure how to describe it)?

I spent a long time thinking about what I'd say, and revis-ing my lines, but in the end I was about as successful as I'd been with my good-bye note to Dad. As in: Not. At. All.

Sample: *Robinson, I think I loved you from the first moment I saw you.* (But I was high on painkillers that day, so I loved everyone.) *When I look at you, I see a better version of myself.* (Wait—so I want to kiss myself?) *I don't know what I'd do without you in my life.* (Um . . . not steal cars?)

It was stupidly, infuriatingly impossible. No wonder I hadn't written anything decent in ages—I couldn't even fig-ure out how to tell a boy that I loved him. That whenever I looked into his eyes, I felt like I was drowning and being saved, all at the same time. That if I had to choose between dying tomorrow or spending the rest of my life without him, I would seriously consider picking imminent death.

I was afraid of what I felt. But was that the only reason it was so hard to admit it to him? Or was I afraid that he didn't feel the same? Yes, I was definitely afraid of that.

Now, as we drove in silence through the wide-open morning, I wanted so much to slide over to his side of the bench seat. I wanted to put my hand on his leg and feel the answering tremor go through him. I wanted to say, *Pull over and kiss me.*

I took a deep breath. I couldn't sneak over toward him, inch by cowardly inch. I was just going to have to go for it. *All or nothing, Axi. Now is the time.*

I closed my eyes, offering a prayer to the gods of young love, Cupid or Aphrodite or Justin Bieber: *Don't let this be a terrible mistake.*

When I opened my eyes again, I saw that the truck was drifting to the right.

"Robinson?" I said, my voice rising as we veered toward the shoulder.

He didn't answer, and I looked over. His face was so pale it looked almost blue. He began to cough—a terrible, racking, wet sound that came from deep within him.

He looked at me and his eyes were full of fear.

And suddenly he was vomiting.

Blood.

"Stop the truck!" I screamed, reaching for the wheel.

We were already on the shoulder, and Robinson somehow managed to hit the brake while still gagging. Cars whizzed past us, shaking the cab with their speed.

"Oh my God, Robinson!" I cried, moving toward him. I was holding out my hands as if I could catch the blood—as if I could stop it from coming out of him and then put it back inside, where it belonged.

The air swam in front of my eyes. I was crying.

After a horrible, endless moment, Robinson stopped coughing. He wiped his red-streaked mouth with the sleeve of his flannel shirt.

"It's not that much, really," he said weakly, looking at his shirt. "I'm okay now."

But I knew this if I knew anything: *Robinson is not okay.*

Then again, it was possible that I wasn't, either.

part Two

26

AND SO NOW, UNDER A COLORADO SKY SO BLUE it hurt my eyes, we arrived at the terrible truth. You can plot your escape, you can ditch your life and your family, and you can race down a two-lane highway in a stolen car. But there are things you can never outrun.

Things like cancer. Because that comes along for the ride.

I managed to get us to a hospital forty-five minutes up the road in La Junta. Robinson lay with his head in my lap, and I ached to run my fingers through his hair and tell him everything would be all right. But because the truck didn't have power steering, I needed both hands on the wheel.

And I wasn't sure that everything *would* be all right, not at all.

The small hospital waiting room was freezing cold, lit with the kind of harsh fluorescent light that makes people look as damp and gray as fish. Robinson shivered and leaned against me. There was a bloom of dark blood on his T-shirt. He buttoned his flannel self-consciously. "Otherwise I look like I've been stabbed," he explained.

"I'm not sure that's a bad thing," I said. There were four other people in the waiting room, and by the looks on their faces, they'd been there awhile.

Robinson shook his head. "I just need to sit down," he said in a raspy voice.

The woman at the desk glanced at me warily as I approached. Maybe she saw the fear in my eyes—or maybe she thought I was homeless or on drugs. I could see my pale reflection in the corner of a mirror, and I couldn't exactly blame her.

"Can I help you?" she asked. Her name tag read DEBBIE.

"My friend is sick," I said, pointing to Robinson, who was huddled on a plastic chair in the corner. The scene in the truck played over and over in my mind. It was nightmarish.

"The doctor has been paged," Debbie said. She inspected my face, frowning lightly. "Do you need to see him, too?"

"I'm absolutely fine," I said stiffly, even though I felt like I might collapse from exhaustion.

I rejoined Robinson, and we sat in the corner for what felt like hours. Eventually, an old man with his arm in a cast leaned over and put his good hand on my knee.

"It's a Saturday morning, hon," he offered. "Most of the doctors and whatnot are fishing."

I bit my lip, hard. We had no doctor. And when we got one, I knew what it would mean: blood workups, fine-needle aspiration biopsies, positron-emission tomography scans.... The thought of going through this again made me want to run and hide.

"Welcome to small-town America, Axi," Robinson said, "where the bowling alley and the Elks lodge have larger staffs than the hospital."

"Don't worry, the doctor is coming," I said. "Hey, in the

meantime, we can watch TV. I know you haven't been getting your daily dose lately."

Robinson nodded. "If only you had a Slim Jim and a box of Oreos, everything would be perfect."

I tried to wipe a spot of blood from his collar. "You really have to eat better."

"I know," Robinson said. "I'm in the ER because of too many Slim Jims and not enough TV." He looked at me slyly.

Oh, if only that were true, I thought. For just a moment I clung to a wild hope that the doctor would give him a spoonful of extra-strength Maalox, and then we could be on our way to the Gateway Arch in St. Louis, or the world's largest ball of twine. But I'd seen his blood, the way it was dark, almost coffee-colored. I knew that meant it came from his gastrointestinal tract—where the cancer had been.

Where maybe it still was.

"Why do they have to pick the Home Shopping Network?" Robinson asked.

I looked up. A lady with long red nails was selling figurines, smiling at the camera with glossy lips and blindingly white teeth. "Come on. Don't tell me you don't love that jade elephant," I teased.

Why were we talking about crap made in China? About junk food? The elephant we needed to talk about was the one in the room: Robinson's *blood*, his *illness*, which wasn't a matter of nutrition.

On the other hand, ignoring that truth was exactly how we'd gotten as far as we had. We didn't sit around and mope. We took charge; we took *off*. We laughed and we drove too fast and we stuck our heads out the window and gave cancer the finger. Because we understood that a person could be dead long before he or she actually died. And no matter what the future held for us, we didn't ever want to be that kind of people.

Robinson blinked drowsily. "I do kind of like the elephant. I think jade's supposed to be good luck. We could probably use a little of that."

His voice was thick with sleep. His eyes closed, and he leaned his head on my shoulder. I squeezed his fingers, still wrapped in mine. Just like he'd said, we were in this together.

"Everything's going to be fine," I whispered. But Robinson had fallen asleep already, and he couldn't hear me lie.

27

THE BITTER IRONY OF MY LIFE WAS THAT TWO years after my sister, Carole Ann, died in a pediatric oncology ward in Portland, Oregon, I became a patient in the same wing. I recognized all the nurses, who'd shaken their heads in disbelief. "Both Moore babies?" they'd whispered. *"Both?"*

If God or fate or karma has decided you're going to get cancer, though, you cross your fingers for a kind like mine. Hodgkin's lymphoma is not uncommon, which means that doctors know a lot about it, and by now they're pretty good at curing it. That's the glass half-full.

"Yeah, the glass half-full...of shit," Robinson used to say. I'd met him for the first time in that place, and every time he'd curse, I'd sort of punch him in the arm, because I didn't like it. But I did like *him*, which made being there a little bit easier.

Don't get me wrong. Even a highly curable cancer is no walk in the park. Yes, the hospital walls were painted pretty colors, the nurses wore Winnie-the-Pooh scrubs, and some of the older kids pretended the ward was a boarding school complete with uniforms of thin blue gowns, fuzzy slippers, and bald heads covered in colorful scarves. But being there and being sick totally sucked.

Until the day I met Robinson. Until the day he found me.

If life were a movie, we'd have had what they call a "meet cute." Sort of like this: I'd knock into Robinson while carrying a giant stack of magazines I'd borrowed from the waiting room. And all those good, trashy weeklies like *Us*, *People*, and *Life & Style* would slide everywhere on the floor. I'd make a joke about studying for my pop culture quiz, and he'd laugh as he helped me pick up the mess. By the time the magazines were back in my arms, we'd have realized we were totally hot for each other, and hilarity and romance would ensue for the next ninety minutes.

In real life, it went like this: in a narcotic haze from a bad reaction to a chemo treatment, I was staring at the TV, convinced that Barney the purple dinosaur was speaking directly to me. When I failed to decipher his message, I fell asleep, waking later to see a beautiful dark-haired boy sitting next to my bed. I knew then that I had died, because unless I had been transported to heaven, there was no way a guy that hot would be smiling at me.

But I wasn't dead. It was Robinson, and he was real. He said to me, "You look like shit. I feel like shit. Let's be friends."

And just like that, we were. That's how magnetic Robinson was: he could tell you that you looked terrible, and you'd still adore him.

Robinson was sicker than I was, but he didn't act like it. He had a rare kind of non-Hodgkin's lymphoma called Burkitt's. The *non* means it's worse.

"Burkitt was the doctor who discovered the cancer in

equatorial Africa," Robinson informed me. "It's a lot more common there." He sounded almost proud of his strange and exotic cancer. Then he grinned. "Burkitt also had this whole elaborate theory about the right posture for taking a crap. He said if you squatted—you know, like a baseball catcher—you'd never get colon cancer. Seriously, you can't make this stuff up."

I looked up Burkitt's immediately. For patients with Robinson's numbers (his cancer was Stage IV) the survival rate was 50 percent.

There were kids on the ward who'd only have to have a foot amputated or a mysterious lump removed, and then they'd live to be a hundred. Why Robinson? Why this disease? But Robinson was philosophical. He said, "Fifty percent? I've seen worse."

We all had.

A 50 percent chance of surviving was a flip of a coin. So the night after I learned what the odds for him were, I sat up in my adjustable hospital bed, held a penny tight in my palm, and squeezed my eyes shut. "Heads, he lives," I said. I didn't even whisper what tails meant. I threw the penny into the air, and when I caught it, I had to breathe deeply for a long time before I could look.

It was heads.

I can't tell you how much weight I put on that coin toss. I believed in it with every single cell of my body. *Our luck would not run out.* That's what I told myself.

But they were only words. My mom could predict rain by the dull ache in her knee. My childhood dog, Sadie, could sense the mailman when he was still two blocks away. In this weird, quiet way, they knew what was coming.

And now, so did I.

Now, in the cold, cold waiting room, Robinson leaned

against me. I could feel his breath. I imagined I could see the faint, precious pulse of his heartbeat, fluttering beneath the skin. He was so beautiful, so alive.

But for how long? I didn't need a doctor to tell me what I already knew. Robinson—my better self, my heart, my life—was very possibly dying.

Our luck would not run out? *Please*, Axi. Everything runs out eventually. *Everything.*

EVENTUALLY, ROBINSON WAS ADMITTED TO THE La Junta hospital, and a nurse took us to a private room. She helped him into a bed, and I hopped up on the empty one beside him.

"Are you going to write this down?" Robinson wondered aloud. "In your journal?"

"I only write down the good parts of our adventures," I said.

Robinson snorted. "You can't write a book without a conflict."

I said, "Who said anything about a book? This is my journal. It's a pink notebook I got at Walgreens for two ninety-nine."

Robinson shrugged. "You never know..."

For some reason, this made me laugh. "Sure, I'll write a book," I told him, "as long as you promise to actually read it."

He held up his little finger. "Pinkie swear."

But before I could lean toward him, a voice boomed from

the doorway. "So—just what do we have here?" We looked up to see a bearded giant wearing a lab coat and staring at us.

He introduced himself as Dr. Ellsworth, and he hadn't even asked Robinson's last name before he launched into a list of questions. Did Robinson use drugs? Alcohol? Had he traveled internationally recently? Had he ever had an ulcer? Was he allergic to any foods? Had he eaten any spinach during last month's *E. coli* outbreak?

Robinson shuddered at the thought of spinach. He answered no to everything.

I was still amazed by the doctor's size. He could have been a circus strongman, but now he was bending over Robinson's chest, listening to his heart and lungs.

He was frowning.

He palpated Robinson's stomach, and Robinson inhaled sharply, wincing. I had to look away then. I couldn't bear to see him in pain.

After several minutes, Dr. Ellsworth spoke. "I'm going to send you to get a CT scan and an X-ray. There are… abnormalities."

Just because I was expecting to hear something like this didn't mean it didn't knock the wind out of me. I drew in a wobbly breath as Robinson said, "Actually, if it's all the same to you, Doctor, I'd rather not have those things."

"You might be a very ill young man," the doctor said.

Robinson watched him, blinking his dark eyes. "Might," he allowed. "But let's just leave it at that. No news is good news, right? In the meantime, I do think I have a touch of the flu or something." He offered the best rakish grin he could muster, which, considering the situation, was pretty impressive.

"You have walking pneumonia," Dr. Ellsworth said. "And pleurisy is likely. I can tell you that right now."

"Please let that be all he has," I whispered. I suddenly thought of the orb Robinson had bought me in Mount Shasta, and I reached for it at the bottom of my backpack. I ran my fingers over its smooth surface. It was both a worry stone and a good-luck charm.

The doctor turned to me. "And you?" he asked. "Are you in need of any medical care you'd like to refuse?"

I shook my head. "I'm just here for moral support," I said.

Dr. Ellsworth walked over to the side of the bed I was borrowing and touched my neck. His fingers were cool. "I see the scar right here," he said. "It's from a radiation burn, isn't it?"

I moved away from his touch, saying nothing. I wasn't a patient here, and I didn't have to answer. It didn't matter what I'd had. I was clear. In remission.

Although, as my dad's friend Critter used to say, *Just because it's sunny today don't mean the shitstorm ain't comin'.*

Dr. Ellsworth crossed his arms over his massive chest. "What's going on with you two?" he asked. "Where did you come from?"

Robinson and I looked at each other. He shook his head almost imperceptibly.

I spoke for us. "We can't say at the moment."

Dr. Ellsworth gave us both sharp looks. "This is not a game. It is my belief that this young man here has a mass in his abdomen. A tumor. Do you comprehend the seriousness of that?"

Robinson tried to sit up. "Hey, Axi. What's the difference between a doctor and a lawyer?"

I knew this joke—it was one of Robinson's standards. And I was only half-surprised he was trotting it out now. Playing along, I said, "I don't know. What?"

"A lawyer will rob you; a doctor will rob you and kill you, too."

Dr. Ellsworth made a sound in his throat—a choked-back laugh? A grunt of annoyance? "I'm trying to help," he said.

"Then bring in a TV," Robinson quipped. "Preferably one with cable."

The truth was, Robinson and I had a routine down. We'd perfected it in the halls of the Portland cancer ward. The nurses loved us. We were the Abbott and Costello of cancer. "Hey, Robinson," I said. "What do you call a person who keeps getting lymphoma over and over again?"

"I don't know—what?" But he was already laughing.

"A lymphomaniac!" I cried.

Robinson whooped and pretended to slap his thigh. "Oooh, that was a good one," he said.

Dr. Ellsworth sighed. "If there were a drug to prevent gallows humor, I'd prescribe it for both of you." But I could tell that he thought we were just a tiny bit funny.

He stepped toward the door. "I'm going to give you some intravenous antibiotics, and I'm going to encourage you to think very hard about those tests I mentioned."

"I don't like tests," Robinson said. "I always fail them."

"Where are your parents, young man?"

I glanced at Robinson. That was a question whose answer I didn't know, either.

Robinson turned away. "I'm a legal adult," he said. "Do you want to check my ID?"

Dr. Ellsworth gave Robinson one more long look, then shook his head and left the room.

Robinson closed his eyes. "I'm just going to take a little nap," he said. "If you can stand to be without my company for a while."

I got up and pulled the thin blanket over him. I didn't

want him to leave me, not even for a minute. "I think I can manage," I said softly.

He said, "You should close your eyes, too."

"I'm not tired," I said, lying again. But I knew I couldn't sleep, anyway; I needed to watch him. To make sure he didn't start coughing again. To make sure the blood stayed inside him, where it was supposed to be. To watch his chest rise and fall, rise and fall.

I sat down by his bedside. I hoped the antibiotics would work their invisible cellular magic, and quickly. And I wished that what Robinson needed was only—to use his terminology—a little tune-up. Because we weren't going to stick around to get six weeks of chemo in La Junta. That wasn't in the plan.

A few minutes later, I looked up to see that Dr. Ellsworth had returned. "We're moving you to a different room," he said. "I don't want you too far from a ventilator. Or the nurses' station."

Robinson looked over at me and offered a faint, sleepy smile. "Precautionary, of course," he said.

"Of course," I repeated. "You just have a touch of what-ever's been going around." Like cancer was contagious, the way doctors once thought it was. Like it was no more serious than the common cold.

I didn't dare look at Dr. Ellsworth. He was going to add *crazy* to Robinson's list of diagnoses, I could already tell. And that was just fine with me.

Because as far as I knew, nobody ever died of crazy.

29

IN THE EVENING THEY SEDATED ROBINSON, because his breathing had become labored and painful. That, apparently, was the pleurisy. Or maybe it was the pneumonia. I didn't want to know. When they said things like "peritoneal fluid analysis" and "low platelet count," I put my fingers in my ears.

Alone, I read every magazine I could find: *Golf Digest*, *Sport Fishing*, and *Fit Pregnancy*. None held any useful information for me, but considering I'm a golf hater, a vegetarian, and a virgin, that was not exactly surprising.

Then I wandered the corridors, noticing again how much one hospital resembles another. They sound the same (the beeps of heart monitors, the hiss of oxygen machines, the murmuring tones of visitors). They serve the same food (syrupy, too-sweet grape juice; soggy dinner rolls; and pink, plastic-looking ham). They even smell the same (odors of disinfectant, recycled air, and bodies and what comes out of them—a mix I can only describe as *lavatorial*).

As terrible as La Junta General was, a tiny part of me

relaxed a little. Unlike the rest of our cross-country journey, the hospital ward was known territory. A place I could navigate. And I guess I was glad to have a roof over my head again.

But as Robinson would be the first to point out, you can't be Bonnie and Clyde in a hospital. You're in a different movie altogether.

"Pace much?" one of the nurses asked with a friendly smile when I walked by the station for the twentieth time.

I smiled. "Sorry. Just stretching my legs."

"No worries, keep at it," she said. "Exercise does a body good."

She looked like she could stand to get a little exercise herself, but she was busy playing FreeCell on her computer. Slow night in the ER, I guess.

I turned down a new hallway and came upon a set of heavy double doors. Pushing them open, I found myself in the foyer of a small chapel.

It was utterly unlike the rest of the sterile white hospital. The front wall was a deep red. There was a plain wooden altar with LED candles flickering alongside it. There was no statue of Jesus on the cross, though—no Mary or Ganesh or Buddha or L. Ron Hubbard, either, or whoever it was people prayed to around here. There was just that red—the red of valentines, of blood. Faint classical music came from invisible speakers.

I sat down on a bench. My parents had taken me to church about three times before they lost interest in shushing Carole Ann and me every other second. Now I was the only one in the room, so I didn't quite know what to do with myself. I put my face in my hands. Anyone who poked a head in would think I was praying.

I thought of Carole Ann and Robinson—and myself,

too. How we'd all been affected by forces that felt terrifying and supernatural but were actually just terrifying and basic. Cancer is abnormal cells dividing without control and invading other tissues. It's that simple. But it was still always a mystery: *Why in the hell is my body trying to kill me?*

Before I went into remission, I hated my body for betraying me. And considering that I was being treated for cancer at the same time I was suddenly growing breasts and having to shave my legs and stick giant pads in the crotch of my underwear—well, it felt like my body was adding insult to injury.

Having Robinson with me on that journey meant everything. We were able to laugh at how weak we were. We had contests over who had the worst mouth sores (chemo causes them; they're awful). We goaded each other to eat food when food was the last thing we wanted.

We'd saved each other, Robinson and me. Or at least, he had saved me.

But why me? Why was I doing so well when Robinson was so sick? When Carole Ann was dead?

What I know about sickness—beyond the fear, the uncertainty, and the nightmarish drudgery of it—is that it builds a wall between the sick and the well. Back in the pediatric oncology ward, Robinson and I had been on the same side of that wall. Now I couldn't bear the idea of any wall between us. I wanted to experience what he was experiencing. I wanted to be with him. For everything.

In a way, I felt like my body was betraying me again—but this time, it was killing me by keeping me well. I knew that wasn't rational. It wasn't like I wanted to get cancer again... right?

I stared at the flickering lights for a long time. When no priest or angel or epiphany from above came to answer my question, I decided to go back to Robinson.

He was getting the intravenous antibiotics for his chest infection. They'd given him morphine, too, because otherwise the medicine hurt too much going in.

Robinson turned toward me and smiled. His eyelids were heavy, his skin pale. "Have I ever told you how beautiful you are?" he asked.

I straightened the edge of his blanket. "That's the morphine talking," I said.

But still I blushed. And I hoped and prayed that it was really him talking.

30

I WAS STANDING ON THE EDGE OF THE CLIFF again, and dream-Robinson was beside me, holding my hand. I knew he was supposed to tell me something that would reassure me, but he was so silent he could have been a ghost.

I took a step forward, about to plummet into the depths—

I woke with a start.

In the darkness, there was soft rock playing from the radio at the nurses' station, a kind of music that Robinson liked to claim was as deadly as cancer. The nurses always had a good laugh at that one.

I was about to close my eyes and roll back over when I saw the shape at the side of my bed. *Robinson.* He moved forward and touched my shoulder. Even in the darkness, I could see that he had his clothes on—not a hospital gown. "Axi?"

I pushed myself up.

"It's time to leave," he said softly.

He placed my backpack at the foot of my bed and held out

his hand to help me up. His fingers were warm and reassuring, as if I were the sick one. Robinson was always so careful with me. I remembered walking the long halls of the Portland hospital with him, the two of us so weak we shuffled like octogenarians.

"Octo-what?" he'd said.

"Octogenarians. People in their eighties."

He'd laughed. "Oh, I don't have to worry about living that long."

I'd stopped in my tracks. What about that coin toss? Didn't that mean anything? "What are you talking about?" I'd demanded.

Robinson grinned. "Axi, I'm going to be a rock star—I'll wear out my body by sixty-five," he explained. "Too many decibels. Too much rock 'n' roll. You can read about me in books someday. I'll be the guy slayed by music. *I knew that dude*, you'll say. *He was cool.*"

Now, in the middle of the night, in the middle of nowhere, I touched Robinson's shoulder. "Are you sure you're okay?"

Faintly, I could see him smile. "I think I've seen enough of La Junta," he said. "We'd better be moving on."

31

I DIDN'T BOTHER ASKING HIM TO LOOK AWAY while I changed into ever-so-slightly-less-grimy clothes. For one, it was dark, and for two, what secrets did I still have from him?

Besides the fact that I loved him, obviously. But maybe it was time to let go of that secret, too, if only I could be brave enough.

Robinson had moved over to the window, his face dimly lit by the orange glow of the parking lot lights. When I was dressed in my jeans and a rumpled sweater, I went to stand beside him.

"Did you know that Cancer is the dimmest constellation of the zodiac?" he asked.

When I shook my head, he pointed to the dark sky. "It's over there. And it doesn't look anything like a crab."

"I didn't know you were such an astronomer."

Out of the corner of my eye I could see his grin. "Axi, I have facets you can't even imagine."

I felt almost dizzy when he said that. Is it possible that

you can love someone more than you love life itself, and yet you're still never going to know for sure everything he's thinking? I wanted—I needed—to see every facet of Robinson that I could, for as long as I could.

"And the crazy thing?" Robinson went on. "Every star that you see out there is bigger and brighter than the sun. They only look small because they're farther away." He was still gazing out the window as if a message were written for him in the sky.

The message is right here, Robinson, I wanted to say. *Look at me, and I'll tell you.*

Still, though, I was mute. I tentatively moved closer to his side and clumsily knocked into him with my hip. For a moment I worried the bump I'd given him was too hard. How fragile was he? But when he didn't seem to notice, I wondered if I should try it again. I wondered if I should grab his hand. I wondered if I should tackle him, throw him to the floor, and kiss every inch of his frail, beautiful body.

I scooted closer to him again, and this time it felt like it registered. He was suddenly more aware of me. He stayed very still as energy seemed to ripple in the air between us. I held my breath, and I think he was holding his, too.

Now is the time, Axi, I thought. *Carpe diem.*

I reached across him to his far hand and turned him toward me. "I have something to tell you," I whispered.

"I'm all ears," he whispered back.

He waited silently, giving my eyes time to search his face: his high forehead, his deep-set eyes, his full mouth.

I opened my lips, but nothing came out. I was the writer, the reader—and now, when I truly needed to say the things I'd been wanting to say for what seemed like forever, words were utterly failing me.

"It's okay," Robinson said softly.

What's okay? I could have asked. *Nothing is okay! We're in a hospital because you could be dying! How many more chances will I have to chicken out before you're suddenly gone?*

If I couldn't say anything, I had to do something. Right this second. Or I might never get to feel the sensation of his lips touching my lips.

I couldn't live without that.

And that was all it took. I wrapped my arms around his neck and brushed my face so close to his that his unshaven chin tickled my skin. And then—I kissed him.

When our lips met, in a rush of warmth and softness, electricity flooded my body. I was sure that I began to glow. That I was full of starlight.

Finally. This was what I'd been aching for. And from the way Robinson's breath instantly melted into mine...I felt for all the world like he'd been aching for it, too.

Why on earth had we waited so long?

Robinson's arms tightened around my waist, and his hands found their way into my hair. A tiny moan escaped from his throat, and he kissed me full-strength, like he'd never been sick and never would be again...like he was more alive than ever.

And so was I.

After a minute, or an hour, we pulled apart, breathless. My cheeks were burning, and my whole body felt like it was vibrating. Like it was singing.

At first Robinson's eyes looked so solemn that my breath caught in my throat. Then, like a light blinking on in the darkness, came the smile that I craved, that crooked grin full of life.

"I love you, Axi Moore," he whispered. "What else can I say?"

I shook my head and smiled, my eyes glistening. I was still so overwhelmed that I couldn't say a word.

If this was what life was like without words—a life of *doing*, not just talking—I just might be willing to give them up forever.

32

IT WAS TIME TO GO. WE HURRIED OUT INTO THE darkness, Robinson's arm wrapped around my shoulders. It was like a hug—as if now that we'd finally really touched, we couldn't bear to let go of each other—but it was also him using me to hold himself up.

I was still glowing. I felt brighter than any of the stars.

Kissing Robinson was like coming to the end of the desert and finding a spring. It was sunshine after years of winter. It was Christmas in June. It was—oh, give me a break, why bother with dumb poetic phrases?

What I felt was joy.

Joy that totally swept away the anxiety of breaking out of a hospital against medical advice. My list of rebellious feats was growing longer by the second.

At the edge of the parking lot, Robinson leaned down and gave me another deep kiss. Then he pulled away, smiling. "Suddenly I feel like I can do anything," he said.

I felt exactly the same way. Everything would be fine. Or even better than fine. Magical. "Just tell me that *anything* doesn't include taking a different car," I said, pressing my hand against his scratchy cheek. "This is excitement enough."

Robinson kissed me again, his lips soft but urgent. At this rate, we'd never leave the parking lot—and maybe I didn't even care, as long as this kept happening.

"I'd never ditch Chuck the Truck," Robinson said after a while. "He needs to see Detroit."

I laughed giddily—clearly the making out was messing with my head a little. "Chuck the Truck?"

"Yes, ma'am," Robinson said. "Second cousin to Charley the Harley."

He laughed at his own joke and climbed into the truck. He started the engine, revving it a few times to warm it up. Then, for some reason, he scooted over into the passenger seat, where I was about to sit.

I quit my giggling. "Um, Robinson?" I said, eyeing the empty space behind the steering wheel.

He leaned back against the headrest. "Yeah, I know I said I felt like I could do anything…but I think it's probably better if you drive right now."

I noticed that his voice had become raspy again, and he had his hand over his chest, as if he were having trouble breathing.

"Then we should turn around and go back to the hospital!" I insisted. "Detroit will still be there in a couple of days."

Robinson shook his head. "No way, Axi. I'm done with that place."

"But what if it's not done with you?"

He patted the seat. "Come here, Axi. Sit beside me."

I went around to the other side and clambered onto the truck's high bench seat. Robinson put his arm around my shoulders, and I buried my face in his flannel shirt. It smelled like the hospital, but underneath that, like him. Like soap and pine and *boy*.

Of course I wanted to leave. I wanted to be alone with Robinson again. I wanted more of what we'd started in the hospital. A *lot* more.

But was this a mistake?

When Robinson spoke again, his voice seemed stronger. It also seemed like he'd been reading my thoughts. "Who cares if leaving here is a mistake? I'd make this mistake again, a million times," he insisted. "We're together. That's what matters. I want to take this trip with you. That's all I want. That's all I need. I'm not going to be irradiated or scanned or biopsied or whatever it is they want to do to me."

I spoke into his shirt because I didn't want to move away from him, not even a single millimeter. "But what if it's a death sentence? To refuse treatment now?" I whispered.

Robinson scoffed. "A hospital is a death sentence. You can cut your finger, get a staph infection, and the next thing you know, you're checking out the grass from underneath. Leaving now, Axi, is choosing life."

I could hear the quick beating of his heart. "But what if it's a shorter life?"

He shrugged. "Well, as Kurt Cobain said, 'It's better to burn out than to fade away.' Although, actually, he was quoting a Neil Young song."

I sat up suddenly. What in the world was I going to do with this infuriating person? "May I remind you that Cobain used it in his *suicide note?*"

"Well, you have to admit he had a point, GG," Robinson said mildly.

I closed my eyes and breathed in deeply, calming myself. Robinson's hand reached out, and his fingers slipped between mine, trying to reassure me.

What if doing what you wanted and doing what was right seemed like two entirely different things? What if by living the life you chose, you somehow doomed yourself—or worse, someone you loved?

After a minute, I opened my eyes. We couldn't know the future or how long it would last. We could only choose to be happy and alive right now.

"Okay, okay, you win, Robinson," I said. "But only on these conditions." I held up two fingers. "One: do not call me GG, remember? Two: you are not allowed to die. Do you hear me?"

Robinson grinned and saluted me. "Yes, ma'am," he said. "Agreed. Ten-four. Et cetera."

We shook on it, as if it were just that simple.

And then I gritted my teeth and started driving.

33

ROBINSON FELL ASLEEP ALMOST IMMEDIATELY. This was fine with me, because I needed complete and total focus on my new assignment: piloting a speeding death-and-dismemberment trap across the country.

Because, FYI, car crashes kill way more kids than cancer does. Those crosses you see on the side of the highway, the little white ones hung with fading silk flowers? They're for people my age. ("People who were texting," my dad liked to remind me—because he never wanted to blame Budweiser for anything.)

I managed not to become a highway statistic in those early hours, but there were occasional...problems. For instance, I pulled into a Texaco for gas but didn't know how to operate the pump, and Robinson was sleeping so deeply I couldn't wake him. After I begged some nice old man to help me fill my tank, I got back on the highway going in the wrong direction. For thirty miles.

After I turned around, I tried playing the radio softly. It barely worked, so I turned it off and had only my thoughts to keep me company:

I never knew how damn big *the United States is.*
Where's the nearest Starbucks?
How come my dad hasn't found me yet?

The miles ticked by, monotonous but nerve-racking. Eventually, I just started talking out loud to keep myself company.

"Don't take this the wrong way," I said, though I knew Robinson was still in dreamland, "but I don't think I ever believed we'd make it this far. Like, wouldn't my dad call the cops when he woke up and found me gone? Or even just call Critter? That guy's a human bloodhound."

Critter had even found the diamond that had fallen out of my mom's engagement ring—in a river. Not that having the diamond back encouraged her to stick around.

"Obviously, I'm not saying I want to be caught. I want to keep going. But I guess I wonder if we've just been really lucky so far? Or is there a certain amount of…disinterest on my dad's part concerning the location of his remaining daughter?"

I took a sip of cold truck-stop coffee. It felt good to talk about it, even if—or especially because—Robinson wasn't listening.

"And then there's you," I said to Robinson's sleeping silhouette. "Where are your parents? Aren't they worried about you? Do they have any idea where you are?"

When I met Robinson on the cancer ward, he'd brushed off all talk of his family. No sad-eyed father sat with him while he got his chemo; no weeping mother held his hand while he was bombarded with radioactive particles.

He was, for all that the rest of us could see, 100 percent alone.

On the other hand, no one was more popular. Robinson could turn a Domino's delivery guy into his new BFF in five minutes. Once I heard two of the nurses talking about how they wanted to adopt him. And of course he could've had his pick of girls, on or off the ward. He was magnetic.

Out of everyone, he'd chosen me. I was his family.

When we were discharged, Robinson followed me to Klamath Falls. "We need to stick together, Axi," he'd said. "Plus, I have an uncle there. Says I can live in his basement."

I didn't question it—all I cared about was not saying good-bye.

I realized now how much he'd left behind in the course of his life: his parents, his uncle, the doctors who wanted to treat him. It was as if he'd run from everyone but me.

"Am I enough, Robinson?" I heard myself ask. "Can I really be everything you need?"

He shifted in his sleep, stretching out his long legs. But he didn't wake up to answer that critical question.

"I wonder," I went on, "if it's possible to go so far that I'll stop being afraid of us not ever coming back." I chewed on my lip for a while, then drank some more bitter coffee. "I thought I'd figured out the risks. I thought I had everything planned out. But I hadn't counted on you getting sick."

I sneaked another glance at him. His eyelashes made a dark curve against his pale cheek, and his left hand twitched, moving in a dream.

There was another thing I hadn't counted on. And that was falling in love, as fast and irrevocably as you would fall off a cliff, and realizing that loving someone might mean to simultaneously want to slug them and hold them and possibly have to watch them die....I hadn't counted on that.

I reached over and touched his cheek. "I love you," I whispered. "Please stay with me."

In his sleep, Robinson turned and sighed.

34

ROBINSON AND I STOOD, OUR FINGERS INTER-
twined, and stared at the ruins: crumbling buildings,
burned-out houses, litter-strewn sidewalks, and the empty
hulk of an old Ford factory.

"Welcome to Detroit," Robinson said happily. He was
feeling much better today, and I was hoping our location had
nothing to do with it. "Motor City. Motown. I could have
been stuck growing up here if my parents hadn't left."

"It was probably a little nicer back when they were growing up here, huh?" I said, all the while hoping it wasn't sym-
bolic that the first place Robinson and I visited together as a
couple (because that's what we were now, right?) was in total
shambles.

With the tip of his boot, Robinson sent an empty can of
Red Bull arcing into the summer air. "Yeah, probably it was."

I took a picture of a mildewed sofa with a bunch of pigeons
perched on it. To our left, a tree was growing out the side of
a building.

"I guess it could be beautiful, in a way, if you were into

romantic decay or steampunk or something," I said. "Or maybe we should imagine it like the Parthenon in Greece. A bunch of grand old ruins."

Robinson nodded thoughtfully. "That old Ford factory is where my grandma and grandpa met and fell in love," he said. "On the assembly line." He gestured off vaguely in another direction. "And down that way was the Chrysler plant where my mom and dad did the same thing."

I bent down and plucked a dandelion from a crack in the pavement. "So I guess this used to be a pretty romantic place then," I said.

Robinson was quiet, gazing out on the desolation. Thinking, maybe, about his family, wherever they were. So it took me completely by surprise when he whirled me toward him. He held me close for a moment, his arms tightening around me. And then he bent down and kissed me, long and deep, until I felt that familiar softening inside, my legs going wobbly. Like maybe if he didn't keep holding me up, I might dissolve.

When he pulled away, he smiled. "What do you mean *used to be?*"

I kept my arms around his waist. I wanted to be as close to him as possible, for as long as possible. "I stand corrected," I said, looking up at him, backlit by the sun, so the ends of his dark hair looked like they were on fire. "Two generations of your family fell in love here. That's pretty amazing." Thinking: *Now three.*

He nodded, but he didn't elaborate. His eyes had that faraway look in them again.

"I guess you come by your car obsession naturally, then," I continued. I wanted him to keep talking, because he was always so tight-lipped about his family that I knew almost nothing about them.

"My dad always said his first baby was his 1967 Mustang," Robinson offered.

"So you grew up here?" I asked.

Robinson began to whistle that Sufjan Stevens song about Detroit.

I jabbed him in the ribs. "Seriously, you're not going to answer? You tell me you love me, but you don't want to tell me where you were freaking born?" I was laughing, but I was a little offended, too.

When Robinson looked down at me again, his face was clouded. "I'm just not...in close touch with my parents these days. It makes me sad to think about them. So I try not to."

Seeing as how he'd had enough hardship lately, I decided not to press the issue. "Just give me a natal city."

Robinson smiled. "You and your fancy words. *Natal.* World, I ask you: Who says *natal* besides Alexandra Jane Moore?"

I jabbed him in the ribs again. There wasn't anyone but pigeons to answer him.

"No, I wasn't born here," Robinson said finally. "Chrysler moved the plant before I was born. My parents went to North Carolina, and that's where I showed up. My dad worked for a steel company for a while, and then he opened up his own auto repair shop." Robinson began to whistle some other song I didn't recognize, ending our conversation.

I sighed. "At this rate, it'll take me fifty years to learn about your childhood."

He reached out and touched my cheek with his fingertips. "Oh, Axi-face, who cares about the past? We have now."

"Axi-face?" I repeated. I took his hand and brought his fingers to my lips. Smiling, I kissed them on their tips, one after the other.

He nodded. "It's new. You like it?"

"I'll get back to you on that." The truth was, I'd like any pet name he came up with. But I wasn't going to admit it.

For a while we just stood there, being quiet with each other, our fingers touching lightly. We watched birds circling overhead, and the clouds shifting. It struck me then that the earth could be covered in trash and wreckage, but you could always find something that seemed clean and perfect. Maybe that was a metaphor for something.

After a while I leaned in to give Robinson a gentle kiss. He took my face in his hands. "So," he said, "can I buy you dinner or what?"

I smiled. "Does that make it a date?"

Grinning back, he shrugged. "Depends. Am I going to get past first base?"

"Pig," I said, laughing.

"Pig!" he repeated. "Speaking of which, let's go eat some."

35

WE PLAYED MOTOWN IN THE CAR—DIANA ROSS,
Stevie Wonder—as we drove downtown. Robinson hummed
and tapped his fingers on the dash, following the drumbeats
and adding little flourishes of his own.

We found a restaurant full of Christmas lights and
orange-velvet banquettes, its walls hung with funky instru-
ments and dozens of black-and-white pictures of Detroit in
its old-timey heyday. Someone was playing the piano in the
corner, loudly, and the place was packed.

"It's like a speakeasy crossed with a TGI Fridays," I said
as we sat down.

"Or, like, if Liberace were a gangster and this was his
living room."

"Or it's the hangout of a pimp who likes jazz and antiques,"
I said.

Robinson grinned. "It's awesome."

We found a table in the corner, and the waiter came by
and set two small glasses full of clear liquid on the table.
"Hungarian moonshine," he said, by way of greeting. "It's

Ed's birthday." He seemed to think we should know who Ed was. "I'll be back to take your order in a minute."

Robinson and I looked at the glasses and then at each other. "Should we?" I asked.

He pretended to look disappointed. "I have so many fake IDs. I really wanted the chance to use another one."

We held up our glasses and clinked them together. "*Sláinte*," I said.

"*Slan-cha?*" Robinson said, frowning. "I've heard that before . . . what does it mean?"

I shrugged. "Dunno. It's just some old Irish toast." But of course I knew exactly what it meant. It meant "health." Because didn't that matter more than just about anything these days?

We knocked our glasses back, and the liquid burned down my throat, making me shudder. "Is that what radiator fluid tastes like?"

Robinson was sloshing it around in his mouth. Then he swallowed. "This is more like rubbing alcohol, I'd say."

I could feel it in my stomach now, warming me. Was it possible that I felt looser, almost light-headed already? "Funny how a tiny little shot makes me feel so rebellious, when I'm already a car thief."

"I believe your term was *borrower*," Robinson noted.

"Because that's going to go over really well with the judge," I said. *"Oh, you were only borrowing that Porsche? No problem, then!"*

"You guys aren't from around here, are you?"

Robinson and I both looked up, startled. Guilty people are jumpy people, I guess. But it was only our waiter, who looked like he'd had a shot or two of the moonshine himself.

"No, sir," Robinson said, polite as can be.

The waiter pointed a finger at us. "Well, when you go

back home, tell your friends how the Big D is doing just fine. I know you went and saw the closed-up factories; everybody does. But don't remember just the dead stuff. Remember this." He waved his arm around the happy, noisy room. "Remember the music and the moonshine. Is that a deal?"

Robinson and I nodded in tandem, and the waiter nodded back, satisfied. "Be back in a minute for that order."

When he left again, Robinson reached for my hand. "He's right. You have to remember the good stuff, Axi."

There was something about the way he said it that made a chill crawl up my spine. Like he was talking about much more than just Detroit. But I smiled and shook his hand anyway. "It's a deal. Scout's honor," I said. "Pinkie swear. Blah blah blah."

Robinson smiled. "You really are beautiful, you know that?" he said.

I looked down at the tabletop, but he reached out and tucked a finger under my chin, tipping my face up so I had to look right into his dark eyes.

"I mean it. Someone should tell you that every single day of your life. And right now, it gets to be me."

"It's always going to be you," I whispered.

He smiled again. "Get over here."

I went around to his side of the booth—and I sat down in his lap. It surprised both of us.

"Axi," he said, his voice soft and throaty. He ran a fingertip along my collarbone. "I never took you for the PDA type."

I shivered under his touch and pressed my forehead to his. When I spoke, our lips were tantalizingly close. "I'm learning how to live dangerously," I said.

He moved a fraction of an inch closer, so his lips almost brushed mine. "And what do you think of it?" he whispered.

I could almost taste him, and I held out for another long, delicious moment before finally pressing my mouth against his. Pushing my fingers into the tangle of his hair. We kissed, and warmth flooded my body.

"I like it," I whispered. "A lot."

I was nearly dizzy. *So this is what being intoxicated feels like.* But it wasn't from the shot I'd taken.

I am here to say that moonshine has nothing on love—and lust.

36

"THE BLUE STREAK, THE MEAN STREAK, AND the Millennium Force," Robinson said. "I want to go on all of them. You only get to go on the Mean Streak, Axi."

He was pretending to be mad at me because I'd told him he couldn't have a Slim Jim until he'd eaten a banana. *Who are you, my mother?* he'd asked. I told him I couldn't watch him eat things made from mechanically separated chicken, aka *slimy pink meat paste*, anymore. Then he'd accused me of being a snotty vegetarian, and I had tackled and tickled him in the cab of the truck until he pleaded for mercy.

Now we were inside the gates at Cedar Point, the roller-coaster capital of the world, nestled away in Sandusky, Ohio. Robinson, the daredevil, and me, the one who gets queasy on swings.

"I feel like the Junior Gemini might be more my speed," I said.

Robinson snorted. "Axi, you've done things lately that were a lot scarier than a roller coaster." He cocked a finger at me, miming a gun.

"Don't remind me," I said.

"So. Shall we?" he asked, and held out his arm.

How could I refuse him? My scalawag, my partner in crime, my heart. He seemed like he was in perfect health. Was he? I didn't know, but now was the time to enjoy it.

We stood in the first line for an hour at least, surrounded by tired parents, their hyperactive eight-year-olds and sullen thirteen-year-olds, and a handful of sunburned retirees apparently willing to risk a heart attack to pull four g's on a single plummet.

Robinson saw me picking nervously at the hem of my T-shirt. "I'm telling you, this is going to be awesome," he said. "You're going to love it."

He reached out and stroked my hair, and then his fingers moved down to my neck, kneading gently, reassuringly.

I almost moaned in pleasure. "Whatever you say..." Suddenly I wasn't thinking about the ride at all anymore. I was thinking about his hands. "Just keep doing that."

He laughed, rubbing my shoulders now, his body long and warm against my back. "Is this all it takes?" he asked. "A little back rub and tough Axi Moore turns into a quivering pile of acquiescence?"

"Ooh, that's a big word for you," I teased, trying to reclaim some measure of my sass. It wasn't easy.

"Maybe a good vocabulary is contagious," he said.

"Mmmmmmm."

"Although it seems like you might be losing yours."

"Mmmmm, lower..."

Robinson pulled me against him then, wrapping his arms around me from behind. "Maybe we shouldn't get too carried away," he said into my ear.

I sighed. "I guess..."

"But you're not afraid anymore, are you?"

I shook my head firmly. I wasn't.

Of course, my heart *did* begin pounding as soon as we climbed into the rear car of the Millennium Force, but I told myself it was because of excitement, not fear. I told myself that compared to all the things we'd done that were authentically dangerous, like stealing cars and riding motorcycles and breaking into people's pools, this was a walk in the park.

When we rose slowly up the hill, the tracks amazingly smooth beneath us, I grabbed Robinson's hand. Ahead of us people were already screaming. My knuckles went white around Robinson's fingers.

"Here it comes," he said.

When it seemed that the car could climb no higher into the faultless summer sky, we came to the top, paused for one silent, anticipatory second—and then plunged down. *Downdowndowndowndown.*

I screamed more loudly than I ever would have thought possible, and beside me Robinson let out a wild whoop of joy. We raced and looped above the park, the wind making my eyes water and the car whipping me back and forth. I never stopped screaming, not for one single instant. And Robinson, he just laughed and laughed, letting my fingernails dig half-moons into his skin.

When we finally slowed down on the last approach and pulled under the awning to stop, I turned to Robinson, an enormous smile on my face. "Wow," I declared. "I want to do that again."

He gave me a triumphant look. "I knew you'd like it. I know you better than you know yourself." Then he reached up. "Give me a little help here, will you?"

I bent down and grabbed his hand, felt the weight of his palm in mine. "Thanks," he said. He brushed my bangs out of the way, and then his lips against my forehead were soft and sweet.

Holding hands loosely, we walked out onto the concourse, which was lined with flowers, streaming with people, and fragrant with the smells of fried food and sunscreen.

"Let's get cotton candy," I said.

"And sodas as big as our torsos," Robinson added.

"And nachos and licorice ropes," I cried, beginning to skip.

Robinson laughed as I tugged him along behind me. "I think the roller coaster knocked a screw loose. Don't you want some kale or something?"

"Tomorrow! Today we're going to act like normal teenagers!"

Because today I actually felt like one. As if nothing made Robinson and me different from anyone else our age—not sickness, crime, or anything. We were carefree. Lucky. Immortal.

"Have I ever told you I love you?" Robinson asked, catching up to me.

"Yes, but tell me again," I said, stopping to press myself against him.

"I love you," he said.

"I love you back," I said.

And then we kissed on the midway as crowds of people streamed around us and the roller coaster cars corkscrewed overhead.

37

"So," Robinson said, "onward to the Big Apple?" We were finally heading for the truck, so exhausted it felt like we ought to take turns carrying each other.

"No one calls it the Big Apple, you know," I said. "That's a tourist thing."

"And we're not tourists?" he asked, lifting one dark eyebrow.

"No, we're *adventurers*," I said. "Explorers."

Robinson handed me the souvenir key chain he'd bought at the last gift shop before the exit. It was a tiny model of the Millennium Force, tucked inside a snow globe. "Since you're a driver now and all," he said, grinning crookedly.

"Of course, I don't have any keys," I pointed out.

"Hey, if you don't want it, I can hook it to my screwdriver or my cordless drill."

But of course I wanted it. It was a present from the boy I loved. "I'm going to get you something, too, you know," I said, giving the snow globe a little shake.

Robinson demanded to know what it was, but I shook my head and mimed zipping my lips. "It's a surprise."

As I climbed into the driver's seat of the truck, I caught Robinson eyeing a sporty black BMW parked next to us. "Don't even think about it," I said. "I can't drive a stick."

"I'll teach you that next," he said. "And then, ATVs."

"Then dirt bikes," I said. "Why not?" Because everything was going to be just fine from now on. Maybe we really did have all the time in the world.

With Robinson as my navigator, I got us onto I-80. We had a long drive ahead of us, and the back roads just weren't going to cut it. I wanted something lined with Starbucks.

"Doesn't time move slower the faster you go?" Robinson asked, staring out at flat green fields and signs for Pacific Pride truck stops.

I thought back to my physics class, which felt like it was about a million years ago (so what does that say about time?). "It's only a matter of nanoseconds or something. Time moves slower the closer you are to the earth, too."

"That gives me an excellent reason not to go mountain climbing."

"As if you needed one," I said.

"True. Somehow the thought of plunging hundreds of feet to my death never appealed to me." He toyed with the key chain, watching the snow sift down over the tiny roller coaster. "Do you ever think about what happens after?" he asked suddenly.

"After what?" I asked, moving into the passing lane.

"After we earn our wings," he said. He looked at me, waiting for a reaction. I kept my eyes on the road. "Don't joke," I said.

Robinson crossed his arms over his chest. "I'm not joking. I'm asking."

"After we 'earn our wings' ..."

"Don't you remember? Nurse Sophie used to say that all the time. She was totally sincere."

I pressed harder on the gas pedal. I was actually going the speed limit now. "Because she believed that when you die, you become an angel," I said. "Whereas you think we just take a dirt nap."

Robinson snickered. "Sorry. That dirt nap thing always gets me."

"It's not funny," I said.

But the truth was, we'd joked about death constantly back in the ward. All of us had, because somehow it made us less afraid. *Oh, I'm sooo tired*, someone would say, *I think I'll go sleep with the fishes.* Someone else would pipe up: *Lately I've been thinking about buying a pine condo.* Or: *Yeah, I'm planning on going into the fertilizer business.*

It was flipping Death the bird. And it made awful things like chemotherapy-induced nausea and hair loss just slightly less awful. But I thought—or hoped—that Robinson and I had left that sort of thing behind us. That such humor was no longer... medically relevant.

"I don't know, Robinson," I said, gripping the steering wheel. "I want to think there's something on the other side, but where's the evidence? No one sends you a postcard from the afterlife."

"Which is totally rude of them," he replied.

"I know, right?" I raised my fist. "Do you hear that, Carole Ann? *Rude.*"

Robinson reached over and put his hand on my knee. "Don't worry," he said. "I'll write you."

I felt like I'd been punched in the gut.

And I wanted to laugh, to show that I knew he was joking. But I wasn't entirely sure he was.

38

WE CROSSED THE WIDE EXPANSE OF PENNSYLVA-
nia while Robinson slept. In the dark it looked like any
other state, and I shot through it at seventy-five.

In East Orange, New Jersey, at midmorning, I sent Robinson into a Pathmark to buy groceries ("healthy stuff," I'd
said, fully expecting him to try to pass off Froot Loops as
actual fruit) while I went across the street to a place called
All That Glitters Is Gold.

Thanks to my dad, I knew my way around a pawnshop.
Which was how, for fifty bucks and the pearl-and-gold
bracelet that had been my mother's, I bought Robinson an
acoustic guitar.

"Where'd you go?" Robinson asked when I pulled up outside the Pathmark. He set the bag of groceries in the backseat, and I was shocked to see an actual banana in it.

"Just a quick errand," I said, trying not to smile at the
thought of the guitar hidden under the tent behind the backseat. "Did you honestly buy fruit and vegetables?"

He leaned over and kissed my neck. "Tell me where you went," he said, his lips ticklish on my skin.

I drew in my breath. "No." Every time he touched me, I felt my whole body begin to hum and shiver.

"Tell me," he said again, moving from my neck to my earlobe, his mouth light and teasing.

"Robinson," I whispered. I'd tell him anything, I'd give up every secret I'd ever had, if he kept doing that.

I pulled him toward me, my mouth finding his. Before I knew it, my fingers were on the buttons of his shirt. I managed to get the top two undone, but then suddenly he moved away from me. He backed up against the car door, rebuttoning his shirt quickly.

I sat up straight, blinking. Confused. Didn't he want it, too?

"What?" I asked. "Why—"

"Security guards," Robinson said, nodding toward the burly guys walking up and down the rows of the parking lot.

There were three of them—two only a stone's throw away. But they could have been sitting in the backseat and I wouldn't have noticed while Robinson was filling up all my senses.

"We should probably go," he said. "We can, um, do some more of that later."

My cheeks were pink with embarrassment. "Okay," I said. As if I didn't want to shout, *Hell yes, we will!*

Robinson smiled. "But you know what? I think I want to drive."

I was so relieved that he was feeling good, so thrilled at the way I could kiss him now whenever I wanted—security guards notwithstanding—that I, small-town girl Axi Moore, didn't freak out at *all* when the New York skyline became visible along the turnpike, with its hills and valleys of silvery skyscrapers. I didn't care that we sat in traffic outside the Holland Tunnel for forty-five minutes, or that Robinson got lost on the way across town to the East Village.

He was driving. He was happy and strong. That made everything okay.

39

TOGETHER, ALONG WITH A CRUSH OF TOURISTS, we walked down St. Marks Place, trying on cheap sunglasses at the outdoor booths and browsing a two-story store called Trash and Vaudeville, where Robinson posed for a picture in a silver pleather biker jacket and I tried on a bright blue wig. We stopped in to St. Mark's Bookshop, and I got a copy of Whitman's *Leaves of Grass* and a book of Dylan Thomas poems.

"Poetry?" Robinson said, looking aghast.

"Just read one," I said.

Robinson opened the Whitman to a random page and cleared his throat. " 'A child said, What is the grass? fetching it to me with full hands;/How could I answer the child?... I do not know what it is any more than he./I guess it must be the flag of my disposition, out of hopeful green stuff woven.' " He looked at me, intrigued. "Okay," he said, "I like that well enough. 'Hopeful green stuff woven.' "

I laughed. "I've got something you'll like better, though." I took his hand and led him down the street to the car.

"Is it my surprise?" he asked excitedly.

"Look under the tent," I said.

When Robinson pulled out the guitar, his whole face lit up. He hefted the weight of it in his hands and plucked a string experimentally.

"Axi, how—"

"Let's go play it," I said. I didn't want to have to tell him that I'd given up my mother's bracelet—the last thing I had of hers—to buy it. And that I wasn't the least bit sorry.

Hand in hand, we walked over to Tompkins Square Park and found a bench beneath a ring of ginkgo trees. Robinson strummed for a moment, finding the chords. They seemed familiar to me, but I didn't recognize the tune until he began to sing.

"*Moving forward using all my breath*," Robinson sang. The song was "I Melt with You."

I haven't talked about Robinson's voice, and this is partly because I can't explain it. It's clear and rough at the same time; it's intimate but also demands an audience. It's usually soft, but somehow you hear it not just with your ears but with your whole body. And with your heart most of all.

People who were walking by began to stop to listen as he sang. Robinson didn't seem to notice them gradually gathering around him, though. His eyes were on his boot, tapping on the cobblestones. Every once in a while, he looked at me, right into my eyes, singing: "*I'll stop the world and melt with you…*"

Soon there was a big circle of people, young, old, and in between. Most of them were parents, with kids carrying stuffed bunnies or pockmarked Nerf footballs or—the older ones—iPhones. And these parents all knew the song, because it was the one they'd danced to twenty years earlier, when they were in high school and in love for the first time.

At first a few of them just mouthed the words, but then, quietly, they began to sing. Then others joined in, too, and they lost their hard, blank city faces and smiled, and in another minute it was a damn *sing-along*. I swear to God, there were people with tears in their eyes, because that's how beautiful Robinson is when he plays.

When the song ended, there was silence. For a moment I felt like the entire city went quiet and took one long, sweet breath. Like everyone, everywhere, was thinking about life, and how it is the happiest and saddest thing, the most wonderful and the most terrible and the most precious.

Then the silence broke. A woman in a bright yellow dress began to clap, and then, just the way the singing had grown, so did the clapping, until the applause was really loud. There was another woman blowing her nose, and a man staring up at the sky and blinking really hard and fast—but most people were just smiling.

An old man stepped forward and placed his cap on the ground. "You forgot to pass the hat," he said.

Robinson looked up, startled. "Pardon?" he said. He was still in the world of the song. He didn't realize there was anyone but him and me.

The old man looked a little like Ernie. He turned back to the crowd and called, "Cough it up for the young performer, all right?"

Robinson and I watched as almost every person stepped forward with quarters and dollars. I saw a woman give her daughter some money, and the girl tiptoed up and put a twenty into the hat. She was about Carole Ann's age when she died, the age she'd be forever. Her hair was even red, like my sister's.

"Thank you," I whispered.

Then it was all over, and the people left. Robinson and I were alone again. The hat was full of money.

Robinson was smiling at me. "We're rich," he said, and he pulled me onto his lap.

And truly, then, it felt like we were.

40

WE DECIDED TO SPLURGE ON A HOSTEL THAT night. It sounded like a better idea than sleeping on a park bench, though we would've had plenty of interesting company had we gone that route.

The Grand Street Hostel was on the edge of Little Italy, where it bleeds into Chinatown, and it looked decent enough from the outside. There were a couple of backpacker types smoking out front, and the guy at the desk was friendly in a stoned sort of way.

But Robinson and I quickly learned that the difference between a hostel and a hotel goes way, *way* beyond the minor distinction in spelling. When the *s* is added, you subtract things like privacy, comfort, and in this case, ceilings. The hostel was a maze of tiny, thin-walled cells, sloppily constructed inside an enormous hangarlike room.

"It's a bit more prison-y than I might have expected," Robinson said.

"No kidding," I agreed, stepping over a lone boot in the hall. "I feel like we should have gotten fingerprinted."

Luckily, we had our own room, with two single beds pushed right up against each other, and about six inches of floor space on either side.

"Well, the sheets look clean, at least," Robinson said brightly. Then he gave me a quick kiss and headed down the hall to the bathroom.

I sat on the corner of the bed and looked up at the non-ceiling. I could hear one end of an unpleasant cell phone conversation from a nearby room. *It's not my fault you got kicked out*, someone said. *Everyone's hated you for years*.

I hummed a little, trying to give this person some privacy. The song was "Tangled Up in Blue," but you wouldn't know it, since I can't carry a tune. I can't play an instrument, either. "It's okay," Robinson used to assure me. "You'll make me a great roadie someday."

I hummed faster and plucked at the corner of the sheet. I realized I was nervous, but also excited. Robinson and I hadn't been alone in a room together since LA, when we ever-so-chastely watched *Puss in Boots*. What would happen tonight, I wondered. How *un*chaste would we be?

This was another thing I definitely hadn't planned for. It was a road I'd just have to feel my way along.

No pun intended.

When Robinson came in from the bathroom, his hair was wet and he smelled like Ivory. His shirt hung loosely on his shoulders, and he was wearing blue plaid boxers.

He placed his folded jeans on top of his backpack. The bed sighed as he sat down.

"Hi," I half-whispered.

"Hi back," he said softly. "Well. What do you want to do now?"

I knew the answer to that question, even if it kind of ... scared me a little. I took a deep breath, willing myself to be brave.

I slipped my shirt over my head.

Robinson sucked in his breath. And then he gently swept the long waves of my hair away from the back of my neck and kissed me there. I shivered, goose bumps rising on my arms.

I could feel his breath, the impossible softness of his lips. I tilted my head back, and he ran a finger down my neck, stopping in the hollow of my clavicle for a moment before tracing each of my collarbones. He kissed along my shoulders, tickling me with the tiniest scratches of his unshaven chin.

We fell back against the bed, and above me, Robinson shrugged off his flannel. Then he bent his dark head down, and we were nothing but lips and tongues and teeth until we had to stop to catch our breath.

Then we lay there, our eyes locked in the half-light. Robinson was looking at me the way you'd look at something you'd lost a million years ago and never thought you'd find.

I gazed back at him in wonder, realizing how much of him there was still to discover: the scar on the inside of his palm, the blue veins in his wrist, the triangle of freckles on his chest, just to the left of his breastbone. These small, secret places. I wanted to know all of them.

But I didn't know how far things would go tonight. I wanted to be slow—and I wanted to go fast.

Robinson cleared his throat. "Do you—?" he began.

"I don't have any protection, if that's what you were going to ask." My voice came out too loud, and I shrank back against him in embarrassment.

He made a noise—a grunt? A half-laugh?

"I don't want to have kids," I blurted.

Then he really did laugh. "Whoa, Axi. Moving a little fast, are we?"

I pulled the blanket up over my face. This was all so new to me. Could I help it if I was doing it wrong?

But still, there was something I wanted him to know. I forced myself to keep talking, though part of me was ready to die of humiliation. "I didn't think we were about to make a baby, Robinson. I meant it as a philosophical thing. Between the Moore family cancer genes and, like, global warming, any kid of mine would be doomed. She'd be born with blue eyes and a ticking time bomb inside her, just like the rest of my family. Talk about getting dealt a shitty hand of cards." I tried not to sound as bitter as I felt.

Robinson was slowly stroking my fingers. "The blue eyes are so nice, though," he said quietly.

I smiled and placed my hand on his smooth chest. His arm was tucked under my neck, and as we lay there, it felt like we were extensions of each other. Like our bodies and our hearts had to be together to make one whole, perfect person.

41

THE NEXT MORNING WE WOKE UP IN THAT SAME position—through some miracle, Robinson's arm hadn't fallen asleep during the night. We got coffee and big, pillowy bagels from the corner deli. We asked for them toasted and dripping with butter—Robinson's favorite. Then we took the subway up to the Metropolitan Museum of Art.

When a panhandler made his way through the subway car, dressed as if it were winter instead of June, Robinson reached into his pocket and produced a crumpled five.

The panhandler bowed as he accepted it. "Money and a beautiful woman. You have everything, sir."

"Well, actually, now *you* have my money," Robinson pointed out.

The panhandler considered this fact for a moment. "But who needs money when you have her?"

"My thoughts exactly," Robinson said. He put his arm around me like I belonged to him.

When we got to the Met, we wandered among the huge,

high-ceilinged rooms, ogling famous works we'd only seen in tiny reproductions: Monet's *Rouen Cathedral*, Van Gogh's *Cypresses*, Georgia O'Keeffe's *Black Iris*, and Jackson Pollock's *Autumn Rhythm*.

And although I was staring at masterpieces, what I kept seeing was Robinson the night before, shirtless, lying next to me. It made it hard to concentrate. Sometimes, when he looked at me in a certain way, I wondered if he was having the same experience. "A pretty girl who naked is/is worth a million statues." The poet e. e. cummings wrote that. (Not that I'd been totally naked. Just...partially.)

Robinson stopped in front of *Madame X*, a portrait of a beautiful woman by John Singer Sargent, and shook his head in wonder. "We sure don't have art like this in Klamath Falls," he said.

"We don't even have *falls* in Klamath Falls," I replied.

I'd thought that maybe a part of me would miss my hometown. Crappy as it was, it was still mine. But I missed nothing—because everything that truly mattered to me was either already gone or right here next to me in the museum, holding my hand.

When we ended up in front of the Egyptian tomb—the one where Holden Caulfield almost has a breakdown in *The Catcher in the Rye*—Robinson bent to wipe a scuff from the toe of his boot.

"I'll try not to take this as a sign," he said.

"A sign of what?" I asked sharply.

"Doom," Robinson answered. "Isn't stumbling across a pharaoh's tomb worse than, like, a black cat crossing your path? You know, King Tut's curse and all those stories..."

I slid my hand into the back pocket of his jeans. "No, Scalawag, don't be silly. We were randomly walking. We could have just as easily ended up in the café or something."

"Which reminds me—"

"—that you're hungry."

"Exactly." He stood up a little straighter, and I could see the way he shook off his moment of worry. "Do you know what else I want?"

"No," I said, but the word caught in my throat, because I did know, of course. I just wanted to make him show me the answer.

Robinson backed me up against the wall and pressed his lips to mine. My arms circled his waist and I arched myself against him. This was what *I* was hungry for...

A group of kids in Camp Treetop T-shirts filed into the room, so we ducked into the tomb to make out in secret. We hardly even cared when a few giggling kids spied us and called some of their friends over.

But we pulled apart and, exchanging some giggles ourselves, quickly made our exit.

42

Our final New York destination: Nathan's Famous. It was all the way out on Coney Island—which is not actually an island but is so far away from Manhattan on the lurching, sluggish F train that it felt like an entirely different world.

When we finally got there, the beach was as wide and flat as a parking lot, the waves small and distant. There were a lot of people, and some of them were actually swimming, which no one in Oregon did without a wet suit. The Pacific is *cold*.

Though Robinson seemed drained, we strolled along the boardwalk past bumper cars and an arcade popping with digital gunfire. People were flying kites and skateboarding and jogging and hawking cheap souvenirs, like huge foam sunglasses and T-shirts that said KEEP CONEY ISLAND FREAKY.

"You want to ride the Cylone?" I asked, pointing to the roller coaster in the distance. "Or the Wonder Wheel?"

Robinson shook his head. "Let's just get the hot dogs."

Because he seemed so tired all of a sudden, I suggested, ever so delicately, the idea of going back to the hostel. But Robinson wouldn't hear of it.

"I need my daily dose of nitrates," he said. "Plus, we're tourists, and it's our job to be touristy."

So we turned up Surf Avenue, where the enormous green sign for Nathan's loomed above the street. There was a big outdoor seating area, with seagulls perched near the plastic tables waiting for scraps. The air smelled like the sea and beer and grease. Not that appetizing, in my opinion, but Robinson's whole demeanor had changed. He looked like a kid on Christmas morning.

"How many should I get?" he asked.

"I don't know," I said, scanning the menu. "Two?" I was going to have to order the Caesar salad, since this wasn't exactly the place to get a tofu dog.

Robinson scoffed at two. "Sonya 'the Black Widow' Thomas ate more than forty. Says right there on the sign."

"But that was a hot dog–eating *contest*," I said. "This is just a meal."

Robinson considered the statement. "True. I'll settle for… four. One with chili, one with sauerkraut, and two plain."

"You're taking your life in your hands," I said disapprovingly.

"Only my gastrointestinal tract," Robinson countered, and I grimaced.

Instead of eating with the rest of the crowd, we took our food back to the beach and sat on the warm, gritty sand. It was littered with cigarette butts and half-buried beer cans. But still! The ocean was a gorgeous blue-green, and the weather was perfect, and we were together.

"Can you believe that two weeks ago we were on a beach in California?" Robinson asked.

"Crazy," I said, taking a stab at a limp piece of lettuce. "We've done so much."

Robinson waggled his eyebrows at me. "Not enough, if you know what I mean."

"Pervert," I said, nudging him with my bare toe.

He bit into his second—or was it third?—hot dog and nudged me back.

I decided to abandon my wilted, greasy salad and lay back in the sand, watching the kites swoop and dive above me. I must have fallen asleep for a little while, because when I woke, Robinson wasn't next to me anymore.

I looked around for a moment, and when I didn't see him, I got up and began walking toward the boardwalk. Maybe he'd gone off to find the Headless Woman or Insectavora, the tattooed fire-eater. Maybe he was buying me a Coney Island shot glass to go with my Cedar Point snow globe.

But he wasn't doing either of those things. Instead, I found him leaning against a fence, shaking.

And vomiting.

I reached out to touch his shoulder, but he waved me away. I took a step back. "You need to see a doctor, Robinson," I pleaded.

After a moment he looked up, his face pale and his eyes red and watering. "Before you go all drama on me," he said, "it was the hot dogs. Not the you-know-what."

"And how do you know that?" I asked.

"I'm *fine* now. And actually, this is totally awesome," he said, wiping his face and trying to smile at me. "I could so beat that Black Widow lady—I'll just eat and barf, eat and barf, and that way I can consume an unlimited number of hot dogs."

I sighed. "You are sick, Robinson. In a lot of ways."

"But you love me," he said, reaching for my hands.

"I do," I said. *So much.*

Robinson fell asleep on the train home, and I practically had to carry him up to our cell in the hostel. He seemed feverish, but I told myself it was just sunburn. Windburn. Whatever it needed to be, as long as it wasn't another infection.

I sat for a long time, listening to the sounds of the city all around us, but mostly just watching him sleep. Were his cheeks less full? His eyes deeper, more sunken? It could be happening so slowly, so subtly, that I hadn't been able to see it...

I lay down beside Robinson and curled my body around his, remembering how I'd refused to tell him a bedtime story back in Las Vegas. I pressed my cheek against his beating heart and vowed I would never say no to him again.

43

"WE HAVE TO GO TO PHILLY," ROBINSON announced.

"We do?"

He nodded. "I'm not saying this trip is a bucket list or anything, but it is extremely important that I eat a Philly cheesesteak."

I handed our room key to the stoned front-desk clerk, and we stepped into the sunshine. "Tell me you're joking," I said, thinking, *He can't keep a hot dog down, so why on earth is he talking about cheesesteaks?*

Robinson shook his head. "Today I want to do everything, Axi. Every silly thing I can think of."

I put my hand on his waist, slipped my fingers under the edge of his shirt to feel his skin. I could feel him shiver at my touch. "As opposed to yesterday, or the day before, when you were a good boy and did only what others told you to do?"

He laughed and wrapped his arms around me. "Okay, you have a point."

I didn't want to spoil the mood, but I had to say what I

was thinking. "We've had a lot of fun, and we can definitely keep on having it. But I think you should see a doctor, just to be sure."

Robinson shook his head again, this time more emphatically. "No can do, Aximoron. Places to go, people to see..."

I looked at him carefully, weighing his stubbornness against mine. If I fought hard now, maybe I could get him to go. Just a minor checkup, I'd say, a quick ear to the lungs and heart, maybe a *tiny* little X-ray and reading of his LDH levels. I'd sit in the waiting room, staring at stale magazines and waiting for good news.

Because maybe it would work out. Who was to say it couldn't?

On the other hand, if Robinson went to the hospital, he would resent me for it. Intensely, and possibly eternally.

Whose trip is it, Axi? I asked myself. *Yours? Or his?* Because in the end, someone had to make the call.

"It's less than two hours away," Robinson said, interrupting my thoughts. "It's not like I'm asking you to drive me to Daytona."

"You're not going to do that next, are you?"

"No, ma'am. Scout's honor."

I sighed. "Fine," I said. "You win."

He smiled his beautiful smile. "I love it when you roll your eyes like that," he said. "It's adorable."

"Oh, stop."

"And when you sort of wrinkle up your nose, like you smell something funny, but it's really that you're trying to decide whether to laugh or be annoyed."

"Oh, *really.* What else do you love about me?" I was annoyed, but it was at myself rather than at Robinson. Or not annoyed, exactly—more like...scared.

We were at the truck now, and I was climbing into the

driver's seat. "Let's hear it," I said. I pulled into the street and pointed us toward the Holland Tunnel. You'd almost think I had a license to drive.

"Well, everything," Robinson said. "But specifically? The list is kind of long."

"You are such a flatterer," I said.

Robinson didn't say anything for a while after that. In fact, we were on the other side of the river before he spoke, and I thought he'd fallen asleep.

"I love how you touch the tip of your nose when you're thinking hard about something," he said, turning to fix his gaze on me. "I love how you tuck your hair behind your ears but it always slips right back down immediately. I love your eyes and your perfect lips. I love that your nail polish, when you bother to wear it, is always chipped. I love how you use fancy words that I have to look up at home. I love the tiny little crescent moon of a birthmark on the tip of your left pinkie. I love the way—"

I didn't need to hear any more. I needed to kiss him. So I pulled over to the side of the road, and there, with the New York City skyline behind us, I did.

"It's going to take a lot longer to get to Philly this way," Robinson said, talking and kissing and smiling all at once.

"We have time," I said. "We have so much time."

44

"SO, SCALAWAG, DO YOU WANT TO GO TO PAT'S King of Steaks or Geno's?" I asked, poking Robinson awake—gently, of course. We'd made it to Philly in under two hours, and now I was parked between the two cheesesteak institutions, which stood a block away from each other like captains of opposing teams.

Robinson yawned and stretched. "You know," he said, frowning slightly, "I'm not actually that hungry right now." For a moment he placed his hand over his stomach—a strange kind of gesture for him. "What I'd like is a nice warm drink."

I looked at him sharply. It was eighty degrees out, and I was sweating against the truck seat. "You're not cold, are you?"

Being cold meant that Robinson might have a fever, and if he had a fever, that meant he might have an infection, and if he had an infection, then he needed to get to a hospital. Stat. Because infections in what doctors like to call an immunocompromised person—a person like Robinson, who'd had high-dose chemo, radiation therapy, and a stem cell transplant—could be deadly.

I reached toward his forehead to feel it, but he brushed my hand away. "No!" he said, a little too loudly. "I just thought some tea sounded nice. Then we go get the cheesesteak."

He got out of the truck and started walking. I stayed where I was, staring at him through the windshield, feeling both mad and worried. What was I supposed to do? Drag him to the ER so they could take his temperature? He wouldn't let me.

So I got out and caught up to him—easily, because he was walking at an old man's pace. Like every step took concentration and effort.

"A little caffeine and I'll be good to go," he said, pointing to a coffee shop at the end of the block.

Please be right about that, I thought. I took his hand.

In the café we found a window table and sank into the worn but comfortable seats. Then a salesman type burst in and commandeered the table next to us, talking on his cell phone and at the same time waving the waitress over, as if it were a matter of life and death that he got served before we did. "...QR codes are going to increase the conversion rate of your sales funnel—" he was saying. When the waitress walked by he shouted, "Large Earl Grey with soy milk on the side and raw sugar, *two lumps*."

Robinson glared at him for a moment. "This is the City of Brotherly Love, jerk," he muttered. Then he rested his head on the table. "Man. I don't know why I'm so tired."

I wanted to scream, *Because you have cancer?*

Instead, I reached out and ran my fingers through his thick, dark hair. I'd almost forgotten what he looked like without it. It took a while to grow back after the chemo, but when it did, he grew it longer.

"That feels good," he said, his voice muffled.

I took a deep breath, steeling myself for what I had to say. "Robinson, we need to get you back to a hospital—actually, *our* hospital. I'll use my credit card and we'll fly home. We can be there in ten hours."

"I don't like planes," Robinson said to the tabletop.

"You have to see Dr. Suzuki. Now. She'll know what to do."

"Every time I hear her name, I think about violin lessons. Have you heard of the Suzuki method of teaching music?"

"*Don't* change the subject."

Robinson lifted his head from the table. His tired eyes met mine. "You say she'll know what to do. But what if there's nothing to be done?"

"There's always something to be done," I said, my voice rising. I didn't like this new fatalistic tone of his at all.

"You've planned everything so perfectly, Axi. Please don't get all freaked out now."

I reached for his hands and gripped them hard. "But when does it end, Robinson? We can't run like this forever."

"We're not going to," he assured me. "We just have one more stop to make. It's the last one."

"One last stop?" I asked. "Where's that? Please don't say you want to go to New Orleans to eat jambalaya or something."

He laughed and squeezed my fingers. "No. My stomach is no longer dictating our travels. But it's ... well, it's a couple of states away."

"A couple of *states?*" I repeated. I doubted Chuck the Truck would make it that far.

Next to us the salesman had begun shouting. "No, Ed, the goal is to *shorten* the amount of time it takes the *probable purchaser* to become a *product owner!*"

Both Robinson and I glared at him now. He'd taken a table that could have seated six, and he was treating it like his desk. Scattered across it were his iPad, a BlackBerry, a leather binder, a copy of the *Philadelphia Inquirer*, car keys...

His car keys.

It was then that I had an idea that would have shocked the old Axi Moore to the depths of her soul. Good thing she no longer existed.

"Axi?" Robinson said, waving a hand in front of my face. "Aren't you going to get on my case for not telling you where I want to go?"

"Yes," I said distractedly. "Later." I was staring at the salesman. *Get up*, I thought. *Get up.*

"The numbers don't add up, Ed," he yelled.

And then, as if what I'd just imagined were totally meant to be, the salesman stood. Still yammering into his Bluetooth, he made his way toward the bathrooms.

I got up and threw a five on the table. "Meet me at the southeast corner of the block," I said, and I was out the door before Robinson had even opened his mouth to ask me why.

Outside, I half-jogged down the street, clicking the automatic lock button on the key chain and watching for the answering flicker of headlights. Would it be the blue Acura? The silver Toyota? I had such a mighty sense of purpose that I hardly noticed the racing of my heart. I was taking care of Robinson. If he needed to go somewhere, I was going to see to it that his journey took place in a reliable vehicle.

I'd crossed onto the next block and was nearing the third without a single chirp of a car. My pulse quickened and my head began to hurt.

I was stealing a car.

In broad daylight.

Fear began to trump my sense of purpose. I started

jogging faster. *Where are you? Flash your lights*, I whispered, like I had magical powers or something. Or phenomenal luck. It didn't matter which.

Finally, when I was about to give up, I heard the beep of a horn answering its remote key. I turned toward the sound and gasped. It was a midnight-blue Mustang GT. A convertible.

I started cackling like a crazy person. Robinson was going to freak out.

Easy as pie, I opened the driver's-side door and jumped in. The seats were tan leather, and the inside sparkled like that salesman spit-shined it every morning. He was going to seriously miss his ride. A wave of remorse came over me, but I shook it off.

The Mustang practically leapt into the street. I pulled up to our truck and quickly tossed our bags in at the same time I called to Robinson, who was leaning against a telephone pole as if standing up on his own were too much work. "Hurry, the bus is leaving."

He walked toward me and his eyes widened. "Wha—"

"Just get in."

It took him another second to wrap his head around the directive. But then he slid in next to me, and I gunned the engine.

And we were gone.

"How—what—I don't—" Robinson stuttered. "Am I—"

"Keys, Clyde," I said, feigning complete nonchalance. "They're *so* much easier than a cordless drill."

"I just don't—" He couldn't even finish a sentence.

"I borrowed them from the loud guy in the coffee shop."

Robinson's eyes widened even further as he looked around the car. He ran his hand over the dashboard. "Four-point-six-liter V-8 with three-fifteen horsepower and three hundred twenty-five pound-feet of torque. Pure American-made muscle. This thing is a beast, Axi." He turned to beam at me. "Just when I thought I could not possibly love you more."

He began to laugh—a strong laugh like I hadn't heard in days. "Seriously, *thank God*," he finally said, gasping for breath. "For a minute, I really, truly thought I'd died and gone to heaven."

45

ROBINSON TOLD ME TO DRIVE SOUTH, SO I DID. For once, no questions asked. I'd do anything he asked me, and I had to admit, the Mustang was a major step up from the truck. It had power steering, air-conditioning, and, according to Robinson, "an aftermarket Bose speaker system that costs more than a new Kia." It just ate up the miles.

He was staring sleepily out the window now, watching the world go by the way I used to do. "Have you noticed," he said once, "how this entire country is, like, in patterns? It goes city, then suburban sprawl, then farmland. And then city, suburban sprawl, farmland again..."

"And you're never more than fifty miles from a McDonald's," I joked.

"That's a relief," he answered.

Later that evening, after speeding through Delaware, Maryland, and half of Virginia, I pulled into a rest stop in the middle of the Blue Ridge Mountains. In the humid twilight, I spread out our sleeping bags near the border of trees.

I didn't bother with the tent, because I didn't want to draw any attention our way. According to the strange logic of the interstate rest area system, *sleeping* is fine, but camping isn't. And although camping at a rest area would be pretty low on my list of crimes and misdemeanors, I saw no reason to be awakened by a cop tapping his flashlight on our tent pole.

I held out the Slim Jim I'd bought for Robinson at the last gas station, but he shook his head. "That Filet-O-Fish we had for dinner is sitting in my stomach like a ball of lead," he groaned. "I think I'm going to have to sleep it off."

"I told you to order the salad," I said. "It was good."

He snorted. "Getting a salad at McDonald's is like going into Car Toys and coming out with a pencil sharpener." He slipped into the sleeping bag, not bothering to remove anything but the belt from his jeans.

"Well, I feel just fine," I said a bit huffily.

"Well, *you* don't have cancer," he snapped.

I sucked in my breath sharply and held it. In the silence that followed, I heard the crickets chirping and the rushing waves of cars passing by on the highway. If I closed my eyes, I could almost imagine it was the sound of the ocean.

I felt Robinson reaching for my hand. "I'm sorry," he whispered. "I shouldn't have said that."

I turned to him, tears now wetting my cheeks. "What, we should just pretend that everything's all right? We should just believe what we want to believe? Is that what we should do, Robinson?"

He was quiet for a moment, his brow furrowed in concentration. "I don't know what we should do," he said softly. "Wake up and drive some more tomorrow. Try to laugh. Love each other. I mean, what else is there?"

"I'm scared," I whispered.

"There's nothing to be afraid of, Axi." He brought my

hand up to his lips and kissed it, right in the center of my palm.

"Again, is that what we *want* to believe? I just feel like we're stumbling forward now, hoping for the best. I mean, where are we going? And where is the road map? The metaphorical one, I mean—the directions. LEGO sets come with directions. Temporary tattoos come with directions. Once I saw an entire Web page dedicated to telling you how to order coffee from Starbucks!"

"Really?"

"Yes! Step one is 'Decide what you want to order before your turn in line.' I'm like, oh, really? Wow! Thank you so much! I never would have thought of that."

Robinson was laughing now. I was glad I'd cheered him up, but I wasn't feeling any better. "Where are the directions for the big things? Because I want them," I cried. "What are the instructions for, I don't know, *life?*"

Robinson's laugh slowly faded. "Axi, if we had directions, it wouldn't be life. It would be an assignment. Grunt work. Not knowing is a major part of the deal."

I knew he was right, but I didn't like it. Sighing, I scooted as close to him as possible, but the zippers of our sleeping bags kept us apart.

" 'As far as the laws of mathematics refer to reality, they are not certain; and as far as they are certain, they do not refer to reality,' " I said.

"Huh?" said Robinson.

"Einstein," I said. "Mr. Fox had that written at the top of his chalkboard."

"I like it," Robinson said.

"Well, I want certainty," I said.

I felt like Robinson and I were caught between two different worlds. There was the world we'd been living in—a world of freedom, beauty, and, *okay*, yes, utterly wonderful and terrible irresponsibility—and then there was the darker, sadder world that I sensed we were about to enter. I wanted to know how to navigate it.

Robinson tilted his head closer to mine. "You can put it on your Christmas list."

I turned away. "Don't patronize me. I don't even know where we're driving to."

Robinson rolled over and stared up at the sky. It was a deep, velvety blue, and little pinpricks of stars were appearing, more and more every minute. "Here is certainty," he said. "I love you, Axi Moore. And I will never not love you, for the rest of my life."

The tears came again, and I didn't bother to wipe them away. "I love you, too," I whispered. "For the rest of my life."

We kissed, wrapping our arms around each other and holding on tight. And then, exhausted, we said good night and closed our eyes to sleep.

Lying there in the summer night, it was almost as if I could feel the earth moving beneath us, turning on its axis. And as I listened to the crickets singing to each other, I wondered if the rest of my life and the rest of Robinson's life meant two entirely different lengths of time.

How do you know anything for sure? I thought. But I knew the answer to that already. *You don't.*

Finally I fell asleep. In the middle of the night, Robinson and I rolled toward each other, our arms crossing. The night seemed to hold us, too, in a big, soft, dark embrace.

Robinson's voice was low and groggy. "Maybe we should get married," he said.

I couldn't speak; my heart was too full. Full of joy and surprise—and futility, too, because they don't let you do that at sixteen. I put my head on his chest, wishing I could melt into him entirely. The best I could do was match my breathing to his long, steady breaths. In a moment, I realized that he was asleep again.

It was possible he hadn't even been truly awake in the first place.

46

IN THE EARLY AFTERNOON, SOMEWHERE IN North Carolina, we took an exit off the highway and ended up in a park, near the shore of a small lake.

"Let's stop for a little while," Robinson said. "I like this spot."

Ringed by trees and rolling hills, the lake was calm, reflecting the blue sky back at itself. I rolled down the window and breathed in the smell of clean, piney air. "It's pretty here," I agreed.

We climbed out of the Mustang and walked toward the edge of the shimmering water. Robinson bent down, selected a flat stone, and then skipped it across the surface—one, two, three times.

He snorted. "Terrible. I used to be able to do twelve."

I stood beside him and snaked my arm around his waist. It felt so good to be off the road—to feel my muscles loosening, my gas-pedal foot slowly uncramping. "Maybe we should rent a paddleboat or something. Take a break. Drive some more later."

It was like he hadn't even heard me. "I used to love coming here," he said.

"What?"

His eyes swept over the lake, but he seemed to be seeing some other thing. Or some other time. "We used to build these crazy rafts and tow them over in wagons. Then we'd see how many kids we could pile on them before they'd sink. We'd get in trouble because you need a permit for a boat. And we'd always argue that we weren't on a boat—we were on a raft made by nine-year-olds out of packing crates and big pieces of Styrofoam."

"Wait a second," I said, dropping my arm from his waist and taking a step back. "Are you talking about *this* lake?"

"Of course," Robinson said. "I was born three miles away."

Before I could stop myself, I shoved him, and he stumbled a little. "I'm so sorry," I said, grabbing his hand. "But wait. You brought me...home?"

"I wanted you to meet my parents," Robinson said, as if this were the simplest, least surprising thing in the world.

I was totally gobsmacked. I didn't even know where we were, really, and now I was about to meet Robinson's parents, who until now had been about as real to me as a couple of unicorns.

"Welcome to Asheville, North Carolina," Robinson said, gesturing to the trees and paths and joggers around us. "Formerly Tuberculosis Central, and now known as the Paris of the South, or, to the writers of *Rolling Stone*, the New Freak Capital of the US."

I shook my head in disbelief. I didn't know whether to kiss him or kick him. "You wait until now to tell me?"

He smiled. "A guy ought to surprise his girl once in a while," he said. "It's romantic that way. Now let's go see the sights, such as they are."

And for the next hour, he showed me around his home-town. I saw the shop where he bought his first guitar; the elm tree that he broke his arm falling out of; the elementary school where he'd started a rock 'n' roll club ("It got huge, even though some super-ancient dudes protested, saying rock 'n' roll was 'the devil's music,'" Robinson said proudly).

Nothing was particularly special—and yet everything was extraordinary because it was a part of Robinson's pre-viously classified childhood. I wanted to stop at every cor-ner, peer in every window. I wanted to stop strangers and ask them to tell me a story about Robinson. He'd opened the door to his past, and I wanted to walk right through it.

Robinson touched my arm, directing my attention toward a drugstore sandwiched between a café and a crystal shop. "Look," he said. "There's even a place like Ernie's. But the coffee's even worse—it's like battery acid. I swear it once ate a hole in my jeans." He shook his head at the memory. "Of course, it could have been actual battery acid that did that. I certainly spent enough time in my dad's shop."

"His shop?" I asked.

"He owns a car repair shop. Robinson's Repairs."

"Wow, he named it after you?"

Robinson shrugged noncommittally. "Sort of."

"What do you mean, sort of? Who else would it be—the Swiss Family Robinson? Jackie Robinson? Robinson Cru-soe? Smokey Rob—"

"Hey, see that?" he interrupted. "That's the streetlight that my brother ran his custom-built Cheemer into."

"Cheemer?" I said. "I don't know what a Cheemer is." Clearly the shop-naming conversation wasn't going any-where.

"A Chevrolet with a BMW engine," Robinson explained. "You know, Chevy plus Beemer? Jay Leno has one."

"Oh," I said, wishing these names meant anything to me. "So it's like an automotive mash-up."

He laughed. "Exactly. It's the car version of that Eazy-E and Johnny Cash thing, 'Folsom Prison Gangstaz.' *I got beat for the street, Ta pump in ya jeep*—"

"You should probably stop," I said. "That guy over there is looking at you funny."

"Like I care," Robinson replied, but he stopped anyway. He seemed tired again. "Drive that way, why don't you?" He pointed vaguely to the east, and that was how I saw the Biltmore House, an enormous Gilded Age chateau built by a Vanderbilt whose name Robinson couldn't recall. It looked like a fairy-tale castle—a place where Cinderella would live happily ever after with her prince.

Where was my happily-ever-after, I wanted to know. Why did that silly girl get one when my chances were so slim?

Without even thinking, I pulled onto the shoulder of the road. I looked over at Robinson as if I were about to ask him these questions.

"Oh, this is perfect," he said. "This is a very special place."

I looked around. We were stopped in the middle of a bunch of trees. "What's so great about it?"

Robinson unbuckled my seat belt and pulled me toward him. He brought his mouth close to mine and whispered, "It's where I did *this*."

And then he kissed me, so long and sweet and tender that I almost cried—because here we were, together, and maybe this was finally the end of the road.

47

THE HOUSE WAS A THREE-STORY VICTORIAN with a high, round turret, stained-glass windows, and an enormous porch. The front steps bowed in the middle, and the paint was beginning to fade and peel. But it was picturesque that way—a little bit of shabby chic.

There were rosebushes everywhere, blossoming in all different colors: snow-white, yellow tipped with sunset orange, the soft pink of a ballet slipper. The roses climbed a trellis on the porch and spilled over the railings, filling the air with their glorious perfume.

I climbed the steps after Robinson, cold with nerves. He gave me a quick squeeze and then rang the doorbell.

For a moment, nothing happened. I heard a voice and barking inside, and then a woman who I assumed was Robinson's mother appeared in the doorway. When she saw who had rung, she opened her mouth as if to shout, but instead she fell to the floor—she just sort of crumpled in the hall, like a marionette whose strings had been cut.

Robinson yelped, "Mom!" And he went to help her up,

but before he got to her, a man who had to be Robinson's dad appeared in the hall. He saw Robinson, and for a second he just gaped at him.

They were acting like they'd seen a ghost.

Awkward! I thought—and they had yet to even notice me, the other unannounced visitor.

Of course, if I showed up at my apartment after vanishing the way I had, my dad would probably assume I was some booze-induced hallucination and slam the door in my face.

Robinson's dad slowly bent down to pick up his wife. It was like they were in some kind of slow motion. When they both were finally vertical again, their shock started giving way to a kind of joy I couldn't remember seeing in my father since I was a little girl. Robinson's mom grabbed her son and squeezed him *hard*. "Oh my God!" she cried. "You're here! I missed you so much!"

Robinson's dad was wiping his eyes, trying to keep it together. He reached out and grasped Robinson's shoulder. "Oscar," he said, his voice full of wonder and relief, "you came back."

Robinson was blinking hard and fast and maybe sniffling a little bit. And I was crying, too, at the sight of their reunion, and at the same time thinking, *Oscar? Who's Oscar?*

The barking began again, and a small brown dog came waddling up as fast as her short legs would carry her. "Leafy!" Robinson cried.

She was as fat as a sausage, and her whole body wagged while her tail stayed still. Robinson got down on the floor, and she proceeded to attack him in an ecstasy of yipping and licking. "Sit, girl," he said, laughing, and she obeyed him for about five milliseconds before launching herself at him again. "I love you, too," he said, rubbing her long brown ears.

Then a tall man who looked almost exactly like an older,

burlier Robinson came into the hallway and said, "What's all the ruckus?"

When he saw Robinson, he rushed forward. He looked like he was going to tackle Robinson, and without thinking I jumped in and shot my arm out, as if I—all five feet five inches and 120 pounds of me—could block his charge.

The man stopped short and said, "Wow, hot bodyguard, man."

I flushed as Robinson and his brother hugged and slapped each other on the back.

Then Robinson stepped away and put his arm protectively around my shoulders. "Everyone," he said, "this is Axi." He looked down at me and smiled. "My partner in crime." And then in front of everyone, he kissed me—a little less chastely than I might have expected.

"Well, well," said his mother, sniffling and trying to smile at me, too. "Axi, I'm glad to meet you." And then instead of shaking my hand, she pulled me close into her rose-smelling neck, and I realized how long it had been since a mother—any mother—had held me. "Oh, I'm sorry, dear," she said, patting the damp spot she'd made on my shirt. She laughed, embarrassed. "I'm a bit overwhelmed."

Robinson made the rest of the introductions. "That's my brother, Jonathan. He's twenty, but he's probably still living here, because he's a bum like that." The affection was obvious in Robinson's voice.

Jonathan pretended to take offense. "I've got my own place," he said. "I'm just over here borrowing Dad's tools."

"And waiting to see what your mother will make for dinner," his father added.

"Maybe," Jonathan allowed.

Robinson said, "And this is my dad, Joe, and my mom, Louise, but everyone calls her Lou."

"And what about you?" I whispered. "Oscar?"

He gave a slightly embarrassed shrug. "You can see why I go by Robinson," he said. Then he pulled me close to him again. "I promise," he whispered, "that's the last of my secrets."

48

AFTER A DELICIOUS DINNER OF LASAGNA, GARLIC bread, and salad, during which there were more tears and more fits of laughter than I could count, Robinson took my hand and led me to the back of the house.

"I wasn't allowed to have girls in my room," he said, "but I'm going to assume my parents are over that by now." He pushed on a rather rickety door, but instead of opening into a bedroom, it led to a porch, with windows on all three sides. The painted wooden floor was scuffed and pitched; there was a wicker love seat along one wall and a double bed shoved against another. Guitars and amps were arranged in the corners, alongside neat stacks of CDs.

"This is your bedroom?" I asked, thinking of my dark closet of a room back home.

"It's the old sleeping porch. This place was once a board-inghouse for TB patients," Robinson said. "People with tuberculosis were supposed to sleep in fresh air, so there are rooms like this all over Asheville."

"I love it," I said, running my finger along the windowsill.

Robinson sank down onto the bed. "I slept on the floor out here for two weeks," he said. "Staking my claim. Finally, they said it could be mine."

I sat down next to him. The sheets were clean and the pillows freshly plumped; either someone had sneaked in to make the bed, or Robinson's mother had kept up his room as if he'd only gone out for a walk. "Your parents are amazing. Why weren't you with them—all along?" I asked.

Robinson frowned. "We went to Portland because of the experimental immunotherapy program with Dr. Suzuki. She's the best there is, right? But my parents were living in this terrible motel and going to the hospital every day, and it was just awful. It was too hard on them. I said, 'Please go home. This isn't what I want. I don't want you to see me go through this.'"

"And they just *left?*" I don't know why it shocked me as it did, considering the way my own mother split town.

"They didn't want to, believe me. But I made them. I said if things got really bad, obviously they could come back. But things didn't get really bad—they got better. The immuno-therapy was helping, and I got discharged from the hospital."

"The same day as me," I said, smiling at the memory of that perfect morning.

"Right. And I'd planned to come back here, but then there was the problem of you."

"The *problem?*" I asked.

He smiled. "The problem of having a giant crush on you and you not knowing it," he said. "But conveniently, my uncle had just moved close to your hometown. You were going to K-Falls, and I decided to follow you. I wanted to be with you."

I flushed. "I'm glad you did. But still—I can't believe they let you do it."

"I told them I'd come back here in the fall. Do senior year at my old school. They understood—I wanted to pretend like I was normal, at a school where no one knew I had cancer. I was just a kid who got to study somewhere else for a while." He smiled. "A semester abroad, in bucolic K-Falls."

I snorted. "You'd better look up *bucolic* in the dictionary."

"I don't have to, because I have you," Robinson said, rolling his eyes.

"Oh, right," I said, nudging him with my foot. But his story still didn't entirely make sense to me. "Why wouldn't you ever talk about your family? Why were they such a huge secret?"

Robinson sighed. "I didn't like talking about them because I felt so guilty. I knew it was selfish of me to be away from them. But I wanted to see things, Axi. I wanted to have a bigger life." He reached up and twisted a strand of my hair around his fingers. "I wanted to fall in love."

I nodded. It wasn't totally insane, I guess. "But you, like, wrote them and stuff?"

"Of course," he said. "They knew I was okay."

"But what about this trip? How'd you explain that?"

He smiled. "I told them school was out—"

"Even though you weren't in school anymore," I interrupted.

"Well, they didn't know that. And they weren't going to check the calendar and see that there were three more weeks of classes I should have been in. I told them I was going to Camp Motorsport. It's a summer camp for gearheads." He paused thoughtfully. "It sounded pretty cool, actually..."

I rolled my eyes. "You're crazy."

"But you love me."

I leaned over and kissed him on the side of his soft mouth. "I do."

A blast of music came from the garage, where Robinson had said Jonathan was fixing up an old Buick into a custom racer.

"Did you know we'd come here, then?" I asked.

Robinson shook his head. "I thought we'd go back to Oregon first. But then..."

He didn't finish the sentence, but I could fill it in. He'd started feeling sick. And he'd wanted to go home.

I understood that. I'd want to run to my mom, too, if I had one who was any use to me. If I knew what *state* she was living in.

I looked out the window then, and I saw all these floating lights. They were yellowish green, flashing on and off. "What are those?" I asked.

Robinson gaped at me. "Haven't you ever seen a firefly before? A lightning bug?"

"A what? No! We don't have them in Oregon."

Robinson sat up and peered out at the lawn. "I had no idea you were so deprived. They're the best bugs in the world because they can light their butts up. It's how they find mates."

"They're beautiful," I said.

Robinson reached up and brushed the hair from my face. "Not like you."

"Don't be corny."

"I'm not. I'm dead serious." He paused. "Dying serious, I should say."

"No, you should *not* say that."

Robinson sighed. "Oh, Axi, I'm tired," he said. "Tell me a bedtime story."

"Sing me a bedtime lullaby," I said with a smile. "Like in Vegas." I had every intention of giving in this time, but not that easily.

"Story," he insisted.

"Song."

"I'll flip a coin," he said.

"No! Don't!" I yelped.

He looked at me strangely. "Why not?"

"Just don't."

"Okay, fine. Then you have to tell the story."

We lay back on the bed. I took a deep breath and began. A fairy-tale beginning. "Once upon a time, there was a girl and a boy."

"So far so good," Robinson said. He rolled over so that his face was in my neck. "The girl was always bossing the boy around," he said, his lips brushing my skin. "She kept telling him to eat better."

"The girl had only the boy's best interests at heart," I retorted.

"Mmmm," said Robinson. Already his voice was thick with sleep.

"She wanted to take care of him," I whispered. "And to be taken care of by him."

I paused, listening to the music coming from the garage. It was Bob Dylan, I thought, but I didn't know the song.

"She knew how lucky they were," I went on, "because they had found each other. She understood that sometimes people had to search for years to find what they wanted. Whereas some—the charmed few—just stumble upon it. Like children on a beach. Some come home with only rocks and broken shells, while others unearth a perfect sand dollar, fragile but beautiful."

Robinson sighed. By now he was sleeping.

"And the girl understood something else—and maybe the boy did, too. Love was magical and infinite. But luck, in the end, was not."

Out in the garage, Jonathan turned up the music, and Dylan's nasal, sandpapery voice finally reached me clearly. *"The future for me is already a thing of the past. You were my first love and you will be my last."*

I clenched my fists against my sides. I looked out the window for a star to wish on, but clouds had come in the evening. The only lights were those of the fireflies, turning on and off, on and off.

49

ROBINSON'S PARENTS WELCOMED ME LIKE A
family member—and they said nothing about me spending the night in their son's room. Joe, who was a his-
tory buff, told me all about the Asheville tuberculosis
sanitariums the next morning. (Even F. Scott Fitzgerald,
my ninth-grade literary crush, had spent time in one.)
Jonathan walked me around the car he was working on,
explaining various things about its engine that I didn't
understand and promising to take me for a ride as soon
as he got new tires. Lou bought tempeh bacon when Robinson mentioned I didn't eat meat, and one afternoon she
braided my hair.

"I always wanted a daughter," she said wistfully. "Those
boys and their cars. I love them to the moon, but it's horsepower this and carburetor that, and I always thought to
myself, *Who's going to help me prune the roses?*"

"I don't have much experience with gardening," I admitted. Dad and I had had a spider plant in our apartment, but it
was probably all dried up by then.

"You'd like it," Lou said. "You're a careful person, I can see that."

Used to be, anyway, I thought.

"It's like the Little Prince says," she went on. " 'You become responsible, forever, for what you have tamed. You are responsible for your rose.' You can't tame a stock car, Axi. It's not the same thing."

I smiled. "I've quoted that book to your son."

"Oscar—I mean Robinson, I guess—could never be persuaded to read it."

And then we walked outside, into the soft summer air, and she showed me how to deadhead the roses so they'd bloom all the way until late fall. When we came back, we had armfuls of blossoms, enough to put in every room.

The point is, life with Robinson's family would have been perfect if only Robinson hadn't been getting sicker, minute by minute. It was as if being back home allowed him to finally stop pretending he was all right. And had there been any doubt about his prognosis—or any denial of what it meant— a visit from his childhood specialist had wiped that away.

"I recommend you call hospice," the doctor had said. Meaning: all you can do now is keep him comfortable. *Until.*

Word spread quickly around town, and visitors began to arrive, bringing casseroles and cookies and boxes of Kleenex. There was a procession of friends, neighbors, classmates, and soccer coaches who had known and loved Robinson.

Robinson held court on the old sofa in the living room, pale and covered with blankets, even though the rest of us were in short sleeves and dabbing at our sweating upper lips. His spirits were high, though he tired easily. And though he was in pain, he rarely hit the button on his morphine IV—he said it made his head feel like a hot-air balloon.

Everyone had stories to tell, like the time Robinson won

the Soap Box Derby race, then just kept going for another half-mile because he'd neglected to give his car a set of brakes. About how he'd "borrowed" the high school's mascot costume to perform a gut-busting bump-and-grind during halftime at the homecoming game. One neighbor told me that Robinson mowed and raked her lawn for her but always refused payment, and a pimply twelve-year-old told me that when he was eight, Robinson had saved him from drowning in Beaver Lake.

It was as if I were seeing Robinson's life flash before my eyes, in the words and stories of the people who loved him.

When he felt good enough, Robinson entertained his guests with tales of life "out West," which he made sound way better than it actually was.

"If Klamath Falls has a boom in tourism, it'll be because of you," I told him one evening. "And they'll all come home disappointed."

"K-Falls has its charms," he said.

"Oh yeah? Name one."

"Her name is Axi Moore," he said. "Sheesh, that was easy. Oh, and Wubba's BBQ Express has that great pulled pork sandwich."

See what I mean? Spirits high.

During the days, I passed around snacks and reheated bowls of pasta or soup in the microwave. Even though we in the house weren't hungry, everyone else was. It was like a dinner party that never ended.

Lou moved through the house as if in a dream, or a nightmare. Joe looked pale and scared. Jonathan, on Robinson's orders, hung a sign on the wall that said NO CRYING ALLOWED—not that anyone was capable of following that particular order. Even fat Leafy whined and barked, as if she had stories about Robinson, too.

"She used to be an agility champ," Joe said once, shaking his head. "Can you believe it?"

"Now she's an eating champ," Jonathan added, tossing her a cracker.

I bent down and rubbed Leafy's feathery ears, and she responded with a warm lick of my hand. I had a sudden pang of longing for my old dog. Or maybe it was a longing for the healthy, loving family I'd never really had. It was hard to tell.

50

"CLOSE YOUR EYES," ROBINSON SAID. HE WAS reaching into the drawer by the side of his bed. I pretended to squint, then opened my eyes wide as he pulled out a pocketknife with a gleaming silver blade.

"When a knife's around, I like to pay attention," I said. "Sort of as a matter of policy."

He laughed, then coughed. "I'm not going to point it at you," he said. "Only this." He gestured toward the sleeping porch's wainscoting.

"What are you going to do?"

"It's a surprise," he said. "You'll see. Just close your eyes."

I watched him dig the tip into the wood, and then I did as he asked. I don't know how much time passed, but I must have fallen asleep, because the next thing I knew, Robinson was nudging me awake. "Look," he said.

Carved into the wall of the porch was a message: B&C4EVER.

"Bonnie and Clyde," he said. He was smiling at me, his perfect, crooked grin. "That's us."

"Forever," I said.

We lay back down, and Robinson wrapped his arms around me. I traced the veins of his wrist, their delicate blue lines showing through his skin like a road map, and I thought of the map in my backpack, the one we'd marked with every stop: LA. The redwoods. Detroit. I thought, too, of my bag of souvenirs. Magical objects—a snow globe, a glass orb—that in certain lights looked exactly like junk.

"I miss you already," Robinson said softly.

"I'm here," I whispered back. "I'll always be here."

"But I won't," he said.

In my chest swelled an ache unfathomably deep and dark. And I said nothing, because I knew he was right. I kissed his face, his lips—and then somehow, we slept.

But in the middle of the night, we woke up, and without words we turned toward each other. Robinson's hands reached for me, and his mouth pressed itself against my neck. I brought his face up to mine, hungry to taste his lips. We kissed, and I heard a low moan—mine. I realized I was trembling.

Robinson smiled, lightly tracing the lines of my brow, my nose, my mouth. "Don't be nervous," he whispered.

How could I not be nervous? I knew what was going to happen. The air was charged with it. We were going to kiss until we were breathless, and then...and *then*...

I moved closer to him, running my hand along his hip and down his thigh. I felt him shiver as I brushed my fingers along the smoothness of his stomach.

He caught my hand and held it. "I love you," he said.

"I love you back," I whispered. And then I slid my fingers out of his so I could touch him again.

We kissed for what seemed like hours—sometimes tenderly, sometimes almost desperately. Sometimes we stopped and just looked at each other. As if we were memorizing our bodies and memorizing this moment. I felt like I was made of nothing but longing.

Then Robinson pulled away, and I watched as he slipped his shirt over his head. His white skin seemed to glow in the half-light. He looked at me questioningly, and then he reached for the buttons on my blouse. He was whispering my name.

"Do you want to—" he asked.

"*Yes*," I said.

We wriggled out of the rest of our clothes, and then I wrapped my arms around his back. I guided him toward me. I wanted to pull him into my body—as if we could become one person; as if, finally, I could protect him.

Robinson was breathing hard and we were kissing. I touched him everywhere, even as I felt myself dissolving. He was whispering words into my mouth, but I couldn't concentrate on what they were, because something inside me was unfurling. I was no longer Axi Moore. I was me and I was him; I was the night and the stars. The two of us lay on that bed and shuddered with desire.

Afterward, he slept right against me, and I stared at our initials in the flickering candlelight. B&C4EVER.

And somehow I knew it was true. We would be together forever.

51

I OPENED MY EYES TO THE SOUND OF BIRDS MAK-
ing a loud and unmelodious racket in the big oaks in the
backyard. I snuggled closer to Robinson, glad they hadn't
woken him up, too. Leafy, who'd taken to standing guard
outside his room at night, came in when she heard the rustling of blankets, and sat at the foot of the bed. She immediately began whining, because she knew I couldn't resist
those big brown eyes of hers. In the four days we'd been
here, I'd already fed her almost an entire box of treats.

"Hush, Leafy," I said. "Be patient."

She wagged her tail and whined more loudly, and when
I didn't immediately go in search of the Milk-Bones, she
began to bark.

"Quiet," I whispered. "Robinson's asleep."

But behind me there was no movement, despite the noise,
and a terrible, panicky feeling came over me. I turned to
look at Robinson's chest, and I saw that it wasn't rising or
falling. *He wasn't breathing.* And suddenly I was backing
out of the bed, my hands clutched to my face.

Leafy began yapping even more loudly—a treat was coming any minute now, she was sure of it—and I didn't bother to shush her because it didn't matter. *Nothing* mattered. I dug my nails into my cheeks, and the tears came out fast and hot. I was gasping for breath, and I couldn't say his name, even though I wanted to scream it out.

Robinson, come back! I'm not ready! I'm completely, totally not ready!

Leafy's barks took on a tone of wild confusion. I grabbed her by the collar and buried my face in her warm neck, and I thought, *Oh my God, how am I going to tell Lou? How am I going to do anything ever again?*

I had a mouthful of Leafy's hair and she was still barking, but more softly now, dissolving into a pitiful whimper.

It was done. It was over.

And I'd been asleep.

52

A HAND CAME DOWN AND TOUCHED MY SHOUL-
der, and I jumped like I'd been burned. I looked up through
tear-blurred eyes.

Robinson's face, seeming to float above the bed like a
ghost's. And then his familiar low voice. He said, "Axi? Are
you okay?"

I nearly fell over. It was him. He was alive. "Do I look
okay?" I yelled. I crawled back up onto the bed and gripped
his hands as if he'd rescued me from drowning. Never in my
life had I been more relieved. "Tell me: *do I look okay?*"

"Your eyes are sort of red," he said, his voice groggy but
teasing. "Are you allergic to Leafy or something?"

"I'm going to kill you," I gasped. I let go of his hands and lay
down next to him in the bed, pressing myself against his side
and trying to calm my breathing. I'd been so close to losing him.

"Oh, you probably won't have to bother," Robinson said.
"Something's already on that job. But don't worry. I'm still
around to torture you."

"Never stop," I said.

"I'll do my best." Robinson patted the edge of bed, and Leafy hopped up, too, though it was obviously not easy for her. I watched him pet her soft head and ears. He yawned and then moved around in the bed, restless and uncomfortable as he woke up to his sickness and the pain it caused him.

I ran my finger along the side of his cheek. "Do you want anything?" I asked.

He didn't answer me. His eyes closed, and I thought he was falling back to sleep. He'd been sleeping so much lately. As his breathing became more regular, I slowly eased out of the bed and went to the door, ready to check on his parents. Then he said softly, "Yes."

"What?"

"I want more time," he said. His lashes were dark against his pale skin.

I bit my lip and felt the sting of tears again. "Okay," I whispered. "Coming right up."

When I was in the hallway, he called me back.

"Axi," he said, half-sitting up again. "Listen, okay? First thing: Leafy does not need another treat, no matter how much she thinks she does. So leave the Milk-Bones in the pantry. Second thing: there's a hole in your shirt, and you should get my mom to sew it. Third thing: like that dumb Mason Jennings song says, there are so many ways to die."

I held up a hand. "Whoa, Robinson—"

He ignored me. "It doesn't matter what the end looks like—what matters is that it came. Bam, you're done. But life, Axi? There are degrees of life. You can live it well or half-asleep. You can go sledding down a sand dune, or you can spend your life in front of the TV. And I don't mean to sound like a stupid after-school special, but you have to keep living the way we did these last weeks. Risk, Axi. That's the secret. Risk everything."

I nodded, trying not to cry again. "Okay. But I might not keep stealing cars."

"That's all right," he said.

"What am I going to do—?" I asked. I couldn't say the final two words of the sentence: *without you*.

Robinson smiled. "You should probably try to not fail physics. And you should keep writing."

I thought of my journal, the sloppy, haphazard notes in it and all the pages to be filled. At least I'd taken some pictures on our trip. "I'll write the good parts."

"No, you have to write the good and the bad." Robinson picked at the edge of the blanket. His eyes were so huge and serious. "You can write all about me, and I'll live forever that way."

What could I say? I sank down onto a chair and put my head in my hands.

"You know, yours was the only book I ever wanted to read. So just write it, Axi. You can do it. You can do anything. I mean, look at you. You're not GG anymore—you're so much bigger than her."

I laughed bitterly. "I don't miss her."

"I loved her," Robinson said. "And I loved the sick girl you were when I met you, and I loved the good student and the bad driver. I loved the car thief, the hitchhiker, the quoter of novels I haven't read, and the hater of Slim Jims…Axi Moore, I've loved every you there ever was."

I walked over to the bed and laid my head on his chest. "I'll always be your girl," I whispered.

"I know," he said.

I watched the way our fingers intertwined, and I thought, *What are hands made for but this? For holding. For holding* on.

53

THE DAYS BLURRED INTO ONE ANOTHER AS ROBinson began to dream more and speak less. Time had lost meaning for him, but I was overcome by a sense of waiting. Something was coming, something that would be dreadful darkness and that would also be relief.

We stayed with him in shifts: Lou in the mornings, Joe in the afternoons, Jonathan in the evenings, and me at night. I read to him from Lou's books: Steinbeck, Whitman, Fitzgerald, Hemingway. She read him *The Little Prince*.

One night, in the middle of my watch, I slipped outside into the warm darkness. The crickets were going crazy, and the lightning bugs were like tiny lanterns flashing a kind of insect Morse code.

Through the window, Robinson looked small and frail under the covers, like a little kid in his childhood bed. Like he ought to be clutching a teddy bear.

I picked a star and wished as hard as I could that somehow I could protect him from what was on the horizon.

We're in this together, Robinson used to say. I remembered the first time he'd ever said it to me, at dinnertime in the cancer ward when we'd been handed a tray of brown slop and green peas. "We're in this together," Robinson had declared. "Axi, we can do this." He'd lifted his fork high in the air, like a sword. "We can eat this...this...whatever it is!"

It was a joke back then; now it was real. We were in this together for just a little bit longer, because what was coming next, Robinson was going to have to go through alone. I would have traded my life for his, but there was no one to offer this to. No one who could make the exchange. No star that would grant my wish.

At three o'clock that morning, I was dozing, my hand on his, when suddenly he was awake.

"The motorcycle," he said, his voice haunted and urgent. "Does it have gas?"

I was instantly at attention. "Yes," I said.

"I think the head gasket's blown—it's seeping oil."

"Your brother's looking into it," I said. Whatever world Robinson was in now, I would play along. "He says not to worry, he'll take care of it. It's going to be up and running right away."

"What about the clutch cable? It's worn."

"He'll fix that, too."

Then Robinson looked at me for a long time. At some point, he seemed to come back to himself. "Axi," he whispered.

"Hi," I whispered back.

He gazed around the room at the Bob Dylan poster, the leaning guitars, all the things he'd left behind when he went away to the hospital. His fingers fluttered, and I reached out to grab them.

I knew what was coming. What I should say.

There was a stone in my throat, but I swallowed hard. "It's okay," I said. "It's okay to go." The final stop.

He brought my hand up to his lips and kissed it, right in the center of my palm. Then he closed my fingers around it, as if the kiss were something I could hold on to forever.

I climbed into bed with him. He shifted, sighing. "Axi," he said.

"I'm right here."

I held his head in my arms. I pressed my mouth to his cheek. *We are in this together.*

"Axi," he said again.

I told him I loved him. He loved me, too, he said—always. And I heard him say my name again. He whispered it over and over until it didn't sound like my name at all anymore. It was only sound, only rhythm. Almost like a song.

"Axi." He sighed. "Axi."

And then, finally, he was silent.

Outside, the song of the crickets seemed to crescendo. I reached into my pocket for the lucky penny I had flipped so long ago in the cancer ward, hoping that it somehow meant Robinson would make it. I'd kept that penny with me every single day after it showed me heads, that he would always be with me.

Now I held it tight, and then I flipped it high into the air and watched it land. But on what, it didn't matter. There was no question anymore, no wish—only the answer, and the emptiness it brings.

epilogue

54

IN BUCOLIC KLAMATH FALLS, EARLY FALL IS
bright and dry. The leaves are already turning brown, letting themselves be blown from their branches into sad little piles on unmown lawns.

My dad is down in the courtyard, searching for the watch
he dropped on his way home from the bar last night. He's
been looking for half an hour already. (If you ask me, I think
Critter found it and took it straight to Jack's Pawn.) Dad
keeps looking up at me, sitting here on the apartment's tiny
balcony, like he thinks that any minute I might vanish into
thin air.

I'm not going anywhere. My first community service session isn't until tomorrow afternoon. See, when I got back
home, the first thing I did was walk to the police station and
turn myself in.

Yup. Once a GG, always a GG.

I think I knew from the moment we stole the Harley that
I was going to have to make amends for our journey. It was
the right thing to do. And even though Robinson's eyes are

likely rolling out of his head right now, I think he might have been smiling down on me, too, when the judge handed me my sentence. Grand theft auto is a felony and usually lands people in jail, but miraculously I was only charged with a misdemeanor and was banned from getting a driver's license until I turn twenty-one, and I'm basically going to do community service until my arms fall off.

It's completely worth it to me. After all, the people who "lent" us their cars gave Robinson and me an incredible gift, and I'll gladly pick up trash for the rest of my life if I have to. In fact, I'm thinking about volunteering for the police department, too.

"Axi," my dad calls up, "shouldn't you be heading to school soon?"

"I'll be down in a minute," I reply. *Ugh.* I'd forgotten about my mandatory physics tutoring session, which starts in an hour. Turns out you can't pass a class when you ditch the last three weeks of it and stop being able to understand the supposedly important laws of physics.

Those laws don't explain why Robinson had to die. They don't explain how I'll keep going without him. So I'm pretty sure I don't care that much about understanding how "the entropy of any isolated system not in thermal equilibrium almost always increases."

But then, like a contrarian voice from the heavens, something from class pops right into my mind: *a body in motion tends to stay in motion; a body at rest tends to stay at rest.* That's the definition of *inertia*, a word that would have made Robinson roll his eyes.

I am in motion. I will stay in motion. Maybe one of those magical forces of the physical universe will kick in and keep me going, no matter how much pain I feel.

Or not.

I wrap my arms around myself, inhaling the scent of Robinson that lingers on his flannel shirt, which I'm wearing. And my tears well up and start to spill out all over again. I'm just really, really tired.

"Hey, Axi, check this out!" my dad calls. I lean over the balcony and he points to a part of the withering rosebush in the yard—one solitary flower still miraculously in bloom. I smile weakly. I was hoping he'd finally found his watch.

"You okay?" he asks.

I shrug. I mean, how am I supposed to answer that question? I saw Dr. Suzuki last week, and my cancer is still in remission. My five-year survival rate? Almost 93 percent.

So technically, yes, I'm okay. *Technically.*

But as I sit here letting the sun warm my face, I know that there's a part of me that's missing. It's as if the doctors had sliced something essential out. A vital part that I was sure I needed to keep me breathing. Not just existing. Even now, sometimes I think I hear Robinson's laughter, and for a moment my heart lifts. But when I turn my head to look, it's never him. It's the wind, or the call of a bird, or a hallucination of my own mad dream.

I think it was love at first sight for both of us; it just took us a little while to figure it out. That was understandable, considering we were being stuck with needles, shot through with radioactive particles, possibly poisoned by the horrific substances the hospital tried to pass off as food, and then, when we got discharged, running away and stealing cars together.

So we had other things on our minds.

Of course, sometimes I think maybe we *did* know our feelings right away, but we couldn't admit them to ourselves. Like we secretly thought, *Okay, cancer is scary, but love is* terrifying.

And it is. But it's also exhilarating and bewildering and miraculous.

Right before Robinson and I left on our trip, I'd written a paper on the French essayist Michel de Montaigne. ("Ooooh, *faaaahncy*," Robinson had teased.) "The greatest thing in the world is to know how to belong to oneself," Montaigne wrote. And while Montaigne was a very smart man, I'm sure, in this particular instance he's full of shit.

The greatest thing in the world is to know how to belong to someone else. The way Robinson and I belonged to each other. We held on as tight as we could, as long as we could. It wasn't enough.

And yet it has to be.

At night when the stars come out, I look up and remember Robinson at the window of the hospital in La Junta, me standing so close to him that it took my breath away. I think about what I didn't say then, which is this: the stars we see aren't even real stars. We see the light that they gave off millions of years ago but that is only now reaching our eyes. We don't see a star as much as a memory.

"Remember the me before this," a pale, sick Robinson said to me. "Remember the me with the guitar."

And since memory is all I have now—unless you count a glass orb, a key chain, a shirt, and a penny that once was lucky—I tried to do what he asked.

"Write about us," Robinson urged. "Tell our story."

And I did it; I told our story. You hold it in your hands.

I just wish I could have done it better. How can you, through my plain and simple words, possibly experience the joy I felt when Robinson jumped into that Los Angeles pool, sledded on the golden sand of the Great Dunes, or kissed me in an ancient temple? How can you understand what Robinson meant to me? His laugh was like a peal of bells. He really did consider Slim Jims to be their own food group. When he played the guitar and sang, whether it was in the cancer ward or in Tompkins Square Park, everyone stopped to listen. He was magic.

"Axi!" my dad shouts from below. "I found it!" He's holding up his Timex and grinning like it's a winning lottery ticket.

"Good for you!" I call down. As if he's the kid and I'm the mom.

I feel like I owe my dad, running off the way I did. He almost drank himself to death, worrying and missing me. I'm trying to make up for the fact that I barely got back in time to save him.

I only wish I could have saved Robinson, too.

But I know Robinson didn't want me to be broken after his death. He wanted me whole, well, and writing. About us.

"Make sure to throw in a lot of words I wouldn't understand," he'd said—using the last bits of his energy to tease me. "And a lot of fancy metaphors and stuff."

I just nodded. I'd do anything he wanted.

Loving Robinson made everything seem brighter and more beautiful. And if life has faded a little since he's been gone, it's still a lot more vivid than it used to be. Now the sun dazzles. That vermilion rose flings its perfume into the air. And the breeze soothes me, if I let it.

Most days I think of him and smile, even if I have to cry my eyes out first. He never stopped believing he was lucky. Maybe not lucky enough to survive, but lucky simply to have lived.

He was my light, my heart, my beautiful scalawag. And I was—I *am*—his GG.

OSCAR JAMES ROBINSON
JUNE 21, 1996–JULY 6, 2013

Missing me one place, search another.
I stop somewhere waiting for you.

—Walt Whitman

JAMES PATTERSON received the Literarian Award for Outstanding Service to the American Literary Community at the 2015 National Book Awards. He holds the Guinness World Record for the most #1 *New York Times* bestsellers, and his books have sold more than 325 million copies worldwide. He has donated more than one million books to students and soldiers and funds over four hundred Teacher Education Scholarships at twenty-four colleges and universities. He has also donated millions to independent bookstores and school libraries.

EMILY RAYMOND is the ghostwriter of numerous young adult novels, including a #1 *New York Times* bestseller. She is the coauthor of *First Love*. She lives with her family in Portland, Oregon.

In Bear Mountain, the days are cold but the nights are steamy...

Please turn the page for the complete Bookshots Flames novel

Hot Winter Nights

by Codi Gary

1

ALLIE FAIRCHILD STARED OUT HER WINDSHIELD at the ramshackle cabin.

Please tell me I have the wrong address.

Scrambling for the MapQuest printout amid the fast-food bags and other evidence that she had blown her diet once again, she read the directions over and over. Finally, sure that she hadn't misinterpreted them, she looked up at what had been described to her as "charming and rustic." She was pretty sure it had been the setting for her favorite horror movie, *The Cabin in the Woods*.

In fact, she half expected to see flesh-eating zombies pop out from behind the thick pine trees surrounding it. When her landlord, Dex Belmont, had warned her that they were a few miles outside of Bear Mountain, Montana, he had definitely been bending the truth a bit. According to her car's odometer, she was a good ten miles from the town limits on a curvy road that had made her stomach queasy....

And in the middle of the freaking forests of Narnia.

Leaning her head on the steering wheel of her Jetta, she

groaned in defeat. After thirty-two years, she had thought that she was making a solid choice for once. She'd planned to come to small-town Montana to turn a poorly run trauma center into one of the best in the country, and therefore erase all of the potholes in life she'd been unable to avoid thus far.

"Hoooooooooooowwwwwllll!"

Allie jumped a foot in the air, shrieking. Outside her window was a huge hound with its mouth practically pressed to the glass, vibrating her door with its deep bellow.

"Bluebell!" a deep voice said loudly, out of sight. The car-shaking sound stopped and the dog sat, its hot breath fogging her window. Allie's hand gripped the front of her blouse, sure her heart was going to pound its way right out of her chest.

Suddenly, her passenger door opened and a man peeked in.

"Sorry if she scared you. She likes to be the welcoming committee."

Allie blinked, taking in a head of tousled, sun-streaked brown hair and green eyes set in a tanned, gorgeous face. The man's smile was wide and boyish, completely dispelling her previous surprise and terror. The muscles of his shoulders stretched the lightweight T-shirt he was wearing, and the brief flash of a tattoo beneath the sleeve tempted her to reach out to get a better look.

"Do you always spring out at people like a serial killer?"

His golden eyebrows rose, but he didn't lose that smile. "Not usually, but we've been waiting for you."

Clearing her throat, she said unconvincingly, "Yeah, that isn't helping your whole stalker vibe."

He held his hand out to her, hovering over the center console. "I'm Dex Belmont. Allie, right?"

This guy was her landlord? Taking his hand hesitantly,

she tried to ignore the pleasant warmth of his palm against hers. He had lured her out to his property with a bunch of misleading photos, after all. None of the shots of this cabin had shown an iffy-looking roof or a porch that was missing a sturdy railing.

"Yeah, I'm Allie, and I have a bone to pick with you—"

"Hang on, before you start picking, why don't I come around and get your door?"

"I can get my own door, thank you very"—he slammed her passenger side door before she finished and was coming around the front—"much."

She reached for the handle at the same time he did, and when he pulled it open, she practically fell out on her face, putting her nose-to-nose with his dog. Big, droopy brown eyes stared at her from inches away, and then a large, wet tongue smothered her nose with slobber.

Mustering whatever dignity she had left, she started to climb to her feet, shaking off his hands as he attempted to help. Swiping at her nose with her arm, she glared up at him. Wow, he was tall. She liked tall.

She shook away her thoughts and said, "This is not at all what you promised me. You told me that the cabin was 'cozy'—"

"Look, I may have tweaked the truth a bit, but you're also here two weeks earlier than I was expecting." He crossed his arms in front of his chest, and Allie tried to ignore the way the muscles flexed as he scowled down at her as if she were the one who had bait-and-switched him. "So, before you start throwing a walleyed fit, how about you take a look inside and I'll tell you about all the improvements I'll be making?"

If Allie was smart, she'd get her butt back in her car and hightail it out of there, but this had been the only place for rent, according to the realtor she'd spoken to over the phone. She could buy a place, but she hadn't been ready for that kind of commitment. She wanted to take a few months and get used to Bear Mountain before she actually bought something.

And the few motels she'd passed hadn't looked better than this.

"Fine. Lead the way, McDuff."

That smile was back in place, doing crazy things to her insides, although her outsides were freezing. She rubbed the arms of her lightweight sweater. "How are you only wearing a T-shirt? I wasn't expecting it to be so cold already."

"We start getting snow around mid-October, but so far we've been storm-free." He glanced back at her over his shoulder and she finally understood exactly what the word *smolder* meant. "And as to my attire, my temperature runs hot. Wanna feel?"

"Get real."

Dex chuckled as he climbed up onto the porch. "You never told me why you decided to move from New York to Bear Mountain. I can't imagine it was for the culture."

Allie hesitated in answering when the first porch step squeaked loudly under her foot. "Are you sure I'm not going to fall through here?"

"Front porches squeak, I promise. The first thing I did was start on the porch, so I've already reinforced and replaced a lot of it." He stood at the top of the steps and held his hand down to her. "I won't let anything happen to you."

Despite the temptation, she ignored his hand and walked past him, her shoulder brushing the front of his shirt. She snuck a glance at the hard outline of his chest, swallowing.

"You were just going to tell me why you left home?"

"I needed a fresh start and figured rural Montana was as good a place as any for a change."

"What exactly will you be doing here?" he asked, holding the front door open for her.

"I'm running Bear Mountain Memorial Hospital."

He seemed skeptical. "You're awfully young to take on such a big job."

"If I'd wanted to work in a state-of-the-art hospital, I could have, but I wanted to go where I could really help people." She didn't want to throw charity events or expensive dinners just to "Save the Otters," like her parents did. "As for my qualifications, I have a double major in business and nursing, with a master's degree in hospital administration. I may look young, but I have experience. I know what I'm doing, Mr. Belmont."

When she turned back toward the door, his arm shot out, blocking her way. He leaned down until their faces were only a few inches apart, and her palms started sweating as her heart thumped.

"Why don't you just call me Dex?"

2

Dex Belmont waited for Allie to hightail it back into her car and take off, but she just stood there, her pretty brown eyes never flickering away. He could tell he affected her, but he didn't know whether it was because he pissed her off or because she was attracted to him, and he was more than tempted to find out which.

That wouldn't be a smart move on his part, especially since she would be living next door. She'd get attached, and once she found out he wasn't the kind of guy for a long-term relationship, drama would ensue.

And he was over drama.

"Are you going to show me the cabin or kiss me, Dex?"

Her question sent a shock wave of awareness through him, and for a second, he thought it was a proposition. Until...

"Fair warning: if you attempt the latter, I know six easy moves that will leave you broken and bleeding on the floor."

Picturing this short, curvy woman bringing him low made him burst out laughing. He dropped his arm and let her pass. "I like the brass on you, Allie."

She frowned as she surveyed the kitchen, and he could tell she wasn't happy with its current state. Hell, he couldn't blame her one bit. The place did look like shit, but he was supposed to have had more time. She'd called him a week ago and said she wouldn't be arriving until the first week of November. Then two days ago, she'd called again from Nebraska to let him know she'd be there two weeks ahead of schedule.

"I know it looks bad, but really, there are no leaks and I'll have it looking brand new in just a few weeks. You know, the few weeks I would have had if you'd given me more notice?"

"Fine, you have a point," she said. "I shouldn't have changed the game plan on you like that, but with all the work I have to get done at the hospital and with the weather report saying that it's supposed to get bad soon, there didn't seem to be any time to waste. Plus, I have to get to know the doctors and nurses, and judging by *some* people's reaction to my age and gender, I can't imagine all of them will be too welcoming."

Dex nearly choked as he tried to hold in his laughter. Including his best friend, Hunter, there were four trauma surgeons at the hospital who were all seasoned military vets. He could just imagine how they were going to react to this curvy blonde with just the slightest New York accent walking in there and pointing out everything they were doing wrong.

Actually, he'd pay money to see that...or at least charge admission.

"Yeah, that's true. If you want to whip that place into shape, you will definitely need a firm hand and a good night's rest, which won't be a problem. She might not look like much, but this cabin's sturdy and safe. I'm putting up the new porch railing this weekend, but like I said, I reinforced the deck, so there's no problem there."

Dex saw that she was staring up at the hole in the ceiling and could feel warmth steal up his neck. Okay, so he felt a little guilty for misleading her, but when Heather Dolan at the real estate office had asked him if his cabin was ready to be rented, he'd jumped at the chance to get a little extra scratch during the winter months. Not that he was struggling, but he liked to have a nest egg, something he'd learned from his parents. It was about the only thing he'd inherited from his mathematician father and psychology professor mother. As a child, he'd had to beg his friends' dads to take him along on their camping trips, while his parents had preferred museums and working on their latest publications.

Of course they had loved him, but they'd never really understood his love of the outdoors. Or his decision to become a search-and-rescue specialist after eight years in the army. He'd stopped trying to explain it years ago, and just let it be. He was happy, financially stable, and doing what he loved. His parents came to visit a couple of times a year and spent most their time doting on his quiet, bookish younger brother. It worked.

That being said, if his mother ever found out he'd been less than forthcoming with his current tenant, he'd be in for a damn long lecture on ethics and honesty.

Maybe that was why he was so defensive with the irritated woman standing before him.

"I'll be fixing that, too," he said.

Allie crossed her arms under her breasts and he tried like hell not to look down as she berated him. "I can't believe you rented this place to me in this condition. Even if I had told you I wouldn't be here in three months, the amount of work this place needs..."

She turned away from him as she trailed off, her gaze scanning the room again, taking in all the things that were wrong with the place. Dex knew for a fact that the repairs weren't as extensive as she assumed. He'd had a contractor out months ago to give him an estimate, but Dex had sent him on his merry way. Dex could do everything he'd listed for a quarter of the guy's "conservative estimate."

"Wow, so you're a construction worker, too?" he asked.

She turned those big brown eyes on him. "No, but I don't need to be to tell you this place needs a lot of work."

"Not as much as you think, sweetheart. A little patch here and a bit of paint there, and it will be grand." His fake Irish accent didn't even crack the skeptical look on her face. He'd never met a woman immune to it before.

"I'm sure you think so, but until you get the repairs done, I'm withholding rent."

Outrage blazed through Dex and he took a step toward her. "Now, just one damn minute—"

"No, *Mr. Belmont*"—the way she exaggerated his name, he knew it was meant to rankle him—"you already admitted that the cabin isn't ready for me. I may have had a change of plans, but when I called two days ago, you could have told me the truth and I would have made other arrangements. As it stands, I am not going to pay you to live in a place that probably has a leaky roof, because you weren't honest. Now, you can tell me to get the hell off your property, and I will be happy to find a hotel while I search for another place to live. Or you can get started on the repairs right away, and as soon as they're complete, I'll reinstate our original agreement."

Then she actually smiled at him like she'd invited him over for tea.

"So what do you say? Do I stay or do I go?"

3

HUNTER GRACIN PULLED ON HIS BLUE SCRUBS,
tying the knot quickly. He was running late this morning,
and couldn't afford to piss off the new director of Bear
Mountain Memorial Hospital. God only knew he'd tested
Bill Featherton, the previous director, more times than he
could count when he'd come here after finishing his resi-
dency in his home state of Texas. It didn't help that old
Bill had been a bullheaded dick too tightfisted to update a
single machine in the place during his reign.

Hunter hoped that the new director was actually here to
work and make a change, and wasn't using Bear Mountain
as a placeholder until he retired.

No one knew anything about this guy except that he was
from New York. Hunter couldn't figure out why some big-city
dude would move to the-middle-of-nowhere Montana. Maybe
he was originally from the area and wanted to come home.

Grabbing his stethoscope and lab coat, Hunter ran down
the hallway to the room where the staff was supposed to
gather for the formal introduction. He could speculate all he

wanted, but if he didn't get his ass front and center before the bigwig started talking, he might not have a job at all.

He pushed in next to Jay Cromwell, who glanced his way briefly before facing forward once more. Jay was a large man of few words, except when he got a couple of glasses of whisky in him. Then he wouldn't shut up. Both of them had served in the armed forces, and it had been an instant bond with them and the other two doctors on staff.

"Rough night?" Jay asked quietly.

"Nah, just forgot to charge my phone, so my alarm didn't go off."

"You're lucky she's not here yet."

Hunter paused as he shrugged into his lab coat, surprised. "Our new director is a woman?"

"Apparently."

Hunter grinned, imagining the kind of woman that would come in and whip their asses into shape. Sadly, in his mind she looked a bit like his fourth-grade teacher, Mrs. Harvel, who had sounded as if she smoked six packs a day and looked like she could bench-press a Buick. Hunter had to admit it would be nice to get a younger woman in town, though. The women they had were either married, too young, or about twenty years older than his thirty-four years. As fun as cougars were, he was ready to settle down. He wanted someone he could have kids and grow old with.

"Holy shit," Jay hissed.

Hunter tried to follow his line of vision, but there were too many people in the way. And then, suddenly, a young blonde in a purple silky blouse and black slacks stepped up onto the stairs, smiling out at the crowd.

"Good morning, everyone. My name is Allison Fairchild and I will be taking over as director of Bear Mountain Memorial Hospital.

"What does that mean for you? Well, for starters, I want to assure you that there will be no layoffs; your jobs are safe. However, we will be working to update the equipment and computer system. My goal is to help Bear Mountain become one of the best trauma centers in the country, and to do that, I'm going to need all of your cooperation to make sure the changes I will be implementing are seamless. I will be conducting interviews with all of you, as a way to introduce myself to you and address any of your concerns. Again, I appreciate you all being here today and look forward to working with you. Thank you."

As she stepped down out of sight, Jay whistled. "Damn, she's a lot more fun to look at than grizzled Bill, am I right?"

Hunter couldn't have agreed more, and as the crowd dispersed, a buzz of excitement continued sparking him as he went about his work, waiting for Allison Fairchild to call him into her office.

Just after lunch, his pager went off and he made his way to the administration floor. When he reached the room that used to be Bill's office, he knocked on the door.

"Come in."

Hunter stepped inside and got a good look at Allie Fairchild. From thirty feet away, she had been pretty, but now, she was gut-punchingly gorgeous.

She stood up and gave him a smile, and Hunter caught the signs of tension around her eyes.

"Dr. Gracin, please take a seat."

"After you, ma'am. I might be a doctor, but I'm a gentleman first."

Her smile brightened. "Thank you. I have to admit, you're the only person who doesn't seem to think my presence is a sign of the apocalypse."

Hunter laughed, waiting until she was fully seated before he did the same.

"I'm sorry if they're giving you a rough time. I think most of us were expecting someone a little more—"

"Male?" Her tone wasn't bitter, simply matter-of-fact.

"Actually, I was going to say aged."

She laughed, opening what he assumed was his file. "I assure you, Dr. Gracin, that although I may not be as 'aged' as you may have hoped, I am perfectly capable and qualified to take Bear Mountain to the next level."

"I don't doubt you one bit, Ms. Fairchild. And if anyone else gives you any trouble, I say to hell with them. We could use some new blood." He gave her his best grin before adding, "Especially someone who brightens up the room."

She looked up from the file, her head cocked to the side. "Are you flirting with me, Dr. Gracin?"

"No, ma'am, that would be unprofessional. But, seeing as how you're new and in need of someone to show you around, I thought I'd offer myself up. I'd be happy to take you to dinner one of these nights, show you all the highlights of Bear Mountain." Hunter leaned forward, lowering his tone and putting every bit of his southern drawl into his voice. "Of course, if we're gonna be friends, I'd insist you call me Hunter."

Hunter thought he caught a ghost of a smile before her expression went blank. "I appreciate the offer, but right now, I need to concentrate on the job and not on making friends."

"But you're thinking about it, aren't you?" Maybe he was counting his chickens, but the brief flash of interest in her eyes couldn't have been all in his head, could it?

"I tell you what, Dr. Gracin. If I survive this week, I'll give your offer some thought." Flipping through a page in his file, she asked, "Now, do you have any other questions or concerns?"

Despite her all-business facade, Hunter wasn't deterred. In fact, he had a really good feeling that he and Ms. Fairchild were going to become *very* close.

4

HUNTER STOOD ON THE SIDE OF THE OR TABLE, searching for the bleeder in his patient's abdomen. Peter York, thirty-nine, had come in with a rigid abdomen, a concussion, and scrapes and bruises along his body after a nasty fall. His buddy had told his intake nurse that they'd been hiking, and Peter had been startled by a bear on the trail. Based on the man's camouflage duds from head to toe, Hunter suspected they were illegally hunting said bear, who had turned the tables on them. Not that it mattered; it wasn't Hunter's business what they were doing up on that mountain.

He just needed to make sure that Peter York made it off the table.

Finally, he found the source of the problem, and once he applied the clamps and suctioned, he could see exactly what needed to be done. As he removed Peter's spleen, he started humming an old Garth Brooks song. Hunter's cool demeanor and speedy hands were what had gotten him offers from several of the best trauma centers in the US, but

Hunter had wanted to go where he was needed. And Bear Mountain had been in desperate need of an excellent trauma surgeon.

Sure, the equipment was outdated and some of the nurses were testier than a mama grizzly with cubs, but he saw more than his fair share of action.

Plus, living in the same town as his best friend, Dex Belmont, had its perks. They had met in the army and kept in touch long after they'd been discharged. With Hunter's family back in Texas, things would have been a lot lonelier without Dex. And as much as he loved his parents, things were better when he and his three older brothers put some distance between them.

Finally, Hunter was able to close up. The clear, steady beeping on the monitors told him that Peter York had a good chance of pulling through. Maybe Peter would even give up bear hunting for good.

After Hunter exited the OR and cleaned up, he passed Allison Fairchild's open office door and peeked in. She was bent over some paperwork, squinting, and even though she was chewing on a pencil like a beaver, he still thought she was the prettiest thing he'd ever seen.

And he was almost positive she was feeling him, too. He just needed to give her time to adjust to life in Bear Mountain.

Hunter found Peter's wife in the waiting area. Noting the wife's pallor, he insisted she stay seated as he sat down next to her.

"Mrs. York, I'm Dr. Gracin."

"Is Pete all right?" Her voice wobbled, and Hunter took her hands in his, squeezing them gently.

"I had to remove his spleen, and he had some serious internal bleeding, but barring further complications, your husband should pull through just fine. He looks pretty beat up, though, so I want you to be prepared for that."

Mrs. York squeezed his hands hard, tears streaming down her cheeks. "Thank you so much, Dr. Gracin."

Then, to Hunter's surprise, the trembling, mild-mannered Mrs. York turned to the man next to her and started raining blows across his head and shoulders. "You idiot! You almost got him killed!"

Hunter tried to intervene, but her little fists were too fast for him to grab. "Mrs. York, this is not the time—"

"Mary! I'm sorry. He wanted to come."

Hunter lowered his voice to a soothing tone. "It's all right. You don't need to do that to your husband's friend." Hunter didn't have a lot of experience consoling women, but her sniffles seemed to subside. As he tried to comfort Mrs. York, Allison chose that moment to walk by the waiting room, pause in the doorway, and stare at him.

Then, a smile stretched across her full lips, taking his breath away.

When she disappeared, Hunter wished he could extract himself and go after her, but he had to do his job.

What the hell did that smile mean?

Dex ordered another round the minute his best friend walked through the door of the Grizzly. The local pub had hardwood floors, cedar walls, oak countertops, and stools at the bar. It had the feel of a log cabin, complete with a big fireplace on the east wall. Locals usually avoided peak hours during tourist season, but after ten, out-of-towners went looking for livelier haunts than the laid-back Grizzly.

"Hey, buddy," Hunter said, taking the stool next to Dex. "How did things go with that new tenant?"

Dex's mouth thinned just thinking about Allie Fairchild

and her ultimatum. "She's a pain in the ass. Told me she wasn't going to pay me any rent until I fixed up the place, since I'd misled her about its *condition*."

Hunter whistled. "And you went for that?"

"My first reaction was to tell her to hop back into her little Jetta and get the hell off my property, but to tell you the truth, she wasn't wrong in her reasoning."

"So you're really letting her squat in your cabin for weeks? Are you going to hire that contractor?"

"Hell, no, I'm not paying for something I can do myself. Little Miss Thang can enjoy her stay, because as soon as I get the place up to snuff, I'm going to renegotiate with a three-hundred-dollar rent increase."

Penelope Davis set their beers down, smiling widely at Hunter. "Hey there. How was work?"

"It was good, Penny, thanks." Hunter gave her his million-watt grin, and Dex almost gagged as Penny blushed. Ever since Hunter had moved to town, all the local women had started falling over themselves trying to catch his eye.

Not that there were very many. At least Penny was cute with her splash of freckles, bright blue eyes, and long dark-brown hair. Yet for some reason, Hunter didn't seem interested in her.

When Penny went down the bar to help another couple, Dex nudged Hunter with his shoulder. "She likes you."

"She's a kid," Hunter said.

"What are you talking about? She's got to be in her twenties."

"And I'm in my thirties, man. I'm looking for someone to settle down and have kids with, not a plaything."

Dex sat back on his stool, staring at Hunter in surprise. "When did this happen?"

"When I turned thirty-four and realized that I wanted

to do something more with my time than drink with you. I want to meet someone, get married and have a couple kids. You know, the whole 'warm apple pie with a side of vanilla ice cream' kind of life."

Just thinking about that scenario made Dex break out in a cold sweat. He wasn't against marriage, but he had a lot more oats to sow before he took the plunge. And he was only a year younger than Hunter.

"Anyone in particular you've got your eye on, then?" Dex asked.

"As a matter of fact, I met our new director, Allison Fairchild, and she is stunning."

Dex choked on the swig of beer he'd just taken and barely managed to swallow before he had a loud coughing fit. Hunter slammed his hand between Dex's shoulder blades. "You okay, man?"

"Yeah, I'm good." Dex wheezed.

"Did you suck some down the wrong pipe or have you met her already?"

"*Allie's* my pain-in-the-ass tenant."

Hunter laughed. "Allie, huh? Small world." Suddenly, he sobered. "You're not interested, are you?"

Dex spluttered, "Hell, no! What gave you that idea?"

Throwing up his hand, Hunter said, "Whoa, I was just asking, man. Didn't want to piss in your patch."

"Believe me, my friend, the last thing I'm interested in is a difficult city girl who won't last the month here. You're welcome to her."

5

TWO DAYS LATER, ALLIE WAS SITTING AT HER desk staring down at the mountain of paperwork and invoices in front of her. The hospital needed so many updates, it seemed as if all she'd done since getting to Bear Mountain was sign checks.

The only bright spot in all the mundane tasks were the few times Hunter Gracin would walk by her open door with a smile or a wave. Not that she was looking for a boyfriend, but she'd be pretty well off with a guy like Hunter. He was successful, grounded, handsome, and nice, and much better than any other candidates she'd met.

Like Dex Belmont.

No, Dex wasn't even in the running. He was too cocky, he'd already proved he was a little shady, and he was totally the kind of guy who would love her and then leave her high and dry. She didn't need another jerk to rock her world; she needed a partner with his shit together.

It was why she needed to really think about every move she made here. Her past was filled with regrettable career choices, and a string of bad relationships. Her mother liked to throw them in her face whenever she mentioned Allie's two older, happily married sisters. Both had married men with impeccable New York pedigrees and were loaded to boot.

While Allie was happy her sisters had found love with men her parents approved of, Allie wanted more than what life had to offer in the city. She still wanted the right guy, which is why she started a checklist of all the qualities she was looking for in a man. Hunter matched it perfectly.

Dex, not so much.

Her desk phone rang, and she picked it up on the second ring. "Allison Fairchild."

"Hello, Ms. Fairchild," her assistant, Rebecca Kirkland, said. "If you still want to lend a hand, they're short a surgical nurse and have a family coming in with multiple injuries. Car accident."

Allie hesitated for a brief moment, taking in the mess she'd be leaving behind. But it would all be waiting when she got back in an hour or two.

"I'll be right down." Allie quickly shrugged out of her business casual attire and changed into the purple scrubs she kept in her desk drawer. With her stethoscope in hand, she ran for the stairs. When she finally burst into the emergency area, gurneys were being wheeled in, one after another. Hunter was directing people and Allie made her way toward him without even thinking about it. Maybe it was because he seemed to be the only one besides Rebecca who hadn't hated her on sight, or perhaps it was watching him with that patient's wife, but she liked him.

And it didn't hurt to make friends.

"Hey, I heard you needed some help down here," she said, coming up alongside him.

He glanced her way with a puzzled look. "I thought you were our administrator?"

"Well, I'm also a trauma nurse, and a pretty decent one, actually."

Hunter gave her a wide grin, his blue eyes dancing with amusement. "Is that a fact?"

"It is a fact, so if you can use me . . ."

"I can use you. Dex should be coming with another critical case any minute."

"Dex?"

Crap, please don't let it be—

The automatic doors opened and in rolled a gurney manned by two paramedics. . . .

And her jerk of a landlord sitting astride the patient, administering chest compressions. Against her will, her gaze was drawn to those strong, corded arms as he pressed down hard with each compression, his face tight with concentration. Tiny beads of sweat gathered at his temples and she had the craziest urge to dab his forehead.

"What do we have?" Hunter asked.

Shaking herself, she slapped on her all-business face. Old habits die hard, but she was determined to focus on cute, reliable men like Hunter, and not dishonest, sneaky, hot, sexy men like . . .

"Fifty-six-year-old male, suspected heart attack," Dex said breathlessly. "He was unconscious in the field, and his pulse was weak and thready up until a minute ago—"

"Are you a paramedic?" Allie asked abruptly.

Dex paused in his compressions as he glanced her way, piercing her with those intense green eyes. "No."

"Then maybe you should get off our patient and let us take over."

Allie realized that she'd said the wrong thing the minute

the air chilled around her. The two paramedics looked at her as if she were an insect, and even Hunter frowned at her.

Dex climbed off, and let one of the paramedics climb up. "Whatever the boss wants."

Damn it, she'd let her emotions get the better of her and acted like an elitist bitch. She'd wanted him gone, but she hadn't meant to sound so cutting.

"All right, Trauma Two, let's go," Hunter said.

As they rushed the man off, Allie hesitated, opening her mouth to apologize.

"Shouldn't you go with them? Make sure they're doing their job right?"

Allie's cheeks burned. Of course he probably thought she was some kind of tyrant, but she really wasn't. She had no idea what it was about Dex that made her want to prick him with every barb in her arsenal. She wasn't usually like this.

But she couldn't tell Dex any of that, because he was already walking out the door.

Pushing him from her mind, she hurried to Trauma Two and found the patient surrounded by Hunter and several nurses.

"We've got it covered," he called out, barely glancing at her while he charged the paddles. Then he yelled, "Clear."

His brush-off was so painful that Allie felt as if he had put the paddles to her. *So much for having one ally.*

Dex found his truck in the parking lot with Bluebell waiting patiently in the backseat. He'd asked Brian Darcy, one of Bear Mountain's firefighters, to follow behind the ambulance in it, and Dex was definitely thankful to live in a small town where people could be trusted. Where people knew him and his background.

Everyone except Allie.

Dex slammed his palm against the steering wheel, letting

loose a string of curses that would have made his grandma blush. It had taken all of his self-control not to lay into Allie Fairchild and her snotty, condescending attitude, but he'd been the bigger man, turned the other cheek.

For all the good it did him. He knew he'd be stewing for days about this incident.

Bluebell leaned over the back of the seat and nuzzled his ear. It was the hound's attempt to calm him, but Dex was too fired up. It wasn't as if he didn't have any medical training, didn't know how to administer CPR, yet he'd let her treat him like an idiot.

He hated that. Growing up with parents like his hadn't been easy. He'd been an ordinary kid who preferred fishing to calculus, and their disapproval had given him a bit of an inferiority complex. He could admit that. And Miss High-and-Mighty New York Princess had hit the nerve like a dart to a bull's-eye.

The only reason he had been at the scene of the accident was that he was driving behind them when the car had swerved off the road and hit a tree. Dex stopped to check on them and found the husband unresponsive, with a weak heartbeat. The wife was crying in the front seat with a head wound, and their two teenagers were in the back with minor injuries. Dex called it in and started on the husband, which was probably what had kept him alive until the ambulance arrived.

But he couldn't tell Allie that or she might have thought he cared about her opinion of him. Which he didn't. At all.

Heading out toward the Bear Mountain Search and Rescue building, he cracked his neck and rolled his shoulders, trying to relieve some of the tension plaguing him.

Suddenly, something small and brown ran out in front of his truck. Swerving, he glanced back to see the little fur ball in the road, unhurt. Few cars came out this way, so Dex stopped and got out, making his way back toward the animal. He wasn't sure what it was until it lifted its head and he saw the floppy ears and long snout.

It was a puppy, and not a very old one by the looks of it. The dog cowered as Dex got closer, and started to slink away.

"Hey, buddy. It's okay." Dex kneeled down a few feet away and held out a hand. "I promise you'll be safe with me."

The puppy responded to his voice by submissively moving forward, and Dex saw the wet trail of urine it left behind. When it was finally within reach, Dex picked up the pup, noting its smelly, matted fur, and looked around. No one lived out this way, which made Dex suspect the little dude had been dumped in the forest.

Dex headed into the woods where the pup had come from, whistling, but there wasn't another sound. Fairly confident the pup was alone, he headed back to the truck and climbed into the driver's side, setting the pup on the passenger seat. Bluebell whined and tried to climb over the backseat, but a firm "Stay" from Dex had her sitting back, her long ears perked as she eyed the puppy.

And as the pup sat back, Dex got a good look at the little guy's stumpy left front paw. Dex couldn't tell what breed it was, but he had a feeling that its owners hadn't been pleased by the pup's deformity, most likely something it had been born with. But why let it live to be six, seven weeks before they dumped it?

Grabbing a blanket from the back, he tucked it around the little guy. "What do you say we get you a bath and some grub?"

The puppy cocked its head and whimpered.

Dex took that as a yes. Pleased to have something to focus on besides Allie Fairchild, he started up the truck and headed to work.

6

IT WAS AFTER NINE AT NIGHT WHEN ALLIE stumbled out of her office. She had put in a fourteen-hour day and she didn't just feel exhausted, she was also ready to get away from people. Since she'd made her snarky comment to Dex, the rest of the staff had been giving her a wide berth, including Hunter.

Speak of the devil, there he was, walking out the front door ahead of her. Allie picked up the pace, wanting to make peace with him.

"Excuse me, Dr. Gracin," she called, racing to catch up.

He paused just outside the entrance and waited for her. He was out of his scrubs and wearing a simple T-shirt and jeans. Jeez, were all the men in Bear Mountain immune to the cold? She was wearing wool tights under her slacks and still freezing her butt off.

"I am really sorry about earlier. Mr. Belmont is my landlord and we didn't exactly have the best first impression of each other, but that's no excuse for being rude and unprofessional. I'll apologize to him, but I wanted you to know that behavior like that isn't normal for me."

Hunter crossed his arms over his chest. "I know Dex can be kind of a dick, pardon my French, but he's saved a lot of lives in this town. People respect him."

"Well, I'll do my best to get along with him and make things right." She gave Hunter a small smile and asked, "So what about you? 'Cause, to be honest, I need all the friends I can get."

"I suppose I could be persuaded to not join the angry mob...if you'll have a drink with me."

As much as she wanted to make amends, Allie was so tired that she'd rather get back to the cabin, crawl into bed, and sleep than try to be social tonight. "Can I take a rain check?"

"How about tomorrow? I have the day off; you have the day off. We could go exploring, maybe have a picnic before the weather gets too cold...."

"How do you know I have the day off?"

"I may have asked Rebecca if you were coming in."

Even when he was mad at her, he'd still asked about her schedule? How endearing was that? "Well..."

"I promise you'll have fun."

Think about the list. Plus, it would keep me away from the cabin so Dex can fix it.

Allie pictured being stuck in the cabin all day with Dex; sweaty, shirtless Dex in a tool belt and swinging a hammer with those strong arms....

"Okay, yeah. A picnic with a friend sounds great."

"For now," he said, grinning.

"What?"

"Friends for now."

Laughing softly, she shook her head. "I get the feeling you don't hear the word *no* a lot."

"Not often, but I promise I'll be the perfect gentleman. Would nine tomorrow morning work for you?"

"Nine is perfect," she said.

"And just to show what a swell guy I am, I'll walk you to your car."

"You know, most men don't call themselves 'swell' anymore."

"What can I say, I'm a throwback." Hunter put his hand on the small of her back, and the warmth of his palm was comforting. It made her feel safe and cared for, a feeling she could definitely get used to.

God knew none of the boyfriends she'd left behind had ever shown her such consideration. And as he took her keys and unlocked her door, she didn't feel the need to remind him she was more than capable of doing so herself.

When she pulled in front of the cabin fifteen minutes later, she glanced over at Dex's house and saw that the lights were still on inside.

Tomorrow morning I can talk to him. Tonight I have a date with my new flannel sheets.

Plus, Allie wanted to get a few more boxes unpacked before bed. She climbed the porch steps and unlocked the front door. She flipped on the light and took one step inside when something big stood up on her counter, staring at her with black, beady eyes.

And she let out a bloodcurdling scream.

7

DEX HAD JUST PUT BLUEBELL AND THE PUPPY into crates when he heard Allie's scream. Grabbing his rifle off the rack above the fireplace, he ran the hundred yards to the cabin, only to find Allie standing on the porch, holding the front doorknob, and shaking visibly.

"Are you all right?"

"There . . . there's an animal in the cabin!"

Dex brushed past her, opened the door and stepped inside. On top of the counter with a mangled box of crackers in its hands was a big, fat raccoon. The animal dropped down onto all fours and arched its back, letting out a high growl.

The door squeaked open behind him, and Allie hissed, "Shoot it!"

"I'm not going to shoot it."

"Then why the hell did you bring a gun?"

"In case." Dex glanced around, looking for any of the coon's buddies, but he seemed to be alone.

"Okay, seriously, there is a wild animal eating my brand-new box of Ritz crackers and you are standing there staring at it! Aren't you supposed to be a big, tough mountain man?"

Dex saw the tufts of fur at the edge of the hole in the ceiling. "Looks like he came in through the attic."

"Well, hallelujah, Sherlock, looks like you solved the mystery of how it got in. Now how about you get it the hell *out?*"

Dex sighed and pulled out his phone. Looking over his shoulder at her, he said mildly, "Just a little friendly advice, but the next time someone comes to your rescue, you might want to be a little more grateful."

"I would be grateful if you were actually helping!"

Dex dialed his buddy, Deputy Luke Teller, who picked up on the second ring. "Teller."

"Hey, it's Dex."

"What's up, man? I was getting ready to knock off."

"Before you do, I've got a raccoon situation in the cabin."

Luke sighed heavily into the phone. "Give me ten minutes."

Dex ended the call and guided Allie back out the door. "A deputy will be out in a few minutes to take care of your buddy there."

"You called the sheriff for a *raccoon?*"

Dex gritted his teeth. "I'm getting a little tired of you treating me like I'm an idiot."

"I don't understand why you can't shoo it or shoot it!"

"Because the sheriff's department, which doubles as our animal control, can tranquilize him and relocate him, whereas if I shoot him, you're cleaning up the raccoon bits."

"Oh." Although it was dark on the porch, the kitchen light streaming from the front door highlighted her flushed cheeks. "I'm sorry."

"I appreciate the apology," Dex said, despite the fact that

it hadn't done much to appease him. He also couldn't ignore the fact that Allie looked cold, if the arm-rubbing and shivers were any indication. "Why don't you come over to my place while you wait? At least it's warm in there. I'll look for something to cover up that hole until I can patch it in the morning."

She seemed to hesitate, so Dex shrugged. "Look, it's up to you. You can stay out here and wait in the cold or you can come sit by my fire." He walked down the porch steps, grinning as he called over his shoulder, "But fair warning: raccoons sometimes jump down from trees onto people's backs when they're feeling threatened. He could have friends watching you right now."

He heard her steps pick up behind him, and started whistling. Hey, he might be a gentleman, but that didn't make him a saint.

ALLIE COULDN'T STOP SHOOTING LASER BEAMS
at the back of Dex's head as he walked into his big kitchen.
She'd known he was probably messing with her about the
raccoon jumping on her, but that hadn't stopped her skin
from crawling. She had never been much of an outdoorsy
person. The one time she'd gone away to camp, she'd
begged her parents to come get her after one night, since
she'd stayed up the whole time jumping at every noise.

"Are you hungry? I've got some leftover pasta. Or I can
make some coffee."

"I'm already jittery, so I don't need to add caffeine.
Thanks, though."

Allie sat down on the couch and studied the large open
living room that bled into a beautiful kitchen. Everything
was rustic, except for the stainless steel appliances. There
were framed arrowheads on the walls, dozens of them, and
the large fireplace roared with golden-red flames, casting
dancing shadows on the cedar walls.

Dex came back in with two glasses of amber liquid and held one out to her. "Here, this will calm your nerves."

"What is it?" she asked.

"It's whisky. Don't tell me you're too good for whisky, too?"

His challenge had the desired effect, and she took the glass, downing the contents in one gulp. Her throat blazed as the liquid raced down, pooling warmly in her belly. Her eyes watered and she tried not to cough.

"Looks like I was wrong about you. You drink whisky like a champ," Dex teased, sitting on the couch across from her.

"What did you... ahem... what did you mean by I'm 'too good for whisky, too'?"

"Nothing. You don't seem to really fit in around here."

"Or maybe you have something against me because I don't fall at your feet—like every other woman—just because you're hot."

He quirked his left brow. "You think I'm hot, huh?"

"Don't get too full of yourself. Pretty is as pretty does. Just because you're nice to look at doesn't mean anything to me."

"Is that so?" He stood up and bent to take her glass, leaning in far closer than he needed to. His face was only a few inches from hers and she fought the urge to pull away, refusing to let him think he was getting to her. "So, what does affect you, Allie Fairchild?"

Allie's heart slammed against her breastbone as she stared into those bright green eyes.

Your eyes. Your shoulders. That sneaky tattoo that continues to tease me...

The sound of a cage rattling and a whimper broke the spell.

"What is that?" she asked.

"That would be Kermit." Dex stood up, making it easier for her to breathe once more. He walked across the room and bent over, messing with something she couldn't see.

"What's a Kermit?"

He stood back up with a fluffy bundle of adorableness in his arms. "This is a Kermit."

Allie felt her heart liquefy into a gooey puddle as Dex brought the puppy closer. When he sat down next to her, she didn't even protest, she was so fixated on the sweetest face she'd ever seen.

"Aw, pumpkin, come here." Without asking, she took the puppy from Dex, snuggling him close to her chest. "You are so freaking cute. Where did he find you?"

"I found him this afternoon. Someone had dumped him, probably because he's got a deformed paw. He was a sad little pup at first, but after a couple of baths and some grub, he finally started to perk up."

Allie held the puppy out, studying the paw, and he scrambled to get close to her again, his little tongue darting out toward her. Laughing, she let him lick her nose and hugged him once more. "What kind of dog is he?"

"My best guess is a sheltie. He looks like a tiny Lassie, right?"

"He does." As Dex reached out and stroked Kermit's head, his hand brushed Allie's collarbone and they both stilled. Staring at each other over the puppy's head, she said, "It was good that you stopped. He might have died out there."

"I'd never leave an animal like that."

"Just like you wouldn't shoot the raccoon when you knew you could have him tranquilized and relocated."

Was it the fire finally warming her or had the temperature suddenly amped up?

"I told you, I didn't want the mess," he said softly.

"I don't believe you. I think underneath the dickish exterior, you're a big old softy."

Was she actually flirting with Dex?

Danger! Danger! Abort!

"That's what you think, huh?" He leaned a little closer, and whether it was the lull of his voice or the whisky clouding her judgment, she did the same.

"Yeah. Am I wrong?"

His lips were so close and he smelled so good that she licked her own.

"Absolutely."

Allie closed her eyes, anticipation humming through her body. . . .

The loud pounding on the front door made her jerk back, and his hound started baying.

Dex sat back, his expression unreadable. "That would be Luke."

Realizing what almost happened, Allie moved away from Dex on the couch. "You should probably get that."

He stood up without another word and went to grab the door. Meanwhile, Allie kissed Kermit on the head, cursing herself. *That's it. No more whisky. No more raccoons. And definitely no more alone time with Dex Belmont.*

9

DEX WALKED OUT OF THE CABIN WITH LUKE, grimly. By the time they'd gone back inside Allie's home, the raccoon was gone. They'd boarded up the hole with a piece of cardboard, but it was only a temporary fix. If the raccoons really wanted in, they could do it with very little effort.

Which meant that Dex either needed to repair it tonight or let Allie stay in his guest room and come over to take care of it in the morning.

Or she could just share my bed.

No, that was a bad idea. He couldn't get involved with her, especially after what Hunter had said the other night. It was one thing to have a casual thing with his tenant—that'd be wrong in itself—but to screw over his best friend?

He wasn't that much of an asshole.

After Luke left, Dex made his way back to his place and found Allie on the floor of his living room, playing with Kermit. When she looked up at him, he forgot for a second that Hunter had called dibs and she wasn't meant for him.

What he really wanted to do was cross the room and kiss her, just to see what she tasted like.

"Did he get it?" she asked.

"No, it was gone and will probably be back, especially now that it knows there's food inside. So I can set up the spare bedroom for you and fix the—"

"You...you want me to stay here tonight? With you?" Shaking her head, she said, "I don't think that's a good idea."

"Look, it's not as if I'm going to sneak into bed with you. It's late and it seems like the simplest solution."

"I think I'll take option two and go back to the cabin. You covered the hole, right? It probably won't come back tonight, anyway."

Dex didn't know whether to be exasperated or exhausted. "You would rather sleep in the cabin and risk another animal encounter than stay in my very comfortable guest room?"

"Yes, I think I would." She stood up with Kermit in her arms. "What are your plans for this guy?"

"I don't have any yet, besides getting him in to see the vet—"

"So if I wanted to adopt him that would be okay with you?"

"Aren't you gone all the time?" Dex asked.

"I can find a pet sitter to watch him while I'm at work."

Dex couldn't say it was a bad idea. Allie did seem taken with him. "He needs his shots."

"I'll get them. I promise, he'll be in good hands."

Unable to come up with a reason to say no, Dex grabbed the crate he'd set up for Kermit and nodded toward the door. "I'll walk you back and get him set up."

"Thank you. I'll return it when I get my own." They walked outside and Allie paused. "Thanks for everything tonight, too. I may have misjudged you."

As they crossed the yard toward the cabin, he shot her a wolfish grin. "You mean I'm not a conniving liar who has no business getting in the way of professionals?"

"Yet another apology I meant to give you. I am sorry I was so horrible at the hospital. I'm not usually like that, it's just—"

"I get it, you don't like me and I was stepping on your turf."

"I'm not territorial and I didn't say I didn't like you!"

He reached past her to open the cabin door, and their chests brushed. Allie sucked in a harsh breath, and when his gaze dropped to her parted lips, it took every ounce of will-power not to do it. Not to give in and press her up against the door and kiss her until she was begging for more.

Of course, with Kermit in her arms like a furry shield, it would be a little hard to do, but if he really wanted to, he could probably manage it.

"So you're saying you do like me?"

"I'm saying that everyone deserves another chance at a first impression." She moved past him, leaving him to watch her hips swing as she walked into the kitchen.

"That's mighty nice of you."

Damn, she made a power suit hot.

He saw her face fall as she surveyed the damage. "It's going to take me hours to clean this up."

"Tell you what. Let's get Kermit set up, and then I'll help you."

"Well, I suppose that's only fair, since it's your fault it got inside in the first place," she said teasingly.

"You know, a simple 'thank you' would work."

"Just speaking the truth."

Dex followed her into her bedroom and set the crate down, surveying the changes she'd already made to the room.

A set of blackout curtains covered the window, and across the dresser were a couple of picture frames. One of an older couple, and another with Allie hugging two other women who looked so much like her they had to be her sisters.

Dex almost asked about it, but figured it was none of his business.

Pulling out the bowl of food and water bowl that had spilled a bit in transport, he said, "He might need a dry towel or something."

"I'll take care of it."

Dex left her bedroom, the image of Allie curled up under her black-and-white bedspread too tempting by half.

Dex got to work on the kitchen, and a few minutes later, Allie walked in. "You know, you're probably tired. I can finish up."

"I don't mind. Besides, I thought this was my fault," he said.

"I just...I want to be clear that we need to keep things between us cordial. You're my landlord—"

"Actually, a landlord gets paid."

Frustration marred her pretty face, and she seemed to be clenching her jaw. "Be that as it may, I'm not looking for complicated. And I feel like if anything develops between us it will be just that."

Why her assumption bothered Dex, he couldn't guess. He deliberately brushed every last bit of cracker into the trash and came around the counter. Standing in front of her, he said, "Actually, things with me would be pretty simple, sweetheart. We'd have fun until one of us got bored and we'd say good-bye. Nothing complicated about that."

Dex saw a flash of something in the brown depths of her eyes. Temptation? Whatever it was, it was gone as soon as it appeared and her expression became hard as steel.

"Well, I'm not in the market for that, either. I need to get settled in and concentrate on work. Nothing more."

His lips a hairsbreadth away from hers, he whispered, "Your loss."

Before she smacked him, he turned and headed for the door. Pausing with his hand on the knob, he had to get the last word in.

"But just so you know, winter is coming and it can get mighty cold round here. If you change your mind and need some warming up, you know where I'll be."

10

ALLIE WOKE UP TO THE SUN BARELY STREAMING
into her bedroom. Hadn't she closed those damn curtains
last night? Kermit was whining, probably because he
needed to go potty and was tired of being in his crate, so
Allie swung her legs off the side of the bed. Her clock on
the nightstand read six-thirty in the morning, and for the
briefest moment, she wondered what had possessed her to
ask for the dog. Now she was going to have to take him
outside at all hours while she housetrained him.

Groaning, she opened his crate and picked him up. The
minute his little body snuggled against her, the grumpiness
melted away.

"What do you say we take you to go potty and have a
bowl of cereal?"

A tiny, excited tongue on her chin was her answer as she
opened the bedroom door and made her way to the living
room. She set him down briefly to pull on her jacket and her
boots by the back door, sweeping him into her arms before
he got the chance to have an accident. Taking him out the

side door, she shivered as the cool morning air bit through her thin pajama pants. She was really going to need to invest in a flannel set and some house slippers. She walked down the back porch steps and let Kermit down.

"Go ahead, pumpkin."

The puppy nosed around at the dirt and leaves for a few seconds before he squatted down to do his business. Allie's gaze wandered around the forest, grudgingly admitting that it was a beautiful place. She could get used to being here.

When Kermit was done, Allie called him over and picked him up. Once they were back inside, she set him down on the hardwood floor and took off her boots and outerwear once more.

"What do you think? Kibble for you, Fruity Pebbles for me?"

Kermit chased after her feet, skidding across the floor when she stopped abruptly once she saw the kitchen.

As she took in the chaos of the crime scene with horror, Allie's emotions twisted between fear and fury. She looked up at the cardboard covering the hole in the ceiling, but it was still in place. How the hell had that furry bastard gotten back in last night? Then her gaze landed on her box of Fruity Pebbles, which had been snug and safe in the cupboard when she'd gone to bed. The cupboard that now hung wide open, like a giant mocking mouth.

Her delicious Fruity Pebbles. The box had been ripped open and its guts shredded. What was left of the colorful cereal was spread across the counter and smashed into what looked suspiciously like raccoon feces.

Allie's entire body surged with molten rage.

"Damn you, you no-good son of a bitch!" Allie threw the chewed-up box of cereal across the room, surprised when she heard a familiar grunt.

She looked up toward her front door and found Dex standing in the doorway. He stooped to pick up the mangled box, giving her a dry look as he tossed it onto the overturned trash can.

"I've been dreaming my whole life about a woman who looks like an angel and cusses like a sailor."

Allie glanced around for something else to throw, but couldn't find anything worthwhile.

"What is it with you? Don't you know that cheesy lines and breaking and entering are *not* sexy?"

The panty-melting grin he shot her almost made a liar out of her. "That's too bad, 'cause that's all the game I've got."

"Obviously! What are you even doing here this early?"

Waving at the tool belt on his hips, he said, "I have the day off, so I figured I'd get started on those repairs. After all, the sooner I get them done, the sooner you start paying me."

"Next time, you need to call and then knock before you just come barging in. I could have been sleeping or in the shower."

"Now you're just teasing me," he said, shamelessly grinning at her.

"Whatever. The first thing you can do is figure out how he got in because your stupid cardboard is still there."

Dex walked over to stand under the cardboard, turning his head from every angle, as if looking for a weakness. "Huh. Maybe he never left the cabin after all. Maybe he's in a cupboard or something right now?"

Allie picked up Kermit, her gaze darting around the room in alarm. "Do you think so?"

"Could be. I'll do a thorough search. Your cupboards, your closets...I should probably check your underwear drawer, too."

She realized he was messing with her, again, and glared

at him. "Ha-ha, I had my door shut, so there's no way he was in my room." A lump crawled up her throat, and she hated that she was about to cry, especially in front of Dex. "Please just find him and make sure he doesn't get in again, okay? I can't stand the thought that he might hurt Kermit if I don't realize he's in here."

Every trace of humor left his face. "I'll fix the problem."

"Thank you." Grimly surveying the mess once more, she said, "I guess I'll put Kermit in his crate while I clean up."

Kermit wasn't happy about being locked up again, but she didn't want him underfoot while she cleaned. Especially if any raccoon poop had gotten onto the floor.

As she scrubbed the counter, her gaze kept straying to Dex as he inspected every nook and cranny. He looked good in the white T-shirt and jeans, the tool belt slung low on his hips. He was wearing a dark ball cap that covered his sun-streaked brown hair, and the shadow of the bill gave his face a mysterious edge.

Hunter. Focus on Hunter, remember? He's the catch here.

"I'll be gone most of the day, so don't worry about me being in your way."

"Working today?" he asked without turning around.

"No, Hunter Gracin is showing me around."

Did his shoulders stiffen or was that just her imagination?

"Oh, well, that'll be good. Hunter's a good guy."

"Yeah, he seems nice."

"Plus, he's a doctor."

Allie bristled at his tone, as if he were insinuating that was the only reason she'd said yes to Hunter. Okay, so he was settled with a career and that was a factor in her decision to go for him, but that didn't mean she was a gold digger. She had money of her own.

"What are you saying?"

"Nothing, I just know that most women want to score a man with money and a high-powered job. Doctors are the ideal, right?"

"I told you, I'm not looking for anything right now. Hunter and I are just friends."

He stood up with his hands in the air. "Whoa, don't jump all over me, sweetheart. I was making conversation. You don't have to explain yourself to me."

"I wasn't explaining myself, I was emphasizing the fact that there is nothing going on with Hunter!"

"Gotcha."

Allie violently tackled the rest of the cleanup, sanitizing the counter. Finally, she announced, "I'm going to take a shower."

The jerk had the nerve to leer at her. "You telling me 'cause you want some company?"

That was enough. Grabbing an apple from the bowl, she hurled it at Dex's head. He barely ducked out of the way in time, but when the edge of the apple skimmed his shoulder, she felt marginally better.

Until she reached the door to the bedroom and she heard him shout, "You've got some weird ideas about foreplay, darling."

Slamming the door closed and locking it with a click, Allie threw herself across the bed and buried her head in the pillow before releasing a frustrated scream.

11

HUNTER CLIMBED THE STEPS TO ALLIE'S CABIN and knocked on the door. It was five minutes to nine, and he was really hoping that she wasn't one of those women who are chronically late.

The door swung open and Dex stared out at him, a hammer in his hand.

"What's up, buddy?"

Hunter arched a brow at him as he stepped inside. "It's awfully early to be working on repairs, isn't it?"

"There was a raccoon invasion last night, so I am being a good landlord and dealing with the issue."

"I thought she wasn't paying you."

"She's not, but she will be soon."

"Hi," Allie said, coming into the kitchen with a puppy in her arms. She was decked out in leather boots, tight blue jeans, and a blue long-sleeved top. Her golden-blond hair fell around her shoulders in loose waves and he was struck again by how pretty she was.

For some reason, Hunter glanced toward Dex, and he stiffened as he recognized his friend's expression.

Hunger.

Dex had been adamant about having no interest in Allie, but...as Hunter took a long time to process everything that was happening around him, he decided that Dex was simply looking at Allie the way he did every beautiful woman.

Relaxing, Hunter stepped forward and kissed Allie's cheek. "You look amazing." Taking the puppy from her arms, he held him up until he was at eye level. "And who's this handsome dude?"

"This is Kermit. Dex found him yesterday and I am keeping him. Isn't he adorable?"

"Real men don't say adorable," Dex grumbled, but Hunter heard him.

"Oh, he's definitely adorable." He waited for Dex to give him shit, but his friend silently climbed the ladder under the hole in the ceiling, ignoring him. "I figured we'd start off by taking a drive around town, and I can show you all the places I love around here. Then we'll stop for a picnic.

"Then I was thinking later we'd go by the Grizzly and have dinner," Hunter said. "So is it all right if we put Kermit in his cage tonight? You're not really living until you've had a pulled pork sandwich and a frothy mug of BearFaced Brown."

"I'm afraid to ask what that is," Allie said.

"It's this awesome potato ale made in Idaho, by the Bear Island Brewing Company. It's tasty, you'll like it."

"I'm in."

"Is it cool if you watch Allie's pup for now, Dex?"

Dex grunted, and Hunter called up again, "You okay?"

"Fine. Why don't you two get the hell out of here so I can work in peace?"

Something had definitely crawled up Dex's ass and died there, but Hunter wasn't going to pry it out of him now. Allie grabbed her jacket, a hat, and gloves and gave Dex a withering look.

After going to the front door, Hunter held it open and waved Allie through.

Once she was outside, he shot one more glance at Dex, who finally looked his way.

"What the hell, man?" Hunter mouthed.

Dex didn't answer him, just went back to hammering. Shaking his head, Hunter closed the door with a *thump*.

Dex slammed the hammer down on his thumb for the third time in an hour and hollered. "Shit!" Throwing the hammer down, he climbed off the ladder and wished that he had something to swing at. He had no idea what had set his teeth and temper on edge, but he was pretty sure the blame sat at Allie Fairchild's sweet little booted feet.

Dex could chalk it up to the feeling of wanting what he couldn't have, but there had been women in the past he'd backed off of for a friend and been happy to. And seeing Allie look so relaxed, with her hair soft and touchable, had thrown him. Especially when he started imagining Hunter running his fingers through it.

She's just one woman. A woman who doesn't even think you're good enough for her, anyway.

The voice in his head was right, of course. What he needed was to keep his mind focused on someone else.

Pulling his phone out of his pocket, he scrolled through his contacts, finally landing on Iris Jacobs, a recent divorcée with a wild streak a mile long.

And his finger hovered over the Call button.

*   *   *

After exploring Bear Mountain for several hours, Allie and Hunter sat at the base of a mountain, eating their picnic lunch. A river bubbled and broke fifty feet away, and the view of statuesque mountains and pine trees was beautiful. The sun was out, and warmed the air slightly, but Allie still kept her coat on. So far, the date had been going very well. Hunter was funny, charming, and a gentleman.

"I found this spot when I was out driving and, I don't know, it just became my place. I haven't brought anyone else up here."

Hunter's words were romantic and right. They were sharing a lovely picnic and the sounds of rushing water from a river nearby were positively soothing.

So why didn't her heart flutter the way it had when Dex had stared at her this morning?

I need to put that man from my mind for one afternoon. Why is that so hard?

"Well, I'm honored," she said.

"If you want to feel even more honored, grab a brownie from the basket. I know it's not manly, but baking is actually the one thing I can do outside of the OR on rare occasions."

"You bake?" A man who was gorgeous, successful, and baked? Hunter was beyond the total package.

Allie grabbed one of the brownies and took a bite with relish. "Mmmm, seriously, you should patent these bad boys."

"That would require sharing my great-grandmother's recipe, which would be a mortal sin," Hunter said.

Allie popped the rest of the moist, chewy goodness in her mouth, humming with pleasure.

"Uh-oh, I forgot to pack something," he said.

Trying to swallow the chewy bite, she took a drink from her water bottle. "What?"

"Napkins." He scooted closer. "And you've got something right"—he reached up and trailed his finger over her lips—"there."

Allie knew what was about to happen before his lips closed over hers, brushing and tasting her softly, as if he was savoring her. Allie kissed him back, opening her mouth to his tongue.

The sound of something screeching overhead brought Allie scrambling away and glancing up toward the sky.

"What the heck was that?"

"I didn't hear anything," Hunter said.

Allie's cheeks warmed at the insinuation. He hadn't heard anything because he'd been too busy kissing her, while she...

She'd been distracted by a bird.

It wasn't that Hunter wasn't a good kisser; he was. There just wasn't any...

Spark.

Yet. She couldn't judge Hunter based on her experiences in her past relationships. Those had been crazy hot in the beginning, but fizzled out quickly. She wanted something that was going to last.

"Sorry, I'm not used to the great outdoors."

Hunter, easygoing and nice, just smiled. "Don't worry about it."

Allie figured she'd blown it after that, especially since he started packing up their food. But after he picked up the basket, he took her free hand and held it all the way to the car. Even opened the door for her and gave her a sweet, chaste peck before closing her door.

Everything was perfect about their date, and yet, she wanted to roll her eyes.

12

DEX ORDERED ANOTHER DRINK FOR IRIS, SOME fruity cocktail with a ridiculous name, and another whisky for him. He'd downed three already, but who could blame him? He'd forgotten how grating Iris's nasal voice was.

He pretended to listen to Iris bitch about how cheap her ex was, nodding and grunting as he looked past her shoulder toward the door.

I should have taken Iris somewhere else.

Except Dex hadn't wanted to go anywhere else, and if he was being honest with himself, it was because he wanted to see how Hunter and Allie's date had gone.

"I decided not to speak to him except through our attorneys. It's better for my stress level that way," Iris said.

"Makes sense," Dex said distractedly.

Iris's hand landed on his knee, moving its way up his jeans-clad thigh, indecently close to his crotch. "Here I am dominating the conversation with my complaining. My ex has the kids this weekend. Maybe we could go back to my place and I'll make it up to *you*."

Dex opened his mouth to answer, but the door swung open, and in stepped Hunter and Allie, both smiling and looking nauseatingly happy.

Until Allie's pretty brown eyes landed on him at the bar with Iris's hand in his lap, and her face crumpled into an unhappy scowl.

Was that look because he was there or because he was with Iris? Suddenly, Dex grinned, feeling better than he had all day. He climbed to his feet. "What do you say we play some pool, darling?"

Hunter and Allie had barely sat down at the bar when Penny walked over to take their order.

"What will it be?" she asked curtly.

Hunter, a little surprised by her attitude, asked, "You okay, Penny?"

"I'm fine, just busy."

Hunter glanced around at the handful of patrons in the bar, and as if following his line of thinking, Penny snapped, "I'm trying to study for my test, okay?"

"What kind of test are you taking?" Allie asked.

Penny seemed to hesitate before answering. "Animal biology. I'm going for my master's in zoology."

"That is amazing. I love animals. I just adopted a puppy that Dex Belmont found abandoned on the highway."

Penny's guarded expression flashed into one of outrage. "God, I hate people! Is the puppy okay?"

"Yeah, except he's got a lucky fin, like Nemo."

Penny's whole face melted into a soft, sweet smile. "Aw, poor sweetheart."

"You know, I need to find a pet sitter for him. I'm at the hospital during the day and I don't want him to get lonely or backtrack on his house-training. I was going to put a flyer up at the vet's office, but maybe—"

"I'll totally watch him," Penny said.

Hunter stared between the two women as they went back and forth, totally ignoring him as they ironed out the details of Kermit's new schedule. His gaze wandered to where Dex was, talking to a few bikers playing pool. Hunter shook his head and stood up. "I'll be right back. I'm gonna go say hi to Dex."

He noted Allie's dark look as she glanced toward his friend. "Okay."

If things continued between Allie and him, he was going to have to deal with the dislike between the two. He couldn't have his girl and his best friend hating each other.

Stopping beside the pool table, Hunter saw that Dex was concentrating hard on his next shot. It wasn't as if Dex couldn't handle himself when it came to hustling pool, but Hunter could already tell he'd had a bit to drink. And these guys didn't look like the type to take losing or Dex's good-natured ribbing well.

"Hey, buddy, what are you doing?"

Dex looked up from his shot. "What does it look like? I'm about to kick this guy's ass at pool."

Iris giggled nervously while the biker holding the pool cue didn't appear amused.

Dex took his shot, knocking two into the pockets, and stood up. Pulling his wallet out and holding some money out to Iris, he said, "Why don't you get us a few more drinks, honey? This won't take long."

Hunter shook his head and moved next to Dex. "Are you trying to get yourself killed? You don't know these guys and—"

"Dude, I'm fine. Why don't you go back to your date and see if you can pull that stick out of her ass?"

It took everything in Hunter not to slam his fist in Dex's jaw. "You're being a real asshole, man."

Dex lined up another shot, not even bothering to look at Hunter again. "Then maybe you should walk away."

Hunter did just that, heading back over to where Allie was watching him, her face a mask of concern as he sat down. "Everything okay?"

"Yeah, it's fine. He's like that sometimes. Whatever it is, he'll get over it."

Drunk or not, Dex was kicking the biker's ass, all right, and the dude did not look happy about it. Neither did his scruffy friend who was leaning against the wall, his arms crossed and bulging.

"Eight ball, corner pocket."

Dex took his shot, and as the ball sank in, both men cursed a blue streak while Iris, who had started to look a little bored two games ago, cheered loudly.

Dex grabbed the money off the side of the pool table, now a couple hundred deep, and slipped it into his pocket.

"I want to thank you, gentlemen, for such a splendid night—"

The biker who had lost, a mean-looking son of a bitch with a shaved head and a long, bushy beard, grabbed the front of Dex's shirt and pulled him forward. His face mere inches from Dex, he snarled. The dude's breath made Dex's stomach turn. "Where the hell do you think you're going? You aren't leaving until we have a chance to win our money back."

Dex smirked, too buzzed to recognize the danger he was in. Or maybe he'd just been spoiling for a fight. "I gave you three chances to win it back. Really, man, you oughta quit before I really clean you out."

Baldy didn't like that. He pulled back his burly arm to swing.

Dex ducked, ripping his shirt, and swung, nailing the guy in the gut with his fist. Dex weaved a bit, off-balance, as Baldy stumbled back against a table.

Suddenly, Baldy's friend was there, shoving Dex. He fell backward, hitting the floor so hard it knocked the wind out of him.

Dex tried to get his bearing back just as another biker stepped forward with a pool cue raised over his head.

"Ah, hell!"

Allie stopped talking at Hunter's exclamation and was left alone and dumbfounded as he jumped up and raced across the room. Allie spun around and saw Dex on the ground. One of the men he'd been playing pool with stood over him, a pool stick in his hand. Allie's gut lurched as she realized he was about to hit Dex with it.

Hunter got there as the man was bringing it down, and grabbed the pool cue out of the biker's hand. He threw it across the room. Allie hollered a warning as the other biker made a move at Hunter's back.

And then Dex was on his feet once again.

"Climb behind the bar!" Penny yelled, hopping over it with a baseball bat in hand.

"What the hell are you doing?"

"Squashing this shit," Penny said, tossing Allie a saucy grin before jumping into the fray.

Suddenly, a chair went whizzing through the air…right toward Allie's head. She barely had time to duck before it crashed into the bar wall behind her. Landing on the floor, she climbed back to her feet in time to watch Penny hit the biker attacking Hunter with her bat.

The rest of the bar was clearing out, including the woman who'd had her hand buried in Dex's lap when Allie had first walked in with Hunter. She'd tried not to let it bother her, but still...

Allie saw Dex being thrown over the pool table, the biker looming over him with his hands around Dex's neck. Hunter and Penny were busy pinning the other guy to the floor.

Allie had no idea what she was about to do, she only knew that she was running. She came up behind the biker and let her foot fly up from behind....

And it connected, hard, against his testicles.

The guy let out a high-pitched cry as he released Dex and fell to his knees, his back still to her. Allie hopped on one foot and nearly burst into tears as the pain in her foot radiated upward. As it subsided, Dex sat up coughing and wheezing, and their gazes locked. The light in his eyes when he looked at her stirred a warm, fuzzy glow in her chest, and she smiled at him through the pain.

And then the biker turned on her, looking seriously pissed off. "You stupid bitch."

As he took a step toward her, Allie realized that she should have taken Penny's advice and hidden behind the bar.

13

DEX DIDN'T THINK AS HE LAUNCHED HIMSELF onto the man's back, slipping his arm around his neck in a choke hold. He'd seen Allie's look of terror and lost all reason, jerking back hard as the guy clawed at his arm. The biker outweighed him by a good fifty pounds, but as Dex felt him start to go limp, he tossed him away from Allie as if he weighed nothing.

Then Dex was on him, throwing his fists until someone jerked him off the guy. Dex took in the blood oozing from Baldy's nose and lips, and his muscles relaxed.

"I'm okay, I'm fine."

Hunter released him and faced him with a look of rage. "What the hell were you thinking? The cops are on their way here and you're hammered. You can't drive—"

"I'll take him home," Allie said softly.

Dex glanced her way as Hunter tried to argue. "You don't have to do that."

"We're going to the same place. It's not as if I'm going out of my way or anything."

They were all standing around, talking about Dex as if he weren't there, and it was starting to piss him off.

Hunter nodded. "Okay, thanks. Dex, give Allie your keys."

Dex fished out his keys and handed them to Allie. Unfortunately, he didn't have time to turn away before Hunter stepped into her, gave her a kiss on the cheek, and said, "Sorry for the way our date ended."

"It's all right. I had fun until about ten minutes ago."

"So, you're saying getting into a bar fight wasn't on your bucket list?" Hunter asked jokingly.

"Yeah, not so much."

Hunter took Allie's hand, threading his fingers with hers. "Next time, we'll just stick to the fun."

Jealousy churned in Dex's stomach. He'd had enough. "If we're going, can we get a move on? I don't really want to spend the night in a cell with these two dickheads."

Both Allie and Hunter shot him a dirty look, but he was beyond caring. His head, his face, and his back...every part of him hurt and the room was starting to spin. The last thing he wanted to do was pass out at the Grizzly.

Finally, Allie released Hunter's hand and stepped forward, putting her arm around Dex's waist. "Come on."

Dex wrapped his arm around her shoulder and leaned on her a little more than he needed to.

Hunter roughly helped the bikers to their feet. He was already pissed about not being able to take Allie home, and now he was stuck here, cleaning up Dex's mess.

Come on, the last thing Dex needs is an assault charge on his record. Allie taking him home was the best option.

Still, Dex hadn't deserved the help tonight. He'd been an asshole this morning and in the hour before the fight broke out. For a moment or two, Hunter had gotten the feeling he was jealous of Hunter being out with Allie.

Trying to push his suspicions aside, Hunter stared into one of the burly biker's dark eyes.

"I'm going to go out on a limb and guess that your records aren't so clean that you can afford another run-in with the cops, so I'm giving you a chance. You can leave town now, no hard feelings, but if you stick around—"

"We're gone," one of the bikers said, shooting his buddies a warning glance. The guy who'd started it with Dex didn't look happy about it, but wasn't going to be stupid.

Once the bikers were out of the bar, Hunter handed Penny Dex's wallet. "This is Dex's. Whatever cash you find, give it to the owner. Dex will come in and work it out for the rest."

"And what about the other damages? Those men caused some, and so did you. Is Dex supposed to get stuck with the whole thing?" Penny asked.

Why is Penny being so hostile?

For some reason, Hunter was furious enough at Dex to almost say yes, but he didn't. "No, I'll settle my part of the damages, too."

"Fine." Penny set the bat down on the bar and grabbed the broom. When she tossed it at him, he caught it in midair. "Then you can start now by helping me clean up this mess."

Allie parked Dex's truck in front of his place, ready to tell him to get out. He hadn't said a word to her the entire drive, which had left her alone with her thoughts and a roller-coaster of emotion.

I was just in a bar fight. A man came at me and Dex stopped him.

Allie opened her door and glanced over at Dex. A bruise was already discoloring his cheek, and the cuts and scrapes across his knuckles were probably going to be sore tomorrow. He looked so peaceful and beautiful despite his injuries. His lips, which had escaped unscathed... she was tempted to lean over and wake him up with a kiss.

Of gratitude, of course. For protecting her.

She needed to stop thinking like that. It was insane. The man was drunk as a skunk and beat up. She needed him to get moving, because there was no way she was going to carry him inside.

"Dex, wake up."

He snorted.

After she got out and went around to the passenger side, she pulled his door open and leaned in. Giving his shoulder a gentle shake, she hissed, "Dex, come on, you're gonna have to walk."

Grabbing his arm and putting it around her shoulder, she grunted as she tried to lift him out of the car.

"What are you trying to do, rip my arm off?" Dex mumbled.

"Yes, that is exactly what I'm trying to do, you idiot. I need your help. I can't carry you inside, so you're gonna have to stand up and walk."

"Whoa, why so snippy?" Dex stood up and leaned so hard against her she nearly stumbled.

"Will you at least try to walk straight? You're a lot bigger than me, and if you don't stop swaying, we're both going down."

They paused at the door, and while Allie searched through his key ring for the house key, she felt his breath rustle the top of her hair. "Is that an invitation?"

As his meaning sunk in, her head flew up and both of them cried out when her temple connected with his chin.

"Ow. No, that was not an invitation, you pervert."

"Why am I a pervert? You say something like that, what am I supposed to think?"

Finally, she found a key that worked. "I was trying to find this so I could get you inside instead of leaving you on your porch."

The man actually pouted at her. "You're cranky."

Allie counted to five, trying to find her patience. As she unlocked the door, both of Dex's arms wrapped around her shoulders from behind and he leaned against her, his face buried in her hair. Her skin tingled at his proximity, and she told herself she didn't like it—loathed it, actually—but she couldn't deny that the feel of Dex's hard, lean body pressed against her back made her heart skip with excitement.

"You smell so good. Why do you have to smell so good?"

God, he was practically moaning against the back of her neck, and her hands began to tremble.

"I guess I could try not bathing," she said, trying to lighten the mood.

"Hmm, but you'd still be you."

What the hell did that mean?

Bluebell bellowed. Allie shuffled across the living room, Dex still hanging on to her.

"Where's your bedroom?"

"End of the hallway." His speech was really beginning to slur and Allie, afraid he was going to pass out on her, picked up the pace. Opening his bedroom door, she angled him toward the bed and loosened his arms.

"Here you go, big guy."

Dex flopped across the bed, the back of his head hitting the pillow with a groan. Allie lifted first one foot and then the other, untying his boots and dropping them to the floor. Then she placed his feet on the bed and moved up, trying to get him to lie straight.

While she leaned over him, his hand shot up, cupping the back of her neck. Before she could make a sound, he'd brought her down and his soft, full lips met hers, moving coaxingly. Her mouth parted instinctively. The kiss was over too fast for her to fully process it, but as he flopped back on the bed, he mumbled something.

"What is it, Dex?" God, why did her voice have to sound so husky?

Louder, this time, she heard him. "You taste better."

Better? Better than what?

But before she could ask him, he let out a deep snore.

14

A LITTLE OVER A WEEK LATER, ALLIE FLOPPED into her office chair with a moan. It felt as though she'd been running around nonstop, and her sensible heels had become torture devices. Kicking them off under her desk, she cracked her toes and flexed the arches, wincing at her sore muscles.

Every inch of her hurt, and while some of it was from being on her feet to oversee the hospital updates, most of it was due to stress.

For the last week, she'd been out with Hunter three more times. They'd gone to a movie, and grabbed dinner twice. He was the perfect gentleman and she liked him a lot.

But she just couldn't stop obsessing about the things Dex had said to her. Or that kiss, which she'd replayed again and again. It was so quick she'd hardly had time to realize what was happening, so why couldn't she forget it?

Not that she'd seen much of Dex since then. Either he remembered everything and had been avoiding her, or he had just been feeling lazy these days. He didn't start work on the cabin until she was gone, and he was never there when she arrived home. Still, he'd gotten the railing up on the front porch and there had been no more raccoons terrorizing her kitchen. She had to give it to him; every time she came home, the cabin looked better than when she'd left.

"How's my favorite hospital administrator?"

At the sound of Hunter's voice, Allie smiled warmly. She couldn't help it. She genuinely liked him.

"Fine. A little tired and my feet are killing me."

Hunter sat down in the other office chair and scooted around until he was next to her. He picked up one of her feet and held it in his lap.

And then, with the pad of his thumb, he pressed into the arch of her foot and started rubbing away all the aches.

Allie melted into her chair, whimpering with every squeeze, every press of his hands.

"Does that hurt?"

"In the best way possible," she said huskily.

For several more moments he continued massaging her feet, and then, suddenly, he was pulling her toward him so her legs straddled him on either side of his chair. Her eyes flew open as her simple black pencil skirt rode up her thighs. His arm wrapped around her waist and he dipped his head toward her lips.

"Someone could come in," she protested.

"I locked the door."

Such a bold move was surprising from Hunter, and as he gave her a hard, passionate kiss, Allie had to admit that it did stir something inside her. But was it really him or his assertiveness that was affecting her?

Allowing herself to sink into the kiss, to lose herself in it, she waited . . . and waited for more.

But besides that momentary flutter, this kiss was the

same as all the others they'd shared. A sweet, pleasant kiss. It didn't make her body hum with need or cause her toes to curl.

Damn it.

Don't be discouraged. There is something here. It might not be an over-the-top, runaway passion, but it will grow.

Allie had never had anything that was real before, nothing that would last. She just needed to be patient.

Allie pulled away and gave Hunter a reassuring smile. "We shouldn't do this here."

"Fine, I'll be a good boy, but what do you think about you and me grabbing a beer after work?"

"I would love to, but I have to get home and relieve Penny. She has to work at the Grizzly tonight."

Hunter stood up, running his hands from her waist down the sides of her thighs as he released her.

"Another time, then," he said, shooting her a wink before he unlocked her office door and slipped out.

Allie got home to find Dex up on the roof, hammering.

"Hey," she called.

He'd barely glanced up when she pulled in the driveway, and his indifference was starting to grate on her. How could he say all of those things and then ignore her? He hadn't even thanked her for bringing him home when he was too drunk to do it himself.

Looking around for something to throw, she decided upon a pinecone. The goal was to toss it up onto the roof next to him to get his attention.

Instead, she'd hit him in the ass, and with more impact than she knew she had the ability to generate.

Dex jumped and looked at her over his shoulder with a glare. "What the hell?"

"Don't you have a job or something?"

"I told you I took some time off to fix all the things on the cabin. Is that why you tried to knock me off the roof?"

"Oh, please, it hardly touched you."

With a shake of his head, Dex turned back to his hammering. Heat crawled along Allie's skin, pricks of anger tightening her muscles as she worked herself into a full-on rage.

What an ass. He couldn't spare two seconds to acknowledge she'd done him a solid the other night?

Screw that.

Picking up another pinecone, this time she threw it with the full intention of hitting him on purpose.

Of course it whizzed over his head instead.

Figures.

"What the hell?" He spun around on his knees. "What's your problem?"

"You are, you selfish jerk!"

Before he could say anything to that, she stormed into the cabin and let out a shriek.

Penny glanced up from the textbook she was reading with Kermit sitting in her lap. "Rough day?"

Dex had no idea what had gotten into Allie, especially since she'd spent more than a week ignoring him. He couldn't really blame her. After the things he'd said to her and then that kiss...

He was actually surprised she hadn't slapped him outright.

He'd been drunk, admittedly, and he hadn't been able to stop railing on himself for being an inconsiderate dick, especially to Hunter. There was no reason for him to be so hung up on this one woman, so he'd made it his mission to do the right thing and stay away from her.

But now, the crazy lady was throwing things at him while he was on her freaking roof.

That shit would not stand.

An hour later, once Penny left, Dex climbed down the ladder and opened the door to the cabin without knocking.

Allie shut the fridge and turned on him, her brown eyes blazing. "I thought we agreed you would stop barging in here without knocking?"

"Actually, you said that. I chose to ignore you."

"Well, that's a big change."

"I want to know what your problem is."

"Oh, I don't know, Dex. Maybe it's the fact that I left my date early to drive your drunk ass home and I didn't even get a 'thank you.'"

"You want me to thank you, I'll th—"

"And, you not only spouted off a bunch of total bullshit that messed with my head, but then you kissed me."

Dex felt his face fall. "You're right. I was drinking, but that is no excuse to disrespect you while you were just trying to help me. I acted like an asshole. I'm sorry."

Allie seemed surprised by his admission, if her excessive blinking was any indication. "Thank you."

"You're welcome. So, are we good? Or are you going to continue to throw things at me like a twelve-year-old?"

Allie blushed. He secretly loved the way she looked when she was flushed, even if it wasn't for the reason he wanted her to be.

I just apologized for being a dick. I need to stop imagining Allie Fairchild flushed and moaning in the middle of my bed.

15

ALLIE HAD NO IDEA WHAT ELSE TO SAY NOW that Dex had apologized. Part of her screamed to show him the door, but that wasn't what she did.

"Are you hungry? I was going to pop a pizza in the oven, because I'm too tired and sore to really cook."

"Why are you so sore?"

"Just a lot going on at the hospital. Stress and I've been running around. No big."

Without saying anything, Dex walked to the freezer and pulled out the pizza. "How about you pour yourself a glass of wine and sit down. I'll put the pizza in the oven."

"No, really. That's okay. You've been doing so much on the cabin that I'm sure you're exhausted—"

Waving his hand at her, he laughed. "It's a frozen pizza, not a four-course meal. Seriously, go sit."

Allie wasn't going to stand there arguing, not when her lower back was crying out at her to sit down. Grabbing a bottle of wine and a glass, she sat on the couch. She poured a glass as Kermit trotted over and tried to jump up next to her.

She picked the puppy up and let him crawl across her lap as she leaned back into the couch with a sigh.

She heard the tread of Dex's feet behind her before his hands even touched the sore muscles of her shoulders.

"What are you doing?" she asked.

"Making you feel good."

The way he said it, with an almost husky edge to his tone, sent a shiver down her spine. For the first time, she didn't fight him. She leaned back into his touch as he rubbed, thumbing the knots in her muscles firmly. It was heaven, and the irony that she'd received two massages from two completely different men in the same day did not escape her.

She was practically asleep by the time the oven beeped, alerting them that it was preheated, and he stopped his administrations. She turned around on the couch to watch him go back to the oven, teasing, "You know, if you ever get tired of the search-and-rescue gig, I think you'd kick ass as a masseur."

"Is that a fact?" He was bent over, his jeans-clad ass with its sexy leather tool belt facing her and spinning all kinds of dirty fantasies in her head. Should she ask him to take it off?

She shook her head to clear her thoughts.

Once the timer was set, Dex came back and her fantasy was realized. The tool belt came off and he set it down on the coffee table before sitting next to her on the couch. Spinning his finger in a circle, he said, "Turn around. I'll work out the kinks in your lower back."

Allie didn't even hesitate, just scooted around, pulling Kermit off her lap and setting him on the floor. She presented him her back and her skin hummed with anticipation as he spread the palms of his hands out and began to knead her sore muscles. His thumb and fingers worked at her, and she relaxed, moaning in utter ecstasy. She didn't even start when his hands crept up underneath her shirt, his rough, cal-loused hands against her smooth skin sending pleasure from her lower back down her thighs.

"God, that feels amazing." Allie hardly recognized her voice, it was so low.

Dex's hands lifted her shirt higher, and the cool air on her back broke through her stupor. She was just about to ask what he was doing when she felt something soft press against her spine.

His mouth. He was *kissing* her.

Another brush of his lips on her skin was electric, and she tensed. Not because she didn't like it, but because the sensa-tion was wreaking havoc on her.

Dex's hands smoothed over her lower back and around her waist, splaying over her abdomen, and still, she didn't say no. Didn't want to say no.

He brought her back against him, his mouth finding the curve of her neck. With a sigh, she reached back, cupping his head with her hand. He twisted her around slowly until he had her draped across his lap, and when his lips closed over hers, it felt like she was being licked by a thousand flames.

Allie opened her lips to his tongue and moved her arms around his neck as he made love to her mouth. Hard and soft, light and teasing, and then his hand was tangled in her hair, pulling slightly until her scalp tingled. The drumming of desire between her thighs made her squeeze them together against the ache, wanting so much more than his kiss.

And then his hand was there, cupping the front of her pants, his finger sliding over her. She arched up into his touch as he rubbed her, and she could feel the warmth of his hands through her cotton panties.

He unfastened the clasp of her pants and slipped his hand inside, and when his finger found the nub of her clitoris, she jerked. He pressed harder, rubbing in tight, fast circles until she was gasping against his mouth, her nails digging into the back of his neck.

Oh, yes, I'm—

As her orgasm rocked her, sending tremors throughout her body, she saw bright, flashing lights behind her closed eyes. She came back down, slowly, and realized Dex was still brushing her lips softly, with gentle pecks that brought her back to reality.

Her eyes flew open, and met his bright green ones.

Good God, what did I just do?

Dex knew the moment was over when Allie opened her eyes. The horror in them was like a sucker punch.

Slipping his hand out of her pants, he refastened her slacks, taking his time without letting his gaze leave hers.

A few moments later, when the oven timer went off, Allie still hadn't moved or loosened her grip around his neck. Reaching up, he pulled her hands down and set them across her stomach with a pat. "I'll go get that."

After Allie scrambled off of him, he got up, silently cursing himself. How could he have let this happen? The moment he'd touched her, he knew he was doing something wrong. He should've left, gone home, taken a cold shower, and forgotten all about Allie—but he hadn't been able to stop. He'd waited for her to say no, to grab his hand, to do something...

But she hadn't. She'd melted into him, kissing him back so sweetly, and his mind had moved onto one track. Touching her, tasting her. Branding her as his.

It wasn't fair. It wasn't real. Whatever this attraction, this passion was between them, he wasn't the guy for her. He wasn't the long-haul, "get married and tuck the kids into bed every night" kind of man.

Hunter was, though. Hunter could give Allie what she wanted.

Dex went to the sink and washed his hands, gritting his teeth while the hard-on pressed painfully against the front of his jeans. Ignoring it as best he could, he slipped on Allie's oven mitts and pulled the pizza out. Once he'd set it on the counter, he cleared his throat.

"Look, I'm sorry. I let things get out of hand." With a dry chuckle, he tried to go for nonchalant. "We can just forget this. Chalk it up to temporary insanity."

Allie stared blankly at him over the couch, her blond hair messy and her lips red and raw from his kisses. She was the most beautiful thing he'd ever seen, and yet, he was going to walk away. They needed some distance.

"Look, um . . . I'm gonna skip out on the pizza. But thanks for the invite. I'll just . . . I'll see you later."

Like a coward, he walked out the door without looking back. Because when he'd see the look of relief on her face, he wouldn't be able to handle it.

16

HUNTER KNEW SOMETHING WAS GOING ON WITH
Allie. Over the last week she had been avoiding him and
he couldn't figure out why. He'd invited her to dinner, left
her flowers, and still, she kept coming up with excuses.

Suspicion clouded his mind, and armed with two coffees
and a smile, he was determined to get to the bottom of it.

He tapped on her office door and poked his head in. "Hey,
you got a second for coffee?"

And there it was, that guarded look. "Well, um...I have a
lot of paperwork to finish."

Hunter's patience snapped and he closed the door behind
him. "Allie, I feel like you're dodging me and I've got to
know. Did I come on too strong or do something?"

"No, I mean..." Allie groaned, putting her face in her
hands. When she finally looked up at him, her face was filled
with regret. "I am so sorry I've made you feel like that...
I've just...I've been confused and needed a little time."

"Confused about what?"

He waited for her to answer, holding his breath.

"Well...last week, Dex..." She took a deep breath, as if she were preparing herself for what she was about to say. "He kissed me...."

Blood pounded in Hunter's ears. "He kissed you."

"Yes, and I feel terrible about it—"

"Did you kiss him back?" Why was he even asking this? Of course she kissed him back; she wouldn't have avoided telling him about it if she hadn't.

"I...yes."

"I see." Taking a deep, shaky breath, he smiled. "It's okay. We weren't exclusive or anything. Are you interested in seeing him, or was this a onetime thing?"

"No, no, it just...happened. And he is definitely not interested in me. He told me that outright."

Hunter's fists clenched. *Asshole.*

It wasn't even the fact that Dex had kissed her—well, it was partly that he'd kissed her—but mostly, it was the lies that got to Hunter. Dex had told him he wasn't interested in Allie. Then he'd made a play for her and didn't say a word to Hunter about it? They'd had drinks several times over the past week and he'd had plenty of opportunity to bring it up.

And then, after kissing her, he'd told Allie he wasn't interested?

Hunter was about to lose his shit.

"I am so sorry." Her words were coming out a little choked.

Giving her a no-big-deal smile, he said, "It's okay. Really, I...why don't we take a little break and you can take all the time you need to figure things out."

Allie's eyes were shiny with tears, but he was too keyed up right now to comfort her.

He needed a break himself, some air.

Hunter left Allie's office and headed downstairs and out

the front door. Taking a few deep breaths, he closed his eyes and let the cold air seep into his lungs. A storm was coming, he could tell by the gray sky and the bite to the wind, and something about those gray clouds was calming. Helped clear his head.

Except then he heard Dex's voice. "Hey, man, what's up?"

Hunter's eyes flew open, and all of his fury, all of the betrayal and hurt that had been churning inside him, boiled up and over as he launched himself at Dex.

17

AFTER DEX HAD FINISHED THE ROOF ON THE cabin, he'd gone into town for a case of beer and some essentials. After two weeks, the cabin looked better than it had in twenty years.

And he guessed he had Allie to thank.

He had to admit, he'd wimped out, the way he'd up and left like that, but Allie hadn't exactly reached out to him, either. Clearly, she didn't want to discuss what had happened.

But he was still her landlord, and now that he'd finished his work, he needed to reevaluate the rental agreement with her. He'd figured the safest place to talk was the hospital, where they wouldn't be completely alone and he wouldn't be tempted to kiss her again.

But when he'd approached the entrance, he'd seen Hunter standing out front by the big oak, looking a little nauseated.

Dex had called out a greeting as he approached, but when Hunter opened his eyes, Dex had paused and took in his molten red face and furious expression.

She'd told him.

"Ah, hell—oomph!"

Hunter tackled him to the ground, and for the second time in two weeks, Dex had the wind knocked out of him.

"You son of a bitch!" Hunter threw a right hook that made Dex's cheek explode. The same cheek the biker had punched, too. Stars popped around Hunter's head as Dex tried to focus. "Lying piece of shit, you're supposed to be my best friend."

Dex recovered his wits enough to raise his arms to protect his face, and as soon as Hunter's weight shifted, he bucked, dislodging Hunter. He climbed to his feet and held out his hands in defense.

"It's not what you think, Hunt—"

"What I think is that I told you I was interested in Allie, and you said go for it. Then, the minute my back was turned, you made a play for her. That's what I think."

Dex couldn't argue the semantics, but it was more complicated than that. "I didn't mean to kiss her, it just—"

"Don't say it just happened. That's a cop-out and you know it. Man up and tell me you want her. Don't be a coward."

"I don't want her, okay?" Dex yelled. "I don't. I am not interested in her, not for anything more than a casual f—"

Dex closed his mouth when he saw her, standing in the crowd he hadn't even noticed. This time, he couldn't walk away from the pain on her face. It became ingrained in his memory.

Hunter grabbed him up by his shirt, and he waited for the blow he deserved. It never came.

Hunter shoved him away from him, disgust oozing from his tone. "You're not worth it."

As Hunter turned and walked away toward the side entrance, Dex glanced back to where Allie had been standing, but she was gone.

                               *   *   *

Allie wiped at her red, wet eyes as she searched for Hunter, trying to avoid every gaze that followed her as she passed. It had only been ten minutes, but she knew people were gossiping, speculating about her and what she'd done to cause two grown men to fight over her in front of *her* hospital.

Seems like she'd figured out a new way to screw up her life. She had been in town for barely three weeks and she'd managed not only to pit two best friends against each other but to discredit herself in front of her staff.

She'd tried to fight the tears, but what Dex had been about to say hurt. She'd known, deep down, that she didn't mean anything to him. That what happened had been a mistake, but having him announce it in front of everyone...

It had been hard to hide the effect that'd had on her.

Allie opened the door to one of the on-call rooms and found Hunter lying back on one of the bunks.

He glanced her way as she came inside and locked the door. "What are you doing?"

Allie held up the first aid kit she was carrying. "I thought you could use some patching up."

"I'm fine."

Allie ignored him and sat down on the bunk next to him. Opening up the kit, she pulled out an alcohol pad and ripped it open. She picked up his right knuckle, cracked and bruised, and gently wiped at the blood crusting. When he hissed in pain, she blew on it softly until he relaxed.

"You don't have to do this."

She smoothed the antiseptic ointment over his knuckle and wrapped a layer of gauze around it. "I want to." Once it was secured with tape, she set it back down along his side. "I'm really sorry. I never wanted to cause problems between the two of you."

"The problem is that he lied to me. It has nothing to do with you." He turned to look at her, piercing her with those blue eyes. "Can I ask you something?"

"Of course."

"Do you...do you have feelings for me? Or was that all in my head?"

"Yes, I do, it's just—"

"You have feelings for him, too? Be honest."

Allie didn't want to answer, but he deserved the truth. "I don't know exactly what I feel for him. Right now, I'm disgusted with him and myself, but—"

"Look, I'm not giving you some ultimatum. I'm not that guy, and despite how things are between us right now, Dex is a friend of mine. I'm not taking myself out of the running, but you don't owe me anything, either."

Then, to her surprise, he leaned up and cupped the back of her head, bringing her down for a hard, fast kiss that caused another stir inside her. When he released her, she was a little dazed by it.

"What was that?" she whispered.

"That? That was something to think about."

18

DEX WAS SITTING ON THE FRONT PORCH OF THE cabin when Allie got home from work. When Allie saw him, her hands tightened on the steering wheel before she turned the car off and stepped out. Her stomach twisted and churned, tying her insides up in knots as she approached.

Dex stood up. "Allie—"

"Don't. Just don't."

His full lips compressed into a hard line, and she could tell his green eyes were blazing in the porch light.

"Fine, I just came by to apologize for earlier. What I said was out of line, and I'm sorry."

"Okay." Allie wished her voice hadn't trembled on the word as she tried to pass him. When he reached out to try to stop her, she said, "Don't you dare touch me."

Dex threw his hands up in the air. "All right, I won't, but we still need to talk."

"About what?"

"About the cabin. I finished the repairs and we need to talk about rent."

Allie gaped at him, completely taken aback. After everything that had happened, he was here for money? She stiffened and said, "Don't worry, Mr. Belmont, I'll have the check to you first thing tomorrow morning."

"Come on, Allie—"

"Good night."

With a heavy sigh, he let her pass, and she pushed through the door, slamming it behind her.

Penny held up a bottle of wine. "So I heard you had an interesting afternoon."

"How did you hear that?"

"My phone's been blowing up all day with questions about you. All the single men in town want to do you, and the women want to know what your secret is. I mean, if you can get two guys like Dex Belmont and Hunter Gracin to have a parking-lot brawl, you've gotta be dynamite in the sack."

"Kill me now," Allie groaned.

"No way! You are stirring things up around here. I mean, the most drama this town sees is on *The Bachelor*. You, my friend, are my new hero."

Allie grabbed two wineglasses from the cupboard and held one out to Penny. "Don't you have a bar to work at?"

"Called in sick. Figured you could use a little more estrogen and a lot less testosterone in your life."

"What I need is a time machine."

"Sorry, all out of TARDISes," Penny said as she poured Allie a glass of wine, nearly full to the brim. "But a few of these might help you block it all out for a little while."

The next morning, Dex slammed his fists into the sides of his punching bag, putting all of his self-loathing and bitterness into every blow. God, he had messed everything up, even his apology. He hadn't meant to talk about rent at all, but when she'd tried to blow past him without giving him a chance to explain, he'd lashed out.

Bluebell let out a loud howl as someone pounded on his front door.

Dex, shirtless and covered in sweat, jogged from his gym room to answer it and found Allie standing on his front step with an envelope.

"Here you go. You are paid up for six months, so there is no reason for us to have any other contact except in a professional capacity."

Dex took the envelope, slapping it against his thigh. "Come on, Allie, I get that I handled all of this badly, but we live next door to each other. We are going to see each other around town."

"Seeing each other out and about is fine. It's the being-alone-together part we have a problem with."

Hoping to break through her anger, he tried to tease her. "Are you saying that you have no self-control when it comes to me?"

Her dark-brown eyes were so cold, his smile slipped. "Actually, at this moment, I wouldn't touch you if you were the last man on earth."

With that, Allie spun on her heels and walked to her Jetta. Dex watched her disappear down the road, and when she was out of sight, he slammed the door. Bluebell was lying across the floor watching him pace, and for some reason, he found himself talking to the dog.

"Why can't she just accept that I messed up? We all make mistakes and say things we shouldn't. It's not as if I set out to hurt her."

Bluebell lifted her head and yawned, but Dex kept talking.

"I mean, I said I was sorry, and she's not exactly innocent. She kissed me back; she let me. . . ."

God, when she'd come on his hand, all he'd wanted to do was rip off her pants and bury himself inside her. To make love to her until she was screaming *his* name. He'd wanted to possess her, to brand her as his. It had scared the hell out of him.

So he'd taken the easy way out and bailed. He'd pushed her away and that made him a horrible guy.

And even more, he was the guy who lost his best friend.

Sitting on the couch, he rubbed his hands over his face, breathing deep. When Bluebell stuck her wet nose under his chin and nuzzled him, he let his hands drop to stroke her soft ears.

"I guess I really screwed up this time, huh, girl?"

19

THE FIRST MAJOR SNOWSTORM OF THE SEASON
raged around Allie as she stood over her car engine, cursing. It was just past nine in the evening, freezing, and Allie
wished for the millionth time that she'd left work before
the storm hit, but with half her staff gone for Thanksgiving, she'd stayed late to help.

I could be back in New York right now.

But even surviving a blizzard was better than taking
snide comments from her mother and long-winded lec-
tures from her father for four days. No. Allie had decided
to weather the storm from the warmth of her cabin. Instead,
her car wouldn't start and the cold was eating through her
clothes, numbing her skin painfully.

Out of the darkness and swirling snow, a buzzing engine
and single headlight zoomed into the parking lot. The snowmobile stopped behind her car, and the bundled-up driver
got up, making his way toward her.

She recognized his strut before he even took off his helmet. *Dex.* She'd actually managed to avoid him for the past

two weeks, even the few times she'd gone out with Penny or Hunter and a few other people from the hospital. She hadn't asked Hunter if the two of them were talking, because she didn't think it was her place.

"Are you all right?" Dex asked loudly. His deep baritone swirled around her in the wind, and she shivered, a reflex she swore was from the cold and not because she'd missed the sound of his voice.

"I'm fine." This was the first conversation they'd had in weeks, and she still wasn't ready for it.

"Sure you are. That's why you're standing outside, staring under your hood in a blizzard, right?"

He had a point. "My car won't start."

Dex ducked inside, flipping on a flashlight she hadn't seen in his other hand. "Your battery is probably frozen. Have you checked it lately?"

"No, I've been busy."

"Well, NAPA is closed by now. Here"—he handed her his helmet—"hop on the back and I'll give you a ride home."

She shoved the helmet back at him, a little harder than necessary. "Thanks, but I'll get a ride from someone inside."

Even in the dark storm, the parking-lot light showed that his green eyes were blazing. "Are you seriously going to make someone drive out of their way in a snowstorm just to spite me?"

"I'll stay with Penny, then."

With a shake of his head that sent snow flying off his hair, he said, "Suit yourself."

But as he walked back to his snowmobile, Allie reconsidered her options. Penny had left Allie's place before the storm hit, meaning Kermit had been locked in his cage for at least four hours. There was no way in hell she was going to ask Dex to check in on him. She didn't need to owe him any more favors.

Thinking about Kermit's adorable, lonely face as he lay locked in his cage, though...

"Wait!" Slamming the hood of her car down and grabbing her purse off the front seat, she trudged through the snow to catch up.

He paused, straddling the snowmobile and watching her with one raised eyebrow.

"Can you please give me a ride home?"

Folding his arms, the helmet still dangling from his hand, he seemed to be considering. Unlike her shivering body, he appeared oblivious to the cold, and it made her hate him more than she already did.

If I really hated him, then I wouldn't think about him a hundred times a day.

"Say 'I'm sorry, Dex, for being rude' first," he said.

"What are you, five?" she asked.

He didn't respond, just sat there with that annoying eyebrow arched, waiting expectantly.

She decided she could still despise someone and be attracted to them. Through gritted teeth, she muttered, "I'm sorry, Dex, for being rude."

Giving her the helmet, he waited until she was on the back of the snowmobile with her arms wrapped around him before he started the engine. As he blazed out of the parking lot and up the road toward home, she held on tight, the wind in her face like a thousand needles piercing her skin. Finally, she laid her cheek against Dex's back and closed her eyes. The ride was bumpy and long, and by the time he pulled into his garage, she was shaking so badly she could hardly stand.

"Why don't you come inside and get warmed up?" he asked.

"No, thanks, I've got to let Kermit out."

"I can get Kermit—"

"It's not going to happen," she said harshly. Taking a deep breath, she tried again with a little less bite to it. "Thank you very much for the ride. Good night."

She turned and made her way out of the warm garage and up the hill toward the cabin, the snow blinding her. Finally, she burst inside and flipped on the light so she could see Kermit, but nothing happened. She continued fiddling with the switch, and finally groaned in frustration. She could hear Kermit whimpering and realized how frigid it was *inside*.

As if the heat had been off for hours.

The dark and the cold were beginning to cause a claustrophobic tightness to wrap around her. She had always hated the dark, because her imagination always went to what might be lurking there. Fumbling in her purse for her phone, she called Dex, trying to make her way toward Kermit's cage by feel.

"Change your mind about coming over?"

"No, but my power is out and I can't see anything. Can you bring a flashlight and flip the breakers for me?"

She could hear his heavy sigh through the phone. "Why don't you bring Kermit and wait out the storm with me? I have a backup generator and a fireplace—"

"God, can't you just, for once, do something nice without acting like it is an inconvenience to you?" Her voice came out shrill and panicked. Silence on the other end had her checking to see if the call had dropped, but no, he was still there.

Way to go. Insult the only person who can help.

"I didn't mean that, I just...I don't like the dark."

After what seemed like forever, he finally spoke. "I'll be right there."

As Dex came through the door, the snow slid down his neck and under his collar, making him shiver. Or maybe it was the freezing, dark room. No wonder Allie hadn't wanted to go searching for the breaker box.

Turning on the flashlight, he shone it around the room until he found her sitting on the couch, holding Kermit.

"Are you okay?"

"Yeah. I couldn't find my flashlight or I would have gone out and tried to flip them myself," she said.

"Well, come stand at the door and let me know if anything happens when I try the breakers. The less time I stay out in the cold, the better."

Allie stood up and he could hear the tread of her feet behind him as she followed him to the door. He went around the side of the cabin and yanked the box open. He started pushing the breakers back and forth. "Anything?"

"No, nothing."

"Shit." Closing the box, he hurried back into the house, as if it would be any warmer there than outside.

"You can't fix it?"

"No, not in this weather. You're going to have to stay at my place tonight, so why don't you go grab a few things—"

"Honestly, I'll be fine. I'll build a fire and add some extra blankets to my bed."

He tried to hang on to his temper, but she was being so pigheaded it wasn't easy. "Damnit, woman! It's only going to get colder out there, which means the temperature is going to drop considerably in here as the night goes on. So, why don't you stop being stubborn and make this easy on all of us, including Kermit. You don't want him to freeze just because you don't like me, do you?"

He could tell she was fighting the urge to tell him to go to hell, just from the expression on her face.

"I appreciate your concern, but I'll let him snuggle with me. We'll be good."

Running a hand over his face, he made the decision that was going to piss her off the most.

Taking Kermit from her, he ignored her protests. "If you want to freeze to death, fine, but he's coming with me."

He marched toward the door as she hurled curses at his back.

"You're a jackass, you know that?"

Pausing at the door, he tossed her an exasperated look over his shoulder. "I'm not the one sitting in a dark, cold room because she doesn't want to accept help. I hope you and your wounded pride are happy together."

He stormed out of the cabin, waiting for a moment to see if she would follow, but she didn't.

To hell with her, then. He'd tried to be a good guy, and she'd thrown it back in his face.

He was done.

20

SEVERAL HOURS LATER, ALLIE LAY HUDDLED IN her bed, shivering under four blankets. Her hooded sweatshirt was pulled up over her head and she'd lost all feeling in her nose. She'd nearly gotten out of bed several times and crossed the hundred yards to bang on Dex's door, but had been worried he wouldn't answer. Then she'd have been even more humiliated and cold than she already was.

Besides, he'd been a jerk, anyway, throwing that line about "wounded pride" at her. Just because she didn't want to accept his help more than she needed to didn't mean she was too proud.

At this point, though, she wasn't feeling terribly concerned with owing him anything. Especially since she couldn't seem to get her toes warm.

A noise coming from the kitchen brought her head up, and her stomach tightened in fear. Had the raccoons found a way back in?

Her bedroom door opened and the dark form in her doorway shone a flashlight in her face, blinding her.

"Ah, what the hell?" she cried.

"You are the biggest pain in the ass I have ever met, you know that?" Dex's deep voice growled. He came around the side of the bed, and without waiting for her to say anything, he picked her up, swaddled in the blankets, and headed for the door.

"You don't have to carry me. I give in. You were right."

"I'm not taking any chances that you'll change your mind. I almost left you here all night to teach you a lesson."

"Why didn't you?"

She silently begged him to say something. If Dex had been worried about her, it meant he had to care for her, even if only a little bit.

Right?

"Because I'm a bigger idiot than you."

Well, that wasn't terribly flattering.

"Get the door for me, will you?" he asked.

She reached down to turn the knob and, once they were through, pulled it behind them. His porch light was like a beacon in the storm and she snuggled her face into the front of his jacket, trying to warm her nose.

"Are you nuzzling me?"

"No, my nose is cold. I'm trying to rub the feeling back."

"Well, try not to get snot on my jacket."

Allie stopped and sniffed. She couldn't tell if her nose was running or not, but why take the chance?

On second thought, after what a jerk he'd been, a little snot was the least he deserved.

Finally, when they were both inside his house, the warm air hit her face and she sighed in pure bliss as her numb skin started to tingle.

"I'm going to set you on the couch and get you something warm to drink. Do you want coffee or whisky?"

"I better stick with the coffee," she said. "Whisky and I don't make the best of friends."

Dex grinned as he gazed down at her, the familiarity in his gaze making her heart ache. "I happen to remember you and whisky rather fondly."

No, she couldn't do this. She couldn't let his teasing or his sexy smile break down her resolve. She couldn't get hurt again.

The thought startled her. The last few weeks she'd been angry, with herself and with Dex, but she hadn't really thought about the fact that she had been hurt by him, too. Because despite some of his less-than-stellar moments, she'd actually started to like Dex. He made her laugh, even when she didn't want to, and he had moments of caring that showed a sweet side of him.

Of course, he didn't have a single characteristic on her list. Okay, maybe one or two, but the point was that no matter what she'd started to feel for Dex, he'd squashed it. She was over it, and the first thing she could do to prove that was to let go of her anger.

With a bit of a sad smile, she said, "After everything that's happened, I think we better not dwell too much on that."

He was silent, making his way around the kitchen. She could hear Kermit whining from somewhere. "Hey, where's my dog?"

"Locked in his old crate with a blanket. He's warm at least, which is more than I can say for you."

Considering how her skin stung as the feeling came back into her fingers and face, she hoped so.

"Why do you always have your dog locked up when I come over?"

"Because sometimes you stop by during her dinnertime."

"Your dog has a set dinnertime?" she asked.

"No, I just usually lock her up with a bone while I have dinner, and then I let her out when we go to bed."

Allie turned to see him in the kitchen, her eyebrows raised. "We?"

"Yes, *we*. You are not the only one who loves your dog. Bluebell usually takes the left side of the bed and shoves me all the way to the right by the time the alarm clock goes off."

Allie laughed at the image of the big bloodhound kicking her master out of bed. Dex gave her a boyish smile in return. The one that set off a hundred fluttering wings in her abdomen.

"Do you want milk and sugar?" he asked.

She told herself to stop thinking about him in that way. Maybe they could move past everything and be friends. "Yes, please, both."

He brought her over a steaming mug. "Scoot closer to the fire if you need to."

"Thanks." She took the mug, the ceramic scalding her skin. Setting it down on the side table to cool, she stared into the burning fire, more than aware when Dex sat next to her. Allie watched him drink his coffee out of the corner of her eye, his full lips on the brim, the sexy Adam's apple bobbing in his throat when he swallowed. She worked up the nerve to say something... well, nice.

"Thank you for coming back for me. I know I didn't give you a reason to with the way I behaved."

"It's fine. I'm sorry for what I said." He drummed his fingers on the mug and then added, "Besides, I couldn't let you suffer out there. It would have gone against my code."

Fighting the blankets surrounding her, she tucked her feet up on the couch and turned to face him. "You have a code? I never would have thought."

"Why?" he asked. "Because I made out with my best friend's girl?"

The words instantaneously killed the ease she was just starting to feel with him.

"I didn't mean it like that."

"I know, but I did. I should never have touched you."

"I wasn't Hunter's girl, though." He stiffened next to her and her cheeks finally warmed as she realized how that had sounded. "I just mean…we had only been out a few times and we weren't exclusive."

He actually turned on the couch to face her, pulling her gaze to his with those intense green eyes. "And now?"

"We're just friends." Clearing her throat, she asked, "Why are you asking? It's not like you're interested. You said I was just casual, right?"

"About that—" he started to say, but she couldn't bear to hear his excuses.

"No, you don't need to apologize again. Not after all this time. I get it. You're one of those guys who has to tap every woman he comes in contact with."

"Not *every* woman. In fact, I haven't tapped anyone, as you say, since you showed up."

Allie's gut clenched. "What the hell are you doing?"

"Being honest?" he said.

How dare he?

Flinging off the blankets, she stood up angrily. "Whatever game you're playing with me, it's not funny or fair. I appreciate you letting me stay here and helping me out tonight, but you were more than clear about what your endgame was with me. And I'm not interested in that. Backpedaling or acting like there's something more going on here because you're horny isn't going to work."

"Hear me out, because I swear I'm not backpedaling right now." He grabbed her hand and looked her square in the eye. "I never would have said what I did if I'd known you were there. Hunter had caught me off guard and I was just running my mouth to get him off my back about lying to him. Besides, you weren't."

"I wasn't what?" she asked.

"Casual. I didn't kiss you because you were just there. I did it because I wanted to." His voice lowered. "I wanted you. I still do."

Her heart thumped loudly in her chest. What the hell did she say to that? While the part of her that was still hurt and angry wanted to get up and walk away, she couldn't deny that the words *I still want you, too* sat poised on the tip of her tongue.

But he'd had a chance to step in and be with her, and he'd blown it.

"I can't." She headed for the hallway, abandoning her coffee and her desires in his living room as she escaped.

"Allie?" he called.

She paused, waiting for him to ask her not to go. To stay up, talk to him, and figure this whole mess out.

"Second door on the left."

Dex sat on his couch, shooting back another whisky as he stared into the fire.

What the hell had he expected her to say? That she wanted him, too, despite everything? And when had he decided to go all true confessions on her, anyway?

Truth was, he'd caught himself making his way to her place several times over the last few weeks. He wasn't sure what he would have said when he got there, because he never made it to her door. One thing was for sure, though: Allie Fairchild hadn't been far from his thoughts.

Which should have been enough to make him stay the hell away from her, except…he didn't want to. For the first time, he didn't think of being with a woman as something to avoid. Allie made him want to be better than a jerk who seduced a girl behind his best friend's back. She was different.

But how the hell could he convey all that to *her* when he could barely process what it all meant to him? He knew that he wanted her and had feelings for her, but what did that mean? And was it enough to make him keep trying to earn her forgiveness, or would it just end up leaving them both disappointed?

And it didn't just involve him and Allie. Hunter had just started to forgive him, and despite Allie's assurance that she wasn't Hunter's girl, how would Hunter feel if Dex admitted he had real feelings for Allie? That she actually got him thinking about all the things that used to send him running?

Dex set his glass down with a groan, massaging his aching forehead with his fingers. God, why was this shit so complicated?

21

ALLIE WOKE UP THE NEXT MORNING DISORI-
ented and exhausted. She'd tossed and turned half the night
before finally drifting off after she'd heard Dex's steps
outside her door. For the briefest moment, she'd imagined
him opening it and stepping inside. He'd tell her again how
sorry he was and offer to do anything to make it up to her.

The fantasy had been enough to put her to sleep, but it still
felt like there was a sledgehammer currently beating inside
her head. Getting out of the bed, she tried to straighten the
covers and then tiptoed into the hallway. She was hoping
Dex was still asleep, so she could grab Kermit and sneak out.

Except she didn't have any shoes. Crap. Maybe she could
slip on a pair of his tennis shoes.

One glance out the big bay windows made her heart sink.
She wasn't sneaking out, at least not in tennis shoes. Outside
was completely white, with several feet of snow covering the
ground and still more coming down in a dense whiteout.

"Good morning," Dex called from the kitchen, startling her.

"Hi. Any idea when this is supposed to let up?" Allie

tried to look anywhere but Dex's bare chest, but was losing the battle. It was just so defined and chiseled.

"My weather app says it's going to continue through tomorrow night. I hope you don't have to work."

"No, but if there is a break in the weather, I'll have to get my phone in case there is an emergency at the hospital."

His deep chuckle rose gooseflesh over her skin as he approached in just a pair of sweats and his bare feet. "Not sure what kind of break you're expecting. It's only going to get worse from here. The only good thing to come out of heavy snow like this is the winter tourists who show up to snowboard, ski, and snowmobile."

Allie loved to snowboard when she was a teenager, but she hadn't been in years. With Bear Mountain Ski Resort just up the road, she supposed she'd get a chance to pick it up again. "I guess that means things pick up for you again, huh? Having to rescue people from snowdrifts or avalanches?"

"Not very often. I was actually hoping for a little peace and quiet."

"Don't you need to make a living?" she asked.

"Well, between acts of heroism, I work for the National Park Service as a ranger. I patrol the area, make sure people aren't being stupid and trespassing."

"A jack-of-all-trades," she said. "Why search-and-rescue?"

"Because I enjoy it. Most people who get lost are found cold or hungry, but relatively unharmed. But when they see me coming, they are damn happy I'm there. I can say I do it for the adrenaline rush, but that's only part of it. I want to help people, to feel needed. Useful. I do it for that look on their face that says I'm the guy they've been waiting for."

Allie paused and stared into Dex's eyes. She understood that. Allie had become a nurse to help people, and an administrator to make a difference. And even though her job function required that she make things better for the hospital system as a whole, she did it because she was helping individuals get the care they needed.

Suddenly, she and Dex were looking a hell of a lot more similar.

Dex made coffee, wishing that he could read Allie's mind. He couldn't imagine she was happy to be stuck with him for at least a day, but she seemed content enough. She'd just curled up on the couch with Kermit, staring quietly at the falling snow outside.

"The coffee should be ready in a minute. How would you feel about some breakfast?" he asked.

"Sure, that would be great. Thanks."

He went about the kitchen, pulling out eggs, potatoes, peppers, onions, and cheese. "Do omelets and country potatoes sound good?"

"Like heaven." She was snuggling Kermit, Bluebell dogging her steps as she walked into the kitchen. "Will she hurt him if I put him down?"

"She might lick him to death, but that's about the extent of her viciousness," he said.

As Allie set Kermit on the ground, Dex was pretty sure she called him an ass under her breath, but he let it go. Maybe it was because she was actually talking to him, or that he had her all to himself for another twenty-four hours, but he started whistling joyfully.

"Do you have family?" she asked.

He stopped whistling. "Sure. My parents and my little brother live in Philadelphia."

"Why didn't you go home to visit them for Thanksgiving?"

Beating the eggs with his whisk, he shrugged. "We're not exactly the warm-and-fuzzy type. I love my family, but I'm a bit of an odd duck to them."

"How's that?"

"Mainly because I preferred camping and fishing to studying."

"Ah," she said. "My parents don't understand me, either. Thought I would have been better off marrying a man with an education than getting one."

"That's too bad." Dex started cutting up the ingredients. "I like that you're smart."

Allie cleared her throat. "Can I help?"

"Sure, just wash your hands and—"

"Yes. Jeez, I was a nurse. I wouldn't touch the food with dog cooties all over me."

Dex grinned. "My apologies, Nurse Fairchild."

"Like I was saying, I didn't want to spend the rest of my life married to a politician or CEO, organizing teas and charity auctions. It took me a while to find my calling, but when I did, nothing was going to stand in my way."

Dex had to admit he was surprised by her admission. Allie might be a stubborn, infuriating woman, but she didn't exactly scream rebel.

"I take it you didn't go home because you didn't want to deal with their judgment?" he asked.

"Exactly." She smiled at him over the green bell pepper she was cutting, and he opened his mouth to warn her right before the knife came down. She cried out and cradled her hand, and he was at her side in a second.

"Let me see." She allowed him to examine the side of her thumb, which had been neatly sliced on its side. He grabbed a clean hand towel from the cupboard and wrapped it tightly to stanch the blood. He noticed her wince and mumbled an apology.

"I have a first aid kit in the bathroom. Come on. You sit on the couch and wait while I grab it."

He held the towel around her finger as he led her toward the couch, leaving her there to retrieve the first aid kit. When he got back, her face was sheet-white.

As he kneeled down, he teased lightly, "You're not going to faint on me, are you? Might have to kiss you if you pass out on my couch. Maybe even cop a feel."

"Pervert." A ghost of a smile played across her lips, even as pain filled her eyes, wet with unshed tears.

He pulled back the towel and the cut started bleeding again. Dex was half tempted to put her on the snowmobile and take her up for some stitches, but it was nasty out there and hardly worth endangering their lives for a stitch or two when he could do them just as well.

"Think you can man up while I clean, stitch, and wrap this? It will hurt like a mother, but I think I have some Tylenol with codeine or might even have a couple of Valium."

"Tylenol is fine. Narcotics make me sick." Weakly, she slapped his shoulder. "That's for stringing together one very sexist sentence."

"What? Woman up, then. For a nurse, you're pretty squeamish. It's cute."

"I can handle other people's blood, but I get woozy when I see my own," she said.

He handed her the pain pill and finished doctoring her thumb. He patted her knee comfortingly. "I'll get you some water."

She covered his hand with hers, and held it to her knee. His gaze rose to meet hers, and he was shocked when she leaned over and kissed him. It wasn't anything more than a peck, but it left him wanting to bury his hands in her hair and bring her back for more.

Instead, he just smiled as he stood up. "You're welcome."

22

"YOU'RE A CHEATER!" DEX'S GREEN EYES danced as he said it, so she didn't take it personally. It was nearly seven in the evening, and since the snow was still going strong, they had spent the day watching movies and playing card games. Dex had been the one to suggest a game of slap-jack, and she couldn't help if she was better at it than he was.

"Am not! I'm just faster."

"You totally pushed my hand out of the way," he said.

"Wow, I didn't know such a big man could be such a sore loser."

"You know what? You're gonna pay."

Allie squealed and jumped up from the table, laughing as she ran. Bluebell and Kermit chased after her, yipping and howling, but she didn't get very far. Dex's arms wrapped around her from behind and he lifted her up, spinning them in a circle until she was dizzy.

"Uncle! Uncle!"

He stopped and turned her to face him, practically wheezing with laughter.

"Do you confess to your dirty, rotten cheating ways?"

"Never!"

God, when was the last time I've laughed this hard?

"Then I have no choice but to tickle you into submission." His fingers attacked her ribs and she screamed, reaching to grab his hands...

And then cried out when her injured finger got bumped.

He stopped wrestling her and gently took her hand in his. "Are you okay?"

"Yeah, I just forgot for a minute," she said, her voice tight with pain. The first pill had made her drowsy, so she'd been holding off from taking another.

"Me, too. I'm sorry."

To her surprise, he raised her hand up and placed a gentle kiss on the palm.

She caught her breath as the spot warmed with the press of his lips and breath. Allie stared at him, their eyes locked, and the air around them practically sizzled.

"Allie?"

"Yeah?"

"Am I going to have to apologize again?" he asked.

"For what?"

He trailed his fingers over her cheek gently, taking a step closer. "If I kiss you right now, am I going to have to apologize later?"

Her heart skipped as understanding sank in. This was it. Did she take another leap and give him one more chance? Or did she pull away?

Dex dropped his hand and started to move back, obviously taking her hesitation as a refusal. With her good hand, she grabbed the front of his shirt, stopping him in his tracks.

"Only if you stop."

The shift in Dex's expression stole her breath away and

in the next moment, his lips claimed hers. Mindful of her
sore thumb, she hooked her other arm around the back of his
neck, giving in to his kiss and the touch of his hands, which
seemed to be everywhere at once. Her arms, her shoulders,
her neck…it was as if he couldn't stop tracing every curve
of her body. With a sigh, she melted into him. This was what
she'd been craving, not the quick, fiery passions of her past,
or the tepid stirrings of Hunter's kisses.

Dex was like a warm wave, rolling in and picking her
up, carrying her through pure bliss. Briefly she wondered if
her issues with Dex had to do with them both fighting what
they wanted. If they had just given in and let things develop
the way they were meant to, would they have gotten here
sooner?

She couldn't deny that she felt it. In his kiss, and the way
his arms held her against him, it was as if he couldn't get
enough of her. And never wanted to let her go.

They stumbled toward the bedroom, their clothes leaving a
trail down the hallway. The last thing he wanted her to do
was change her mind, especially as every brush of her bare
skin against his felt like an electric shock.

In the most fantastic way.

No one else existed in this room but the two of them. He'd
shut out Bluebell and Kermit, ignoring their protests, too
caught up in the way Allie slid her bra down her arms, her
full breasts falling beautiful and free.

And all mine.

The possessive thought didn't even stall him as he tossed
his last bit of clothing, his boxer briefs, across the room, and
pulled her to him. His mouth found the pulse at her neck,
and moved down over her shoulder and across her collarbone, worshipping her body. Dex wanted to explore every

inch of her until she came apart in his arms while he was buried inside her, rocking them both into oblivion.

The tips of her fingers slid into his hair, bringing his gaze up to hers. The look on her face was gentle. Smiling. Soft.

Love.

And that's when Dex realized why he'd never been the type to commit, why he'd fought so hard against settling down.

He'd been waiting for Allie.

She was stubborn and obstinate and a giant pain in the ass...but she was also funny, caring, and her beauty was so arresting that sometimes he had a hard time looking away from her.

As he kneeled before her, his lips made their way down her torso. He lost himself in the symphony of her pleasure, working his mouth over her sensitive flesh until she shattered against him.

Lifting her onto the bed and laying her down across his comforter, he took it all in. He'd spent the last five weeks imagining what she'd look like sprawled across his bed with her arms open for him.

Now he didn't have to fantasize anymore.

Once he had the condom on, he crawled up and over her, claiming her mouth once more as he flexed his hips. Her legs wrapped around him and he slid home, groaning in ecstasy as her warmth engulfed him. Rocking against her, he got lost in the taste and feel of her, the sweet sounds of her little moans as he buried his head in her neck, relishing the squeeze of her muscles around his cock as she came again.

When he followed her down, he knew. It had never been this good, felt this right.

It was all Allie.

And this time, he wasn't going to mess it up.

23

ON SUNDAY MORNING, DEX WAITED IN THE parking lot of the hospital for Hunter. It was hard to stop smiling, considering how he'd spent the last three days with Allie. Besides making love, they had talked... about their childhoods and their friends. His time in the army and her failed attempt to appear on some reality singing competition when she was eighteen. Who knew being snowed in could be the most fun he'd had in... well, his whole life.

It was the second day since the snow had stopped and he needed to be back at work, especially since the avalanche danger level was high. He'd snuck out from under Allie's soft body, resisted her sleepy attempts to lure him back to bed, and stopped off in town for two coffees. One would be a peace offering for Hunter. Dex was hoping he'd get to keep his friend, but he wasn't counting his chickens yet.

Hunter pulled up next to him, and when he climbed out of his car, he gave Dex a nod.

"What's this?" Hunter asked.

"Coffee, with a side of 'We need to talk.'"

Hunter came around the front and took the proffered cup. "Aw, are you breaking up with me?"

The joke didn't have the same tone to it, not after the last five weeks. There was a definite edge to it, and Dex wasn't going to bullshit his friend. Not anymore.

"Look, I know that I've screwed up, especially with things between us, but I gotta be honest—"

"You slept with Allie."

Hunter didn't sound ready to throw the scalding coffee in his face, so he took that as a good sign.

"It's not like that. I..." *Ah, hell, spit it out.* "I care about her, Hunt. I didn't know it, or at the very least, wasn't ready to admit it, but I do. A lot."

Hunter took a drink from the coffee cup before saying, "Well, that's it, then."

"If you want to take a swing at me...wait, what does that mean?"

"It means I knew after you kissed her I had lost. I just figured you'd lost, too, when you acted like a total prick. But she gave you another chance?"

"Not at first. Her battery died and her power was out, so she stayed at my place—"

"I don't need details, really. Good for you, though. It seems like she makes you happy."

"She does, I'm not gonna lie. I'm really lucky." Dex was at a loss. Of all the ways he'd expected Hunter to react, cool and collected hadn't been among them. "Well, thanks, man. I appreciate it."

"I'm not going to do cartwheels, at least not anytime soon, but I also am not going to hold a grudge against you for falling for someone." Then Hunter grinned as he added, "Besides, with you off the market, the next hot, single woman that rolls into town will be all mine. No contest."

Holding his coffee cup out to his friend, he gave a toast. "Here's to love."

Hunter's eyebrows shot up his forehead. "Love, huh?"

Dex shrugged with a sheepish smile. "What can I say? She had me the first time she glared at me."

While Hunter laughed, Dex's cell phone rang. "Belmont."

"Dex, we got a couple of snowmobiles at the base of Bear Mountain. You think you can catch up and tell them they gotta call it for the day? At least until we can get some of the snow packed and adjusted? I'm afraid all that noise is gonna bring down the whole top."

"Yeah, I'll take care of it."

Fifteen minutes later, Dex and Bluebell had parked on the side of the road, just under the mountain, when a thunderous sound made his blood run cold.

He looked up and watched as a tidal wave of snow slid down the steep, rocky peak toward the bottom. Dex pulled out his binoculars, but he didn't need them to see the two machines racing away from the base, trying to beat the avalanche.

They disappeared into the snow and Dex sprang into action. As long as they had an air pocket, Dex had fifteen, twenty minutes to find them before they suffocated.

He called 911 and gave them the location as he pulled his snowmobile and sled out of his truck. Arming his own beacon, he secured Bluebell on the snowmobile, her vest and beacon activated as well.

"All right, girl, let's save some lives."

Allie had overslept a little, and used up all of Dex's hot water during her shower, but since he wasn't home, she figured it was fine. Besides, her cabin's power was still out, so he was kind of stuck with her.

Allie didn't really think he minded, especially given the

things she had planned to do to him tonight after she got home from the hospital.

It was going to be her first day back and she figured she was about to have at least one heavy conversation with Hunter. She wasn't going to explain or make excuses, she was just going to be honest about her feelings for Dex. Considering she'd made no romantic moves toward Hunter for weeks, she didn't think he'd care, but still…she was a little stressed about the whole thing.

It took her longer than usual to get to the hospital, because she had to wait for Penny to show up to watch Kermit. She'd agreed to let Allie borrow her car for the day, but insisted they go shopping for a four-wheel drive for her this week.

Allie didn't have a problem with that at all.

She walked into her office and had barely shrugged out of her coat when Rebecca knocked on her door.

"Allie, prepare for incoming. We've got two snowmobilers who got buried in an avalanche at the base of the mountain."

"Thanks, Rebecca, glad to be back. Do they have it covered?"

"Yep, Dr. Gracin is standing by. Just wanted to let you know."

"Thanks. Did you have a good weekend?" Allie asked.

"I did, actually. Just normal family stuff. Hey, what happened to your hand?"

Allie had almost forgotten about the cut. "Oh, I sliced my thumb while cutting vegetables. No big deal."

"That's exactly why I don't cook. Well, I'll let you get back to it. I'm sure you've got lots to catch up on."

She did, and now it looked like she'd have to wait until Hunter wasn't knee deep in avalanche survivors to deal with one of those things.

*   *   *

The first kid had managed to break the surface of the snow by the time Dex reached him, although he was holding his left arm limply against his chest.

"You okay? What's your name?"

"I'm Graham, and I think I broke my arm. But my brother, Chris, I can't find him."

All right, time for Bluebell to earn her kibble. "Bluebell, find."

Bluebell jumped from the back of the snowmobile and sank into the snow. Dex used the snowshoes he'd strapped on to make a path less deep. In the distance, he could hear the sirens signaling help was coming.

Before too long, Bluebell gave an excited howl and started digging, diving headfirst into the snow.

An EMT on another snowmobile pulled up, and Dèx waved, pointing to Graham. "Possible broken arm. The other rider is buried. If you get him out of here, we'll work on this."

Dex grabbed his snow shovel and started digging with Bluebell, yelling for Chris. After what felt like hours of work, he heard a voice hollering from below and Dex started using his hands. "Chris, start moving toward the sound of my voice. You're getting closer, man, just a little farther."

Finally, Chris broke through the snow, gasping, his arms flaying. "Get me the hell out of here!"

Taking the guy's arms, Dex pulled, dragging him out. Chris lay on the ground, breathing heavily. "Thank God, I thought I was going to die down there."

"Are you hurt?"

"Just my head. I think I flipped a couple of times."

"Okay, I'm going to strap you to the sled. Can you walk?"

Chris stood a little unsteadily, and Dex helped him to the

sled before strapping him in. He waved toward a couple of EMTs headed back out.

"Let's go, Bluebell."

Dex took off, heading toward the road. He saw the EMTs spin around and kick up snow. Other people were jumping up and down excitedly, and at first, Dex thought it was in celebration.

And then he felt it. The handlebars were shaking in his grip.

Because the ground was trembling.

Glancing briefly over his shoulder, he saw the second avalanche descending the mountain, gaining on their tail. His heart dropped out of his chest and hit the bottom of his stomach with a sickening thud.

"Shit. Hang on," he shouted, knowing Chris probably couldn't hear him. He pushed the speed, silently chanting, *Come on...come on.*

He was so close to safety, but he could feel the cold air at his back, the leaden snow reaching out for him. So he took a deep breath.

And waited for impact.

24

WHEN HUNTER GOT THE CALL, IT FELT LIKE someone had taken a sledgehammer to his gut, making him want to hurl.

The second thought that raced through his head was Allie. Did she know?

At a full run, Hunter rushed into her office. She looked up from the paperwork littering her desk, much like she had the first time he'd seen her, only this time Hunter was there as a friend and nothing more.

"Allie..."

"Hey, aren't you waiting on an incoming trauma?"

"Yeah, but Allie, you should know—"

"Actually, if you got a minute, I should go first. I am so sorry, but I think it should come from me—"

His voice boomed in frustration. "Shut up and listen!"

Her jaw dropped in surprise, and while she was speechless, he finished. "There was a second avalanche while Dex was bringing in one of the patients."

The blood drained from Allie's face. "Oh, my God. Is he okay?"

Allie stood in the middle of the intake door, waiting for Dex, her whole body quaking with adrenaline.

Two ambulances carrying the injured teenagers pulled up, and as they unloaded them, wheeling them in side by side, Allie overheard one tell the other, "Man, that guy was a fucking badass. You should have seen him...."

The doors closed behind them, so she didn't catch the rest of the conversation, but she didn't need to. She knew enough about what happened to know exactly what she was going to do to said "badass."

Dex's truck pulled into the parking lot and he climbed out, all six-foot-plus feet of him perfectly healthy. Allie couldn't decide what she wanted to do to him more: kiss or kill him.

He caught sight of her and broke into a trot, a broad smile on his face.

"Allie, you are not going to believe what happ—"

Swinging her fist, she punched him as hard as she could in the arm. "Are you crazy? I heard all about it, you idiot! Why didn't you wait for help before charging off like the Lone Ranger?"

"Jesus, what is wrong with you?" he asked, rubbing his arm.

"You! You could have been killed."

"If I hadn't gone when I did, those guys would have been caught under a second avalanche and we might not have found them at all."

"And I'm glad that they're okay, but you"—she shoved him in his chest, frustration raging when he didn't move—"almost ended up buried. Do you know what the hell went through my head when Hunter told me that if you had been seconds slower you wouldn't have made it?"

"Allie, you know what I do for a living. It's not always going to be abandoned puppies and vehicle accidents."

Gripping his shirt now in her tight fists, she tried to shake him. "I know that, but you can't just jump into shit without thinking. Not now. Not after everything we've shared." Her voice broke, and she choked up, blinded by tears.

"Allie, sweetheart, I'm fine. I'm here."

His arms slipped around her, bringing her into his body, and she sagged against him. Her face buried in his shirtfront, she wrapped her arms around him and whispered, "I'm still mad at you."

"I know."

Dex knew that people were peeking out at them, but he didn't care. Allie's anger had surprised him, but nothing had prepared him for the hysterical woman clinging to him.

So many things went through his mind while he was waiting for the snow to overtake him, but at the forefront of his mind were thoughts of Allie. He was damn lucky to be here, to tell her how he felt about her.

In fact, he'd been so exhilarated to have made it, he hadn't even considered she might be upset.

"Okay, I need to say something for a minute. You're missing a few key facts about what went down. First of all, I watched the avalanche happen, so I knew where to find them. With an air pocket, someone buried in the snow can live fifteen, twenty minutes. So, time was ticking. Second, I had my beacon on, so even if I'd been buried, they would have eventually found me."

"That's"—sniffle—"not comforting."

"Woman, will you shut up and let me get this out?"

Reaching between them, he tilted her chin up so he could smile down at her. "And lastly, no matter what, I was going to make it back, because I had something important to tell you."

She wiped at her tearstained face and looked back at him.

He kissed her lips, salty with her tears, and whispered, "That I love you."

Then she hit him square in his shoulder.

"Ouch! I tell you I love you and you hit me *again?*"

"You just have the worst timing. I'm ranting at you for scaring me and you think that's a good time to drop the L-bomb?"

Dex deflated slightly. "Hey, if you aren't there yet, it's okay."

"What? Of course I love you. Why do you think I'm so pissed? We just got started and I thought—"

Dex didn't let her finish, cutting off her anger with his mouth until she was leaning into him. When they finally broke apart, he pressed his forehead to hers and whispered, "I promise to be more careful in the future."

"You better, or next time, I will beat the shit out of you."

Dex chuckled before whispering in her ear, "Have I ever mentioned my dream girl looks like an angel and cusses like a sailor?"

"Hmmm...you may have mentioned that once. If she shows up, I promise to step aside."

"Awfully gracious of you. Angelic, perhaps."

Allie pulled away from him, shaking her head. "There you go with the cheesy lines again."

"I can stop if you want."

"Never, never stop."

Dex never intended to in the first place.

CODI GARY likes to write sexy contemporary romances with humor, grand gestures, and blush-worthy moments. When she's not writing, she can be found reading her favorite authors, squealing over her must-watch shows, and playing with her children. She lives in Idaho with her family.

Books by James Patterson

FEATURING ALEX CROSS

Cross the Line • *Cross Justice* • *Hope to Die* • *Cross My Heart* • *Alex Cross, Run* • *Merry Christmas, Alex Cross* • *Kill Alex Cross* • *Cross Fire* • *I, Alex Cross* • *Alex Cross's* Trial (with Richard DiLallo) • *Cross Country* • *Double Cross* • *Cross* (also published as *Alex Cross*) • *Mary, Mary* • *London Bridges* • *The Big Bad Wolf* • *Four Blind Mice* • *Violets Are Blue* • *Roses Are Red* • *Pop Goes the Weasel* • *Cat & Mouse* • *Jack & Jill* • *Kiss the Girls* • *Along Came a Spider*

THE WOMEN'S MURDER CLUB

16th Seduction (with Maxine Paetro) • *15th Affair* (with Maxine Paetro) • *14th Deadly Sin* (with Maxine Paetro) • *Unlucky 13* (with Maxine Paetro) • *12th of Never* (with Maxine Paetro) • *11th Hour* (with Maxine Paetro) • *10th Anniversary* (with Maxine Paetro) • *The 9th Judgment* (with Maxine Paetro) • *The 8th Confession* (with Maxine Paetro) • *7th Heaven* (with Maxine Paetro) • *The 6th Target* (with Maxine Paetro) • *The 5th Horseman* (with Maxine Paetro) • *4th of July* (with Maxine Paetro) • *3rd Degree* (with Andrew Gross) • *2nd Chance* (with Andrew Gross) • *1st to Die*

FEATURING MICHAEL BENNETT

Bullseye (with Michael Ledwidge) • *Alert* (with Michael Ledwidge) • *Burn* (with Michael Ledwidge) • *Gone* (with

Michael Ledwidge) • *I, Michael Bennett* (with Michael Ledwidge) • *Tick Tock* (with Michael Ledwidge) • *Worst Case* (with Michael Ledwidge) • *Run for Your Life* (with Michael Ledwidge) • *Step on a Crack* (with Michael Ledwidge)

THE PRIVATE NOVELS

Missing (with Kathryn Fox) • *The Games* (with Mark Sullivan) • *Private Paris* (with Mark Sullivan) • *Private Vegas* (with Maxine Paetro) • *Private India: City on Fire* (with Ashwin Sanghi) • *Private Down Under* (with Michael White) • *Private L.A.* (with Mark Sullivan) • *Private Berlin* (with Mark Sullivan) • *Private London* (with Mark Pearson) • *Private Games* (with Mark Sullivan) • *Private: #1 Suspect* (with Maxine Paetro) • *Private* (with Maxine Paetro)

NYPD RED NOVELS

NYPD Red 4 (with Marshall Karp) • *NYPD Red 3* (with Marshall Karp) • *NYPD Red 2* (with Marshall Karp) • *NYPD Red* (with Marshall Karp)

SUMMER NOVELS

Second Honeymoon (with Howard Roughan) • *Now You See Her* (with Michael Ledwidge) • *Swimsuit* (with Maxine Paetro) • *Sail* (with Howard Roughan) • *Beach Road* (with Peter de Jonge) • *Lifeguard* (with Andrew

Gross) • *Honeymoon* (with Howard Roughan) • *The Beach House* (with Peter de Jonge)

STAND-ALONE BOOKS

The Moores Are Missing (with Loren D. Estleman, Sam Hawken, Ed Chatterton) • *Triple Threat* (with Max DiLallo, Andrew Bourrelle) • *Murder Games* (with Howard Roughan) • *Penguins of America* (with Jack Patterson with Florence Yue) • *Two from the Heart* (with Frank Constantini, Emily Raymond, Brian Sitts) • *The Black Book* (with David Ellis) • *Humans, Bow Down* (with Emily Raymond) • *Never Never* (with Candice Fox) • *Woman of God* (with Maxine Paetro) • *Filthy Rich* (with John Connolly and Timothy Malloy) • *The Murder House* (with David Ellis) • *Truth or Die* (with Howard Roughan) • *Miracle at Augusta* (with Peter de Jonge) • *Invisible* (with David Ellis) • *First Love* (with Emily Raymond) • *Mistress* (with David Ellis) • *Zoo* (with Michael Ledwidge) • *Guilty Wives* (with David Ellis) • *The Christmas Wedding* (with Richard DiLallo) • *Kill Me If You Can* (with Marshall Karp) • *Toys* (with Neil McMahon) • *Don't Blink* (with Howard Roughan) • *The Postcard Killers* (with Liza Marklund) • *The Murder of King Tut* (with Martin Dugard) • *Against Medical Advice* (with Hal Friedman) • *Sundays at Tiffany's* (with Gabrielle Charbonnet) • *You've Been Warned* (with Howard Roughan) • *The Quickie* (with Michael Ledwidge) • *Judge & Jury* (with Andrew Gross) • *Sam's Letters to Jennifer* • *The Lake House* • *The Jester* (with Andrew Gross) • *Suzanne's Diary for*

Nicholas • *Cradle and All* • *When the Wind Blows* • *Miracle on the 17th Green* (with Peter de Jonge) • *Hide & Seek* • *The Midnight Club* • *Black Friday* (originally published as *Black Market*) • *See How They Run* • *Season of the Machete* • *The Thomas Berryman Number*

BOOK**SHOTS**

Black Dress Affair (with Susan DiLallo) • *The Killer's Wife* (with Max DiLallo) • *Scott Free* (with Rob Hart) • *The Dolls* (with Kecia Bal) • *Detective Cross* • *Nooners* (with Tim Arnold) • *Stealing Gulfstreams* (with Max DiLallo) • *Diary of a Succubus* (with Derek Nikitas) • *Night Sniper* (with Christopher Charles) • *Juror #3* (with Nancy Allen) • *The Shut-In* (with Duane Swierczynski) • *French Twist* (with Richard DiLallo) • *Malicious* (with James O. Born) • *Hidden* (with James O. Born) • *The House Husband* (with Duane Swierczynski) • *The Christmas Mystery* (with Richard DiLallo) • *Black & Blue* (with Candice Fox) • *Come and Get Us* (with Shan Serafin) • *Private: The Royals* (with Rees Jones) • *Taking the Titanic* (with Scott Slaven) • *Killer Chef* (with Jeffrey J. Keyes) • *French Kiss* (with Richard DiLallo) • *$10,000,000 Marriage Proposal* (with Hilary Liftin) • *Hunted* (with Andrew Holmes) • *113 Minutes* (with Max DiLallo) • *Chase* (with Michael Ledwidge) • *Let's Play Make-Believe* (with James O. Born) • *The Trial* (with Maxine Paetro) • *Little Black Dress* (with Emily Raymond) • *Cross Kill* • *Zoo II* (with Max DiLallo)

For Readers of All Ages

Maximum Ride

Daniel X

Game Over (with Ned Rust) • *Daniel X: Demons and Druids* (with Adam Sadler) • *Daniel X: Watch the Skies* (with Ned Rust) • *The Dangerous Days of Daniel X* (with Michael Ledwidge)

Witch & Wizard

Witch & Wizard: The Lost (with Emily Raymond) • *Witch & Wizard: The Kiss* (with Jill Dembowski) • *Witch & Wizard: The Fire* (with Jill Dembowski) • *Witch & Wizard: The Gift* (with Ned Rust) • *Witch & Wizard* (with Gabrielle Charbonnet)

Confessions

Confessions: The Murder of an Angel (with Maxine Paetro) • *Confessions: The Paris Mysteries* (with Maxine Paetro) • *Confessions: The Private School Murders* (with Maxine Paetro) • *Confessions of a Murder Suspect* (with Maxine Paetro)

Middle School

Middle School: Escape to Australia (with Martin Chatterton, illustrated by Daniel Griffo) • *Middle School: Dog's Best Friend* (with Chris Tebbetts, illustrated by Jomike Tejido) • *Middle School: Just My Rotten Luck* (with Chris Tebbetts, illustrated by Laura Park) • *Middle School: Save Rafe!* (with Chris Tebbetts, illustrated by Laura Park) • *Middle School: Ultimate Showdown* (with Julia Bergen, illustrated by Alec Longstreth) • *Middle School: How I Survived Bullies, Broccoli, and Snake Hill* (with Chris Tebbetts, illustrated by Laura Park) • *Middle School: My Brother Is a Big, Fat*

For previews and information about the author, visit JamesPatterson.com or find him on Facebook or at your app store.

JAMES
PATTERSON
RECOMMENDS

JAMES PATTERSON

Suzanne's Diary for Nicholas

SUZANNE'S DIARY FOR NICHOLAS

This is one of my favorite romance novels I've written, perhaps because it hits so close to home. When my son was younger, my wife kept a diary for him as a keepsake of our memories as a family. This became the inspiration for *Suzanne's Diary to Nicholas* in which a new mother named Suzanne writes a love letter to her baby son, Nicholas. In it, Suzanne pours out her heart about how she and Nicholas's father met and about her hopes for marriage and family. But she could never have predicted that her diary would be read by a woman named Katie Wilkinson, who realizes that the perfect man she so desperately loves may also be the same husband and father described in the diary...

JAMES PATTERSON

Sundays at Tiffany's

What if your imaginary friend
from childhood was your one true love?

and GABRIELLE CHARBONNET

SUNDAYS AT TIFFANY'S

Love stories are harder to write for me because you can't rely on suspense and adventure in order to make them fast-paced, engaging reads. But I always want my readers to have a good time, so if I'm going to write a love story then you can be sure it'll be a page-turning love story. That's exactly what I hope readers will get from *Sundays at Tiffany's*. In it, Jane Margaux is in love with the perfect man. Michael is handsome, comforting, and funny. There's only one catch—only she can see him. An invisible friend who left Jane on her eighth birthday, Michael is back over twenty years later for reasons neither of them know...yet.

I'd like to recommend a new reading experience to you. It's called BookShots.

BookShots are a whole new format of books—they're 100% story-driven, no filler, no fluff, and always under $5.00. And, at 150 pages, they can make reading more convenient. They can be read in an evening, on a commute, while exercising, even during breaks at work on a cell phone.

On the following pages are some BookShots romances. I hope you'll try them. I know you'll enjoy them.

Welcome to BookShots and the reading revolution.

50
*She's got a sexy
little lust list...*

Hidden
Desires

JESSICA LEMMON

50 HIDDEN DESIRES

It may seem like Holly Larsen has it all—the lavish life-style, the lucrative dream job, the supportive family—but she doesn't. Personally, I know that none of those things can amount to anything when you don't have someone to love. And finding a soul mate is hard for Holly Larsen, whose heart is set on Dalton Thomas, even though he's completely off-limits because he's her brother's best friend. At her wits' end, Holly does something remarkably daring by preposi-tioning Dalton with a sexy little lust list. Feel like trying something daring too?

James Patterson's
BOOKSH★TS
Flames

The
McCullagh Inn
in Maine

New York Times Bestseller
Jen McLaughlin

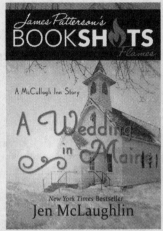

James Patterson's
BOOKSH★TS
Flames

A McCullagh Inn Story

A Wedding
in Maine

New York Times Bestseller
Jen McLaughlin

JAMES PATTERSON PRESENTS

A McCullagh Inn Story

A Princess in
Maine

New York Times Bestseller
Jen McLaughlin

BOOKSH★TS
Flames

THE McCULLAGH INN SERIES

Picture this: A quiet country inn in Maine, complete with a roaring fire and warm home-cooked dishes at every meal. Sounds like a typical James Patterson novel, right? Hah! Except once you settle into Jen McLaughlin's sweet town of Hudson, Maine, you'll be thrown into a riveting, twisty mystery in each book. Because that kind-faced innkeeper? She's got a dark past. And it lurks at every corner, ready to attack.

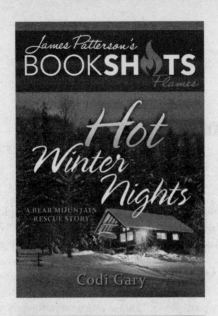

James Patterson's
BOOKSH🔥TS
Flames

Hot
Winter
Nights

A BEAR MOUNTAIN
RESCUE STORY

Codi Gary

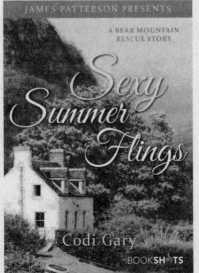

JAMES PATTERSON PRESENTS

A BEAR MOUNTAIN
RESCUE STORY

Sexy
Summer
Flings

Codi Gary

BOOKSH🔥TS
Flames

BEAR MOUNTAIN RESCUE SERIES

Trauma centers can be the deadliest places—so you can imagine why I wanted to set one of the BookShots series at one. But as I developed the plots for the Bear Mountain stories, I realized that they can also be places of hope, salvation, and, most importantly, love. Worlds collide in Bear Mountain, Montana, where the characters feel like neighbors, but the action will keep you on the edge of your seat. And each love story will keep you guessing to the very end.

BOOK**SHOTS**

THERE'S A REVOLUTION IN READING—IT'S CALLED BOOKSHOTS.

BookShots are a whole new kind of book—100% story-driven, no fluff, always under $5, and written and co-written by James Patterson himself.

At 150 pages or fewer, BookShots can be read in a night, on a commute, even on your cell phone during breaks at work.

FOR SPECIAL OFFERS AND THE FULL LIST OF BOOKSHOT TITLES, PLEASE GO TO: WWW.BOOKSHOTS.COM